WINTER SAGE

BELOW THE SALT SERIES

BOOK FIVE

ELIZABETH ROSE

Published by Oliver-Heber Books

0 9 8 7 6 5 4 3 2 1

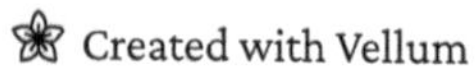

CHAPTER 1

HORN & HOOF TAVERN, GLASGOW, SCOTLAND, 1374

The fires of hell weren't half as strong as old Callum MacKeefe's homemade Mountain Magic. Lord Robin Blake knew now that he never should have taken up the offer of drinking with Laird Storm MacKeefe at his family's Horn and Hoof Tavern in Glasgow. The small place was crowded as usual, most of the occupants being from the MacKeefe clan, of course. Robin had come to visit his cousin Lark at her insistence. And also to see his Uncle Storm. The MacKeefes surprised Robin, all gathering to celebrate his new title and position as Lord of Shrewsbury Castle. This was something he hadn't expected at all.

Then again, the MacKeefe clan didn't need much coaxing to drink and celebrate. This only gave them reason to do just that. For three days now, actually. The Scots kept on arriving at the tavern, not allowing Robin to leave until he'd had a drink with each one of them. So, every day it started a new celebration all over again. If he kept this up much longer, he'd never get back to Shrewsbury. Not to mention, he'd never be able to sit in a saddle again, let alone stand.

Robin downed the rest of the whisky in his tankard, already feeling his head spinning. Damn, it was much too early in the day for this. It wasn't even noon yet, but the tavern was fully operating, and the MacKeefes were present and drinking.

He really should have eaten something first. If it hadn't been for the damned drink gnawing at his insides and making him want to retch, he was sure he would have most likely keeled over or passed out by now. One day of drinking and celebrating had been more than enough for Robin. But now, being the third day of downing the most potent whisky in all Scotland and England combined, the only thing he wanted to do was to leave this place and get away from these crazy Scots! It was easy to see now why some of the clan were referred to as the Madmen MacKeefe.

Men, women, and even children occupied the tables of the Horn and Hoof, having started arriving about an hour ago. It made Robin wonder if the tavern ever closed. Old Callum served meals, drinks, and had rooms upstairs for travelers and the nobles to sleep. It was also where the whores conducted their business. Robin had never had a Scottish lass before and really wouldn't have minded. However, his need and want to return home was stronger than even his desire to bed a wench right now.

The regular patrons of the tavern sat on high stools up at the drink board where old Callum served them himself. Then there were the usual tarts trying to make a living with the drunken men, seducing them in every dark corner. A musician played today, strumming his lute and singing loudly. Some of the words were not suitable for the ears of the children present. It made Robin uncomfortable. My, these Scots were a jarring bunch. Much different from the English. One of the drunken men and a whore were dancing dirty in the middle of the room, creating quite a stir with their vulgar moves.

"Grand-da, bring us another drink," Storm shouted across the room, holding up his empty tankard, waving it above his head to get the old man's attention from behind the drink board. Callum MacKeefe, the proprietor of the tavern and also Storm's grandfather, was a small, skinny, wiry, and ornery old man with long, white hair. His fingers were knobby, as well as his knees. Some of his teeth were missing, and the ones that remained were tinted yellow. Wrinkles covered his entire face and arms. His beard reached down to the center of his chest. His eyebrows were so bushy that it made him look like a madman. Callum MacKeefe had to be the oldest living person in all of Scotland and England combined. At times he laughed uncontrollably for no reason at all, sounding as if he were completely mad. The rest of the time he was just downright cantankerous to anyone who got in his way.

Callum prided himself on his advanced age, saying his homemade whisky was to thank for his longevity. Robin didn't know if that was true. It seemed more likely to him that the man was just too grumpy to die. Or perhaps too crazy!

"Nay, no more, Uncle Storm." Robin held a hand to his mouth and belched. Unfortunately, this only enabled him to feel the burning twice-over in his throat now. "I need to start back for Shrewsbury before the weather changes. Callum said a storm is coming. He told me he can feel it in his bones."

"Och, Robin. Dinna mind my grand-da and all his mindless clishmaclaver," said Storm. "The old man just likes to talk and complain, that's all. Do ye really have to leave so soon? I'm havin' a great time visitin' with ye."

"Thank you for celebrating my new position with me, but yes, I really should go. I've already sent my squire and guards back home two days ago to tend to things at the castle for me. I am the Lord of Shrewsbury and really can't stay away any longer. There is too much to be done. Besides, it is still early in the day and I need to use the daylight to my advantage while I travel." He started to get up, but a hand on his shoulder pushed him back down on the wooden bench.

"Stay put, laddie. After all, ye've only had one tankard of Mountain Magic so far today. Ye are just gettin' started." Callum stood next to him with a bottle in his hand, meaning to refill Robin's cup.

Some of the customers started clapping in a rhythmic beat as one drunken sot stretched out his arms to the side and spun in circles with a bottle balanced atop his head. Callum's head jerked upward and the corners of his mouth pursed down in a stiff scowl. "Stop that, ye fool! Ye spill a drop, Angus, and I'll personally bash ye over the head with the bottle, and ban ye from the tavern for a fortnight," Callum threatened the man. "And ye two," he called out to the vulgar dancers, waving his boney finger in the air. "This is a respectable establishment. Those moves ye are grindin' out are no' fit for the eyes of the bairns, let alone a herd of goats. Now go upstairs and use a room if need be, but I dinna want to see that type of behavior down here again. Get!" he screamed, stamping his foot on the floor. It caused the whore and the Scotsman to run to the stairs, making their way to the upper rooms. Two children with wide eyes watched them from a nearby table while their mother tried to distract them.

Next, a patron entered the tavern, stopping momentarily at the threshold to give the huge man at the door a coin. The MacKeefes as well as nobles ate and drank for free. Everyone else had to pay a half-penny to enter. It was a security measure for the proprietor in case any men well in their cups caused damage while they were here. As the man dug his coin out of his pouch, a large dog ran into the tavern, sneaking past him. The man guarding the door, a rough-looking brute, took the proffered coin and bounced it atop a wooden board to make sure the money was real. The hound's head whipped back and forth as it hurried from table to table, sniffing the air and begging for scraps of food.

"Och, nay, ye dinna. No' again. Someone, get that mangy mutt out of here," complained Callum, his hands waving above his head as he spoke. The dog ran over and put its paws up on the table next to Robin, knocking over the tankards, frantically sniffing the air. Callum quickly snatched up the bottle of his coveted whisky from the table, holding it to his chest in a means of protection. The hound lapped up the spilled ale, not seeming to care it was anything but water. Then the animal proceeded to devour a trencher, old stale crust of bread, snitched from one of the men near the end of the table. The animal stank so bad that Robin covered his nose with his hand. Its fur was matted with mud. There was no doubt the dog was a stray. Callum swung the bottle at the dog, causing the animal to dart under the table and sit at Robin's feet. The hound quickly rested its chin on Robin's lap. Once again, Callum tried to fill Robin's cup.

"Nay, really. No more." Robin's hand slashed out to cover the opening of his vessel. "I'd rather not, Callum. I need to get back on the road anon."

"Hrumph," sniffed Callum, no doubt insulted by Robin's refusal. "What's the matter, Sassenach? Dinna ye like my Mountain Magic? Or is it just that ye canna handle the drink? I'd expect more from the lord of a castle. After all, if ye canna hold yer whisky like my grandson, Storm, ye'll be a piss-poor leader indeed."

"Huh?" asked Robin in surprise at the old man's outrageous assumption. Between the effects of the whisky he'd drunk, Callum's accusing words, and the stench of the pesky dog, Robin found it hard to focus. "Nay. Yes. I mean, it's... it's... tasty," said Robin, not able to come up with a better word to describe his experience from these past three days. He also had no idea what he could possibly say to the old man to calm him down.

"If it's so damned tasty, then have some more." Once again, Callum tried to push his famous fire-water on Robin.

"Nay, Grand-da. Leave my nephew be," said Storm in a commanding voice. "Lord Robin doesna want it. However, I'll take a wee bit more, if ye please." Storm MacKeefe, laird and chieftain of the clan, smiled, puffed up his broad chest, and held out his tankard for more. Callum gladly filled it to the brim. Then Callum grunted at Robin, throwing him a disgruntled look when he noticed the dog at his feet with its head on Robin's lap. "I swear, if someone doesna remove that damned mutt from my tavern, I'm goin' to be servin' it in my next batch of pottage."

"My, those are harsh words," said Robin, his hand going to the dog's head to pet him. "After all, he's just a poor, innocent dog."

"Hrmph!" snorted Callum. "That poor, innocent dog as ye call him, stole another of my chickens from out back this mornin'. Plus, he got into the trash three times last week and made a mess everywhere. I dinna want the animal hangin' around. Get rid of him, Storm!" Callum scoffed and kicked at the dog under the table. When he did, the hound grabbed the bottom of the old man's tunic in his mouth, growling and yanking at it.

"Nay! Stop that. Release him," Robin told the dog, not wanting Callum to start swinging at the poor thing again. Suddenly, an odd thought entered his mind. He wondered what kind of meat had been used in that pottage he'd eaten last night. Then he decided it was probably better that he didn't know. Miraculously, the dog released Callum's tunic and ran back under the table, sitting at Robin's feet once again.

Callum let out a long string of nasty curses and headed back to the drink board, shaking his head. The children at the nearby table watched him with open mouths.

"That's the first time I ever heard that dog growl," commented Storm, raising a brow. "Come to think of it, I've never heard him bark before now, either."

"He was just protecting himself, that's all," said Robin, rubbing his finger over the dog's nose. The dog whimpered, looking up at Robin with sad eyes. Robin's heart went out to him and he barely even noticed the animal's odor anymore.

"More likely he was protectin' *ye*, Robin," said Storm.

"What do you mean?"

"I mean, he's never done that for anyone else. I think the hound likes ye," continued Storm.

"Really? Nay. I don't think so." Robin smiled at the dog, liking the fact that someone cared for him, even if it was only an animal. "Were you protecting me? Really?" he asked the hound. The hound's long tongue shot out to lick his nose. Then he let out a deep sigh.

"The mutt is probably tired from stealin' all those chickens, gobblin' down trenchers, lappin' up ale, and spillin' over trash barrels," said Storm with a deep chuckle. "Plus, I think the animal likes upsettin' my grand-da." He raised his tankard to his mouth once again.

"Uncle Storm, I don't know how you can drink so much of that Mountain Magic and not fall over," said Robin. "It's truly amazing."

Storm chuckled. "Robin, ye need to remember, I'm a Highlander. Highlanders drink Mountain Magic out of tankards, while lesser Englishmen suffer to drink it out of cups." He sat up straighter, looking very proud. "I'm able to handle it. But ye're just a Sassenach. It's too much for ye. I've grown up drinkin' old Callum's liquid fire. Mayhap someday, ye'll be able to handle more, but dinna expect to ever be like me. Dinna feel bad about it, lad, ye canna help it."

"Storm, are you telling your tall tales again?" Storm's wife, Lady Wren, walked through the crowded room to join them. She was English and part of the Blake family. Wren's brothers were Lord Corbett Blake, as well as Robin's father, Madoc. Her sister was Lady Echo, who was the mother of Robin's cousin, Eleanor.

"Nay. I'm no' tellin' tales, Wren." Storm buried his nose in his tankard after having been caught bragging. "Why would ye say that, dear wife?"

"Because I heard what you said, Storm, so don't try to deny it."

Robin felt bad for Storm and came to his rescue. "Uncle Storm was just telling me that he can drink this potent whisky and not be affected since he is a Highlander. I'm just a Sassenach and am not used to it," explained Robin, still petting the dog under the table.

"I see." Wren crossed her arms over her chest and looked down at her husband sitting with his head lowered. "Storm must have forgotten to tell you that he passed out for days after drinking it, not even able to go after me when I left to look for my family before we were married."

"You passed out, Uncle Storm?" Robin's gaze shot over to the Highlander in surprise. Mayhap the mighty Storm MacKeefe wasn't so infallible as he'd like everyone to believe.

"That was a long time ago and is no' important," mumbled Storm, not able to look directly at his wife. "Well, I'd better get rid of the dog before Grand-da serves it up in a pot of stew." Storm put down his empty tankard and reached for the dog, but he nuzzled up closer to Robin.

"Whose dog is he?" asked Robin, curiously.

"No one's," said Storm. "He's just a stray that sneaks into the tavern every time someone opens the damned door."

"Well, what are you going to do with him?" Robin stood up. The dog followed. He wagged his tail, looking up at Robin, sitting down right in front of him once again.

"I dinna ken what to do with him," said Storm with a shrug. "Every time I take him to our Highland camp, he ends up back here at the tavern. The hound is kind of like a bad plague that ye canna shake."

"Mayhap we can take the dog to Hermitage Castle," suggested Wren, bending over to pet the animal. Everyone knew Wren loved animals and had a true connection with them.

The MacKeefes had a Highland camp and also a castle that they'd seized in the Lowlands, near the border. That is why both Storm and his father, Ian MacKeefe, were chieftains. They took turns as laird of the castle and camp, switching off.

"Nay, Da wouldna like that," said Storm. The long silvery-blond braid at the side of his head swung back and forth as his head shook. "He thinks we have enough dogs as it is. Besides, the castle hounds are all trained to hunt. This one is only skilled at beggin' or stealin'. He willna be a good fit with the others."

"I'll take him off your hands," offered Robin, bending down to rub the dog behind both ears. "I mean, if you really don't want him." He was a large dog and his matted, dirty coat made him look even bigger. If he were to stand up on his hind legs he would surely be as tall as Robin.

"Ye want him?" asked Storm in surprise.

"Aye," answered Robin.

"I think that's a great idea," said Wren. "Now that you're lord of a castle, Robin, you probably need some hounds."

"I have kennel dogs for hunting that I inherited," said

Robin. "But I like this one for some reason, even if he is only a mangy, dirty, smelly mutt. I think I'll take him home with me, if you don't care."

"Good! It'll save me the trouble of decidin' what to do with him. The hound is yers," said Storm with a satisfied nod and an outstretched arm. "That should keep my grand-da from killin' the dog, not to mention keep him off my back. However, I'm no' sure what ye're goin' to do with the animal. I mean, I've never seen the dog do anythin' but beg for food. When he's no' stealin' Callum's chickens from the coop."

"Mayhap you're right, but I don't mind. Besides, if I leave him here he's likely to choke on a chicken bone. Even though Callum would consider it a blessing, I don't." Robin swore he saw the dog smiling when he said that. Or mayhap it was the whisky making him daft, he wasn't sure. "What is the dog's name?" asked Robin, standing up straight now.

"He doesna have a name," said Storm. "But Callum has been callin' him Bandit, since he steals food."

"Bandit? Nay, I can't name him that. That is the name of Rook and Rose's dog," Robin told them.

"Then what will you call him?" asked Wren.

"I'm not sure," Robin answered, with his hand to his chin in thought. "Since Storm said the dog was protecting me, I think I'll call it Griffin. Yes, that is what I'll do. Griffin is his name now."

"Griffin? Like those ugly flying gargoyles atop the pinnacles of churches?" asked Storm, making a face. "Well, I canna say he doesna look like one, but that's a horrid name to give to any animal."

"How can you say that, Storm?" asked Wren. "After all, you once named your dog Mools, which means *from the grave*, so how is this any worse? You shouldn't judge Robin's choice." Wren scowled at her husband. "Robin, never mind my husband. I like the name. Griffins are protectors, so it makes good sense to me."

"Thank you," said Robin, looking down and smiling at his ugly dog. He didn't care what he looked like. All that mattered was that he was his now. He would be a lord of a castle with his own hound. He liked the thought of it.

"Robin, I hear you have invited all of us to your new castle for Christmas," said Wren. "That is so kind of you."

"Yes, Aunt Wren. I want the entire family together for Christmas. I hope you will accept my invitation," said Robin.

"We wouldn't miss it for the world." Wren smiled sweetly.

"And neither would we want to miss it." Robin's cousin Lark walked up with her husband Dustin. She held the hand of her young daughter, Florie. Lark was Storm and Wren's daughter.

Children and women were welcome at Callum's tavern, as well as any Scot, Highlander or Lowlander. Even the English could drink here with no problems attached. It was more or less a neutral ground where all sides could gather in peace without a battle commencing. Most of the time, that is. It was known that Highlanders often liked to fight for no reason at all, even amongst themselves.

"That's right," said Dustin. "Even though we only got here a few months ago, we're living in both England and Scotland, now that we're married. To be sure we'll be there for Christmas," he assured Robin.

"Great," said Robin, stretching his arms over his head, followed by a wide yawn. "Well, I'd better be on my way now. I don't like being away from the castle this long. I mean, being a new lord and all, it is important that I watch over everything closely."

"Ye're no' travelin' by yerself, are ye?" asked Lark. "Robin, that is dangerous."

"I'll be fine," said Robin, tapping his sword at his side. Once he'd stood up he felt a little dizzy. Now he wished he hadn't drunk more Mountain Magic today, since he wouldn't have his guards or his squire to travel with him.

"Lord Robin, Lark is right. You shouldn't be traveling on the roads by yourself. It's not safe," warned Dustin. "Take someone with you."

"Stop worrying. I'll be fine," said Robin. He headed for the door with his new hound right on his heels.

"Storm, do something," he heard Wren tell her husband.

"Dinna worry about his safety, Wren," Storm told his wife with a chuckle. "After all, Robin's got the mighty guardian and protector Griffin with him now. The hound is sure to protect him, as long as the enemy doesna have any food to take his interest."

CHAPTER 2

The damned weather turned bad quicker than Robin had expected. After a few days into his journey, getting closer to home, the snow started falling faster. The wind howled, blowing right through him, chilling him to the bone. Although he was dressed appropriately, he felt as though he would freeze before he arrived back at Shrewsbury Castle.

Robin pulled his cloak tighter around him, trying to keep his hood over his head as his horse trudged forward in this winter weather. Griffin led the way as if the dog knew where Robin was heading. With his thick coat the animal wasn't affected at all by the storm. It had already proven to be a good choice to keep the hound with him. After all, it gave him someone to talk to in order to pass the time.

"We're getting closer, Griffin. Just keep on going," he called out. "We'll be home soon." Robin inwardly cursed himself for staying at the tavern with the MacKeefes so long. He never should have let them influence him. If not, he'd be home already sitting in front of a warm fire.

The dog did the oddest thing next. Griffin stopped and

looked off the side of the road and barked. Then he started to growl.

"Come on, Griffin. I'm in a hurry to get home. Keep on moving."

Robin continued to ride, but stopped when he realized the dog was not following him. He sighed and turned the horse around. Griffin continued to bark and growl, looking down toward the water.

"What is the matter with you?" Robin thought he heard something on the wind that sounded like a voice. He cocked his head and listened. Sure enough, it was the sound of a girl who seemed to be screaming for help. His gaze shot upward and he sought out from where the sound came. It came through the brush and from over near the lake. Robin spotted movement. "Come on, Griffin. Someone needs our help," he told the dog, kicking his heels into the sides of his horse, hurriedly making his way toward the water.

"Nay! Leave me alone. Don't hurt me, please." Sage Hillock dropped her basket of herbs and her hand flew to the dagger strapped on her belt. Two of the three bandits that emerged from the thicket headed straight toward her. The third made his way to where she'd left her horse and wagon. "Please, don't take that! I need it."

Sage was a healer, using herbs and gifts from the earth to help those in need. She often worked at the monastery, where ill travelers stopped for healing. The sick were sometimes brought there, hoping that a prayer from the monks or a blessing from the priest would cure them. If not, they often looked to Sage to help aid their malady. She had learned the skill of healing from her late mother.

Sage had been out collecting herbs to replenish her supply. Thyme, sage, and wild marjoram were hardy plants that survived through even the winter months. It was a blessing to be able to find the live herbs hidden under the snow. She had been trying to hurry to beat the approaching winter storm, concentrating on her work rather than on other aspects of her surroundings. If she had been paying more attention, mayhap she would have heard the men approach. Sadly, they sneaked up on her. She was out by herself today with nothing but her dagger to use for protection. Before she knew what happened, the ruffians were standing before her with blades drawn, threatening to kill her.

"You thought you could hide from us, didn't you?" snarled one of the men, getting off his horse and coming closer. He held up a sword, which made her realize these weren't just common thieves. Nay, with blades like this, they were most likely mercenaries. These men were hired to kill, and had no qualms in carrying out the task for money. There was no doubt in her mind that they were sent to kill her, not just rob her. Sadly, she knew the reason.

Sage's gaze shot back and forth and she tried to come up with a plan to save her life. However, there was no way she could outrun three armed men. Neither could she get back to the horse and cart since these men blocked the way. She was trapped with her back to the frozen lake.

"I didn't do anything. Now, leave me be." She held out her knife and backed up, feeling the edge of the frozen water beneath her feet now. The men came closer. She hesitated to move onto the ice, not knowing how thin it was or if she'd fall in.

"Mayhap you haven't harmed us, but you are responsible for Lord Burchard's death, and now you will pay," said the second man.

Damn, she was right about them. They worked for the nobles. Nobles who accused her of killing their lord, even though she had tried her best to heal him. Just her luck. This was the last thing she needed today.

"Nay, I didn't kill anyone. Not purposely, I swear. It was just an unfortunate turn of events."

"Is that so?" snarled the first man, with hatred in his eyes. "Well, this is one event that will be just as unfortunate to you, wench." He lifted his blade, ready to strike her down.

"Help! Someone help me!" screamed Sage, praying for a miracle right now, not wanting to die today. She was alone in a storm and backed up to the frozen lake. She couldn't run if she tried. Her fate was doomed. Sage's body shook and it wasn't from the cold. This couldn't really be happening! Thoughts of her siblings back home flashed through her head. She had to survive in order to raise them. With no parents, she was all they had now. She couldn't leave them this way.

"What's that?" shouted the second man, looking back toward the road.

"Someone's coming!" yelled the man by the wagon. "He looks like a damned knight and he has a hound with him."

Sure enough, Sage heard the sound of a barking, snarling dog. A flash of matted brown fur sped by, and she turned her head to watch. A big, ugly dog jumped up at the man who was about to strike her down. The hound knocked him to the ground. Sage jumped to the side to keep from being hit by the man's falling body.

A knight in a cloak, sitting atop a horse, rode up as if he'd heard her cry for help and was coming to her rescue. She couldn't believe her luck had changed so quickly. Mayhap she wouldn't die today after all. The knight swung his sword at the second man, managing to nick his arm.

"Run!" cried the coward, taking off for his horse. By now, the first man was on his feet, swinging his sword at the dog.

"Don't even think of hurting the girl or my hound," warned her savior in a deep voice.

From atop his horse, the knight clashed his sword against the attacker's blade. Then the third man rode up, bringing her attacker his horse. From his horse, the gallant knight turned to fight the mercenary. When he did, the man on the ground reached up and stabbed the knight in his upper leg.

"Arrrgh," cried the knight, turning and swinging at the man on the ground now. Then he quickly turned back to fight the man on the horse.

"Be careful," Sage called out to the man helping her, as his horse got dangerously close to the water's edge. The lake looked to be frozen, but she knew it was unpredictable. The weather hadn't been cold long enough to support the weight of a man and his horse.

The dog continued to bark, jumping on the attacker who lay on the ground. Between the hound and the knight, they thankfully managed to scare off her attackers. The bad men still sat their horses and rode hard in the blowing snow, making their way back to the road. The storm turned even worse, making it hard to see now.

Unfortunately, the horse beneath the knight slipped on the frozen lake, rearing up and throwing the injured knight down.

The man hit the ice hard. Dropping his sword, his body slid across the surface toward the center of the lake. Somehow, the horse managed to get to the safety of the shore. The dog stood at the edge of the lake barking, looking intently at its master.

Sage was about to stick her dagger back into her waistbelt when she heard the sickening crackle of ice and then the sound of a body splashing into the frigid water.

"Nay!" She looked up to see the man's arms flailing

around. He had fallen through the ice, and could barely keep his head above the water. There was blood coloring the surface snow, making her realize he was hurt worse than she had thought.

"Hold on! I'm coming to help you," she called out, frantically wondering just how she could do this without falling through the ice herself. She looked back at her horse and wagon, having an idea. Then she took off at a run.

Robin's body hit the frozen water hard, taking him by surprise. He'd been so focused on helping the girl fight off her attackers that he hadn't realized his horse had wandered on to the lake. Frightened, the horse had reared up, throwing him, and almost falling. But the animal managed to get his footing and make his way to safety, even if Robin hadn't.

Trying to catch himself, and from the force, Robin hadn't been able to hold on to his sword. He dropped it and it went sliding across the ice as well. And just when he thought things couldn't get any worse, he heard the sickening sound of the ice breaking beneath him.

"God's eyes, nay," he mumbled, just before getting sucked through the hole into the menacing water. The cold liquid filled Robin's ears as he went under, holding his breath and hoping not to drown. Thankfully, he managed to emerge from the water right where he fell in, and didn't get trapped beneath the frozen surface.

He'd succeeded in saving the maiden from her attackers, but now he was the one about to die. He needed help. Robin needed the girl's aid now, and he hoped to hell she'd give it. Frantically, he gripped the edges of the ice only managing to break off chunks, falling back into the water once more. His leg that had been stabbed by the ruffian hurt like the devil. The ice, as well as the water around him, turned bright red from the amount of blood he was losing fast.

When he looked through the blowing snow for the girl, his heart sank. He saw her running away instead of coming to help him. So much for gratitude. From now on, he was done rescuing damsels in distress. Hell, it wasn't worth it. He was also done drinking Mountain Magic with Highlanders, because that is what started this ball of destruction rolling, and it didn't look like it was going to stop any time soon.

"Dammit," he ground out, being pulled down by the weight of his wet cloak and clothes. The water was so cold that he could barely feel his limbs any longer, or he would have tried to remove his clothing. His eyes started to shut on their own. A voice in his head told him to fight to stay conscious. His life depended on it. If his eyelids closed now, they would stay that way forever.

With his hands on the edge of the ice once more, he tried to pull himself up to safety. Sadly, he slipped again, going under the water for a third time. It was becoming more than he could bear. This time, he felt as if it would be the last time he'd go under before he drowned. His new home would be the bottom of the lake instead of back at Shrewsbury Castle. Damn, why did his life have to end this way? He had hoped at least for a noble death, dying on the battlefield protecting the king. Not this stupid way to die. Such a waste of a life. His life. It was over.

This time when Robin made his way up to the surface it was different. To his surprise, through the water he saw an angel. At first, he figured it was the angel of death coming to claim him.

Through his blurred vision, he saw the glowing face of an ethereal being above him. This angel had long, flowing hair down to her shoulders, and was peering into the water directly at him. When his head broke the surface, he instantly realized his mistake. She was no angel at all. This was none other than the wench whose life he'd just saved. The same one he'd seen running away. Part of him was relieved he wasn't dead, but another part of him felt extremely angry. He supposed guilt ate away at the wench and she'd had a change of heart to help him after all. So be it.

The girl grabbed his arm, pulling him higher, partially out of the water. She lay flat on the ice above him with a rope tied around her waist. The rope seemed to trail over the lake behind her. When he noticed the horse and wagon at the shore, he realized her rope was tied to the wagon. In her hand was another rope with a loop tied on one end. The other end seemed to be around her waist as well.

"I'm going to put this around you to pull you up out of the water," she explained. "Please, work with me. It won't be easy. I can't do this without your help."

"I'll t-t-try," he said, his teeth chattering together as his body shivered beyond control. Damn, he'd always hated winter. Somehow the girl managed to get the rope around him, putting the loop over his head, fastening it under his arms.

"I c-c-can't f-f-f-feel my b-b-b-ody," he told her, not sure how he'd be able to help at all.

"Hold on. Don't give up. I'll have you out of here in a minute, I promise." Her voice was soothing and calm which made no sense at all to him in this harrowing situation.

If only he could believe the girl's words, mayhap he wouldn't feel so vulnerable or so doomed right now. But believing promises was for the weak or ignorant. As a warrior he'd learned that promises were naught but words of deception springing from the lips of those who meant to betray him. God's teeth, he hoped this wasn't true because this wench was all he had to link his hope to at the moment. His life was in her hands.

"H-h-how?" he asked, wanting to know her plan. After all, he had no strength to pull himself up, and the girl was too small and weak to do it by herself. Regrets filled him for not leaving the Horn and Hoof sooner and for not traveling with his guards or squire. Regrets that would not change the past, nor promise his future.

"Don't worry. Just hold on to me and do not let go until we reach the shore. Understand?"

"R-r-reach the s-s-s-hore?" he asked in confusion, since none of this made any sense to him right now in his clouded state of mind. The fake angel's words were all he had to go on, and he hoped to hell it was enough. Hope. That was no better than a promise. It was also a word he never used since he didn't believe in miracles, even though a miracle was what he needed right now.

Then, to his surprise, the girl whistled and shouted over her shoulder at the horse.

"Gah! Go. Make haste, Harriet," she called out, calling the horse by name. He honestly thought it was all a bit foolish until the damned animal actually started to move forward slowly, taking the wagon as well as both of them with it.

Robin felt himself quickly slipping from consciousness and fought like hell to keep his eyes open. Her crazy plan was working! Mayhap the girl was really an angel after all. The horse slowly pulled the girl backward over the ice, her body sliding toward the shore. Since the girl had tied the end of his rope around her as well, his body was lifted from the water. His full chest rested on the ice now, his arms grasping hers as best he could.

Sadly, his fingers were so numb that his hold started to slip.

"Nay! Hold on to me," she commanded. "If you let go, there is no way you'll ever leave this water. We might both break through the ice, and I assure you, I am not ready to die yet. You saved my life from those ruffians, now you have to help me save yours. Do you hear me? Answer me!" she shouted. "I asked you. Do you hear me, Knight?"

Her words were gruff, forceful, and demanding, jolting him out of the peaceful slumber trying to consume him. As she shouted at him, it quickly brought him back to consciousness and the matter at hand. In this state, he almost found himself afraid to defy her, since she seemed so determined and angry at the same time.

"Y-y-y-yes. I hear y-you," he answered in a mere whisper. He somehow managed to tighten his grip on her arms.

Then, thankfully, his wet body sloshed totally out of the hole and he was dragged across the ice along with the girl. He and his heavy, wet clothes slid across the frozen surface of the water, being pulled by the horse back to the shore.

The sound of a barking dog split his head, making his brain hurt worse than his wound. He and the girl made it to safety, although he never would have believed this would happen. Mayhap his disbelief in miracles was unwarranted after all.

Immediately, Griffin ran up to him and started licking his face.

"Don't do that, dog! Your tongue might freeze to his face," the wench yelled at his hound. She got to her feet and ran over to stop the horse from pulling them farther. "You need to get up," she told Robin, hurrying over to him and putting her shoulder under his arm to assist him. "You'll ride in the back of the wagon. I will take you to the monastery, out of this storm where I can tend to your wounds. We will get through this, and everything will be all right. Things from now on are only going to get better."

She was bossy and commanding for a woman, and seemed to like to talk a lot. But he was in no shape or position to deny the help of anyone right now. All he wanted was to feel his limbs again. She helped him to stand. It was a struggle to walk, but somehow the girl managed to take him over to the back of the wagon. It took all his strength and focus just to walk the few steps, since his legs were too stiff and frozen to bend. He collapsed into the wagon, glad to feel something solid beneath him. The wench quickly lifted his legs and pushed them inside the wagon as well. Her fingers accidentally dug into his wound and he cried out.

"Oh, no! I'm sorry," she told him, looking at the blood—his blood on her hand as she held it up to her face. "It seems that the wound on your leg is worse than I thought." She leaned over to inspect the wound. "I'll have to do something about it now. It won't wait until we get to the monastery."

The next thing Robin knew, the girl was ripping away the bottom of her gown.

"Lie down," she commanded. "I'm going to bind your leg to slow down the flow of blood."

"Hell, don't bother. I think the blood is frozen in my veins," he grunted.

"Hush, and let me help you." She put her hand on his shoulder, pushing slightly.

When he did lie back, Griffin jumped into the wagon with him. The dog settled down next to him, whining and resting his chin on Robin's chest.

"I'm going to wrap your wound for now. When we get out of this storm, I'll administer herbs to aid the healing," explained the girl.

All Robin could do was nod. He heard a strange tapping noise and realized it was his teeth chattering in his head.

Staring up at the snow blowing around them, he still wasn't convinced he wouldn't die before they even reached shelter.

"I've tied your horse to the wagon, so it'll follow us," she explained, jumping out of the back of the cart and stopping. "You're shivering," she said, reaching over and yanking his wet cloak from him. Then she took off her own cloak and placed it over him for warmth.

"Th-th-thank you," he managed to whisper.

"What's your name?" she asked curiously as she closed up the back of the wagon.

"R-R-Robin," he told her.

"I'm Sage," she replied, picking up a basket of herbs from the ground and placing it in the back of the cart with him. "We'll go now."

"W-w-wait," he said, making her stop in her tracks.

"What is it?" she asked.

"My s-s-sword," he managed to say. He didn't want to leave without it. A knight without his sword was vulnerable and useless. He needed his sword, even if he couldn't swing it right now to ward off a flea.

"Oh, yes. I believe you lost it by the shore when you were fighting my attackers." She turned to face the water. Then she lifted her gloved hand to shade her eyes to look for it through the blowing snow. "I think I see it," she said into the wind.

In a flash, she'd retrieved it and was back with it, placing it next to him in the wagon. As she looked over the side of the cart he could see her pale green eyes. The wind blew her long, strawberry-blonde locks up in the air around her. Her cheeks were so red and rosy that he wasn't sure she hadn't been bitten by the frost.

"Your hands. They're so cold that they're beginning to turn blue," she said, removing her oversized gloves that were more like mittens that trailed all the way up to her elbows. "Here.

Wear these." She shoved his frozen hands into her warm gloves, and already he felt the feeling returning to his fingers from her body heat still clinging to the insides of her gloves.

"S-S-Sage," he repeated her name, trying his hardest to smile.

"Robin," she answered, her eyes interlocking with his.

That's the last thing he remembered before his eyes closed and he fell into a dream world where fires burned hot and the warm cider flowed freely in front of a raging hearth. In his mind, the warmth of his beautiful angel named Sage was pressed up close to his body. In his dream, he held her in his arms, never wanting to let this beautiful, wonderful woman go.

CHAPTER 3

"Someone help me!" cried Sage, as she barreled into the courtyard of St. Erasmus Monastery, stopping the horse and quickly climbing out of the wagon. "I have a wounded and half-frozen man who needs our aid."

"Sage, why are you yelling?" Brother Pascal, the elderly abbot of the monastery, ran out of the chapter house, followed by several other monks. The man hurried over to the wagon, pulling the hood of his dark cloak over his head to protect him from the winter storm. Another door opened across from them. This was the building where the nuns lodged. St. Erasmus was a double monastery that housed both monks and nuns, who shared the adjoining commodities as well as the church. Together they worked side-by-side as a community, growing food, herding sheep, and providing services and care for the poor and to those in need.

Sage ran to the back of the wagon, removing the cross-board. "This man saved my life, but fell through the ice doing it," she explained quickly. "He also has a sword wound on his leg. He needs immediate care."

"Sage, where are your cloak and gloves?" scolded Sister Alberta, hurrying over with several nuns in her wake. The plump woman hid her hands under her cloak for warmth.

"I gave them to the knight," said Sage with a nod, noticing the man was no longer moving. His eyes were closed and she prayed he wasn't already dead. "His name is Sir Robin, but that is all I know about him."

Robin finally groaned and stirred slightly, opening his eyes partially and then closing them once again. Sage's heart jumped in her chest. She let out a deep sigh when she thankfully realized that the knight still lived. His dog jumped up, wagging his tail and barking at the monks and nuns.

"What's this?" asked the abbot, backing away, seeming leery of the dog.

"He's the knight's hound. He's friendly and won't hurt you," she said, scrambling up into the back of the wagon. "Please, someone help me get Sir Robin to the infirmary, quickly. He has lost a lot of blood and is nearly frozen to death. He keeps slipping in and out of consciousness. I sadly fear for the worst."

Sage helped to drag Robin's cold body to the end of the wagon, where the monks picked him up to carry him inside.

"Sage, he doesn't look good," whispered Sister Alberta, as the men headed across the courtyard carrying Sir Robin. The other nuns agreed. "I'm not sure how much we'll be able to do for him. Do not get your hopes up, my dear."

"We've got to save him," she told them, feeling anxiety coursing through her. She wrapped her arms around herself, feeling the cold more than ever now. "You are nuns. Please, pray for him if nothing else. It is imperative that this man does not die."

"Sage, you are a healer," said another nun, Sister Helen.

"You should know better than us that this man is nearly dead." She shot a worried glance at Sister Alberta.

"She's right, my dear," said the older nun. "We will do what we can, but God has a plan for everyone. Mayhap this man is supposed to die at this time."

"Nay!" cried Sage. "Don't say that. I cannot allow him to die. He risked his life to save me and I will return the favor or die trying, I swear." She reached over and rubbed her hand over the dog's head. The hound still stood on the wagon and cuddled up to her, already making her feel warmer.

"Then get your bag of healing herbs," said Sister Alberta with a sigh. She looked back over to the monks. "Once he's inside, strip him down and get those wet clothes off of him right away," she called out. "Sister Beatrice, bring more blankets to the infirmary. Quickly. We have no time to lose." The small group of nuns hurried after the monks.

Sage collected the basket of winter herbs from the back of the wagon, and ran behind the others. The mangy mutt followed closely at her heels. Tears filled her eyes. It was not Sir Robin's destiny to leave this world today. Nay, he couldn't perish this way. She wouldn't let that happen. Sage had to keep this man from dying and was determined that is what she'd do. Not only because he saved her life, but even more importantly, because she didn't want to be blamed for a man's death.

Not again.

Robin drifted off to the place where the sun shone brightly and a soft breeze kissed his face like the gentle touch of a lover. He couldn't remember where he'd been and had no idea where he was right now. All he knew was that it was warm here. And peaceful. Yes, that was all that mattered.

But things changed quickly when he felt the jaws of a beast sinking into his leg. He tried to look down, but couldn't turn his head. Then he tried to yell, but the words wouldn't come. Just the pain. The never-ending pain.

His eyelids flickered open and he screamed out, trying to brush away the beast with his arm.

"Keep him still," came the shrewd voice of a woman.

"We're doing our best to hold him down," came a male voice next.

That's when he saw the fire on the hearth next to him. He lay atop a table while two monks held his arms, and another two his legs.

"What the hell is going on?" he managed to grind out through gritted teeth.

"Please refrain from swearing in front of the monks and nuns."

He turned to see who was speaking, his eyes finally focusing on the face of his angel. But that thought quickly fled his mind when biting pain coursed through his leg once again.

"There. That should do it." The girl held up a needle with thread leading down to his leg. She took a pair of shears and snipped the thread loose.

"What in God's name are you doing?" he asked, biting back the pain.

"Please, Sir Robin. No blasphemy," scolded a nun.

"Let me go! Release me, I say."

The girl nodded and the monks all released him, quickly stepping back.

Robin pushed up to a sitting position. The action caused his head to spin. When he looked down he saw the stitches in his thigh. He sat there basically naked, covered only by his braies.

"Y-you stitched me up?" he asked, trying to clear his head

and figure out what the hell had happened. He vaguely remembered saving a damsel in distress, but the details of what followed after that were still a bit fuzzy.

"You were hurt warding off my attackers," said the girl, applying a cream to his leg. "Then you fell through the ice. Don't you remember?"

"The ice," he repeated, his body wracked with a shiver just from the thought. "Aye. I remember the cold water. How could I forget that?" He narrowed his eyes and stared at her. "I also seem to remember you running away instead of helping me, right after I saved your hide."

The girl stood up wiping her hands on a towel, scowling at him. "In case you've forgotten, I was the one who pulled you from the freezing water and saved your life. I brought you here to the monastery and stitched you up so you wouldn't die."

"Oh." His thoughts flooded his mind and he realized it was true. "That's right." He cleared his throat. "Thank you," he said, looking down at the floor. Then he lay back down, closing his eyes, trying to breathe away the pain. Suddenly, he remembered something. "Griffin!" he shouted, bolting back up to a sitting position, wincing when the stitches yanked at his skin.

"Don't move so quickly or you'll break open the sutures," warned the girl, quickly inspecting his leg again. She grabbed a long cloth and wound it around his leg to cover the wound.

"My dog," he said. His gaze scanned the room. "Where is he? Oh, God, please don't tell me he fell through the ice and died."

"Your dog? That is what you're worried about right now?" The wench had the audacity to raise a brow at him as if she thought he were crazy.

"Yes. My dog. Now tell me, where is he?"

She finished wrapping his leg and stood up. "Your dog, Sir

Robin, is just fine." She looked over at one of the monks and nodded. "Please, let him in now, Brother Isaac."

A monk opened a door and the big mutt bolted into the room, running right over to Robin. Robin's frown instantly turned into a smile.

"Griffin!" he shouted, so happy to see the dog. He held out his arms.

The hound jumped up and put his paws on the table, licking Robin on the face over and over again.

"All right. That's enough," said the girl, pulling the dog away. "Sir Robin, I've stitched, dressed, and wrapped your wound, and now you need to rest." She covered him with a blanket and turned to go.

"Wait," he called out. "What is your name?" he asked her, sitting up once more. The blanket slid down, exposing his bare chest.

"What?" She looked at him oddly and blinked several times in succession. "I told you my name at the lake. You really don't remember?"

"I'm sorry. There is a lot right now that is still hazy to me. I've been through a harrowing incident, you realize. You can't really expect me to remember something like a name at a time like this." He brushed back his long hair, moving it out of his eyes.

"You've been through a lot?" she asked, her tone telling him that she was perturbed by his comment for some reason. "Sir Robin, I remembered your name, even though I've been through just as much or even more than you today. If I must remind you, I was attacked by three men, not to mention at risk of losing my life a second time when I pulled you from the icy water. And I gave you my cloak and gloves, exposing my bare skin to the elements of nature. Yet, you think remembering my name is naught but a trivial thing?"

Egads, the wench was bold to talk to him, a noble, in this manner. Plus, she was rambling on again, her words all jumbling his brain. He noticed all the nuns and the monks staring at him, making him feel worthless. He didn't want the girl to outshine him right now. Plus, he didn't want to seem disrespected. For his sake, he needed to remember her blasted name, and he needed to do it fast. As hard as he thought about it, he just couldn't remember. He saw her basket of herbs on the table, and for a mere second, he thought he remembered something. She was a healer and named after an herb. Or had he just dreamed that? Either way, he had to try.

"Of course, I remember your name," he told her, flashing a smile. His dog rested his chin on the edge of the table, looking up at him with sad eyes that seemed to say even he was disappointed in Robin. All the nuns and monks in the room stood silent, staring at him. Well, he was definitely not cold anymore. Now, his embarrassment made him feel as if he were on fire.

"Really," she said, more of a statement than a question. She crossed her arms over her chest. "Then tell me, what is my name, Sir Robin?"

"You—you were named after an herb," he said, to test the waters to see if he was right.

"Yes, that's right," she said with a nod. "Which one?"

"Which one?" he asked, chuckling lowly, trying to remember some of the damned herbs that his cousin Rook's wife, Rose, grew in her garden. Parsley. No, that couldn't be it. Mint. Nay, that would be stupid. And it certainly wasn't chives. There must be an herb that sounded like the name of a girl—he just had to remember it. Then, it magically popped into his head. He petted his dog and smiled widely. "Your name, my dear, is Rosemary."

He could tell by the scowl on her face and the low whispers of the nuns that he'd guessed incorrectly. He was about to say

Basil, even though that was a boy's name, when she answered for him.

"Sage," she told him. "My name is Sage Hillock. It's really not that hard to remember."

"Sage," he repeated softly, still petting his dog, focusing on the animal instead of her disappointed face. "That's right. That's what I meant to say."

Silence filled the room, making him feel even worse now. He'd just lied in front of so many nuns and monks and he was sure they knew it.

"No more talking. You need to rest and heal," said one of the nuns, thankfully coming to his rescue. "Get some sleep."

"Sleep?" he asked, looking downward. "On a table? Really?"

"Nay, silly, you'll get a bed in the infirmary that's just through that door." Sage walked back to him. Even though she didn't seem to want to do it, she held out her arm. "I'll help you to walk since I just stitched up your leg and I don't want you to break the sutures open."

"I don't—" Robin was about to tell her he didn't need or want her help. After all, he was a knight. A man. He didn't accept help from a mere commoner, especially not a woman. But when he looked down into her eyes, all thought scattered. He felt as if he were looking into the eyes of an angel, for real this time.

Sage Hillock was so beautiful and smelled like sweet flowers. Or mayhap herbs. Her eyes were clear and pale green, reminding him of the sea. He saw a deep sadness lodged within them. He also felt as if this woman was still scared, even though she was in sanctuary here at the monastery where no bandits could touch her. He didn't understand why she didn't seem more relieved.

"Yes, of course," he said, lowering his feet to the ground, standing and leaning on the girl as they headed to the adjoining room. Her body heat against him felt delicious. He would normally be having lusty thoughts, being so close to such a beautiful woman, but instead he felt the girl's worried nature and this concerned him. Somehow, he felt as if she held fear that wasn't for his life but for her own. It made no sense at all, since she was perfectly safe now.

"What is worrying you?" he asked, hobbling to the infirmary, leaning on her for support.

"Nothing," she snapped, shutting him out.

He needed to try another approach. "I'm surprised you were out picking herbs by yourself. Especially on such a cold winter day."

"I'm a healer. It's what I do. It doesn't matter what the weather is, I still need my supplies."

"I see, Winter Sage," he said with a chuckle at his own jest, but she didn't share in the humor.

"I don't find this funny," she retorted.

"I just find it odd that you still seemed so scared, yet you are safely tucked away in a sanctuary here."

"Sir Robin, I am not a noble with an entourage of soldiers around me at all times, like you."

"Yes, I had so many soldiers traveling with me to help me fight off your attackers, didn't I?"

They entered the infirmary and headed to an unoccupied bed.

"That's right, you were alone," she said in thought, stopping at the side of the bed and taking her arm from around him. She looked up into his eyes. "Why were you traveling alone, my lord?"

"I—I wasn't. Not really," he said, not wanting to admit to doing such a stupid thing as staying with the Highlanders drinking, and sending his men ahead of him. "I had Griffin with me." He plopped down on the bed and groaned, his hand going to his wound.

"Don't touch it." She bent over and pushed his hand to the side. "It'll heal faster if you leave it alone."

"I've had wounds before, my dear. I am a warrior. A knight. I assure you, I know what to do," he said, feeling belittled by her words. "I've fought in King Edward's army many times on the battlefield. Neither is this the first time I've been stitched back up, you realize."

"Interesting," she said, staring down at his bare chest as she handed him the blanket once again. "I didn't notice any other scars on your body when we stripped you down and washed you."

His eyes shot up to her. He wasn't sure if he felt more violated that she'd seen and washed his half naked body, or that she was seeing through his lies once more. True, he'd fought for the king on more than one occasion. But fortunately for him, he'd only had stitches once before. And of course, she hadn't seen the scar because it was still covered.

"You act as if you don't believe me," he said, challenging the wench.

"Mayhap I don't." Her nose went up in the air. "After all, you did lie about knowing my name before."

"I'll have you know that I do have a scar. It's on my ass. Did you want me to show you?" He leaned to one side and started to pull his braies down. The nuns gasped and covered their eyes. The abbot hurried over and stepped between Robin and Sage.

"There will be no need for that, Sir Robin," said the monk. He held out his arm. "Brother Francis, quickly, bring me a robe for Sir Robin."

Sir Francis hurried over with the robe folded neatly in his arms, giving it to Robin.

"You can wear this for now, Sir Robin," said the abbot. "The nuns will have your own clothes cleaned, dried, and returned to you soon."

"Thank you," said Robin, smiling wryly at Sage who still looked angry with him. "When is the next meal? I'm famished."

"Don't worry, you will be fed," said Sage.

"By your hand?" he asked, toying with the girl. He threw her a seductive glance but she didn't seem to like his suggestion.

"Nay, I will be leaving the monastery. And unless you feel too weak, I'm sure you are capable of lifting bread and ale to your own mouth, Sir Noble."

"Leaving?" asked Robin, his curiosity piqued. "Where are you going?"

"I don't live here, only work here on occasion, as well as use the herb garden," she told him. "I'll be heading home, of course."

"But we're in the middle of a winter storm," he pointed out, suddenly feeling as if he wanted the girl to stay. "Besides, it's not safe out there. Your attackers might return."

"He's right, Sage," said one of the nuns.

"I agree with Sister Bernadine," said another. "You must stay, at least until the storm lets up."

"Yes, Sisters Bernadine and Alberta are correct," said the abbot. "You must stay."

"Nay. I can't stay. I must get home immediately. It's important." Sage told them, wringing her hands together.

"You're frightened," said Robin, watching her. "What is so important at home that you'd risk going out in a storm by yourself?"

"I'm not frightened." Her hands slowly fell to her sides. "And nothing any of you can say will keep me from leaving."

She turned to go, making Robin extremely uncomfortable. If he could follow her right now, he would, but that wasn't going to happen. He was lightheaded, and knew if he didn't rest, he'd most likely burst open his stitches.

"Then at least take Griffin with you," Robin called out, causing the girl to stop at the door and turn around.

"Griffin?" she asked.

"My hound," said Robin with a nod. "He'll protect you. After all, you saw how he acted around your attackers. I'd feel better if you at least took him with you."

The dog looked up with sad eyes and whined.

"I don't think so," she said, but Robin wouldn't listen.

"Go on, Griffin. Protect Rosemary—I mean Sage. Watch over her and keep her safe. I'll see you again soon."

As if the dog really understood him, it turned and trotted over to Sage, sitting obediently at her side.

"Well, if you insist," she said, reaching down to pet the dog.

She started out the door and Robin stopped her once again.

"Sage," he said, watching as she looked over her shoulder at him and smiled.

"Yes?"

"Bring back my hound in one piece."

She frowned.

"And I'll want to see both of you back here safely, because if you don't return, you know I'll come after you."

He must have said the right thing at last because she smiled at him before heading out the door.

God's eyes, he hoped she'd return with his dog. But more than just wanting to see his dog again, Robin couldn't stop the longing inside him to see Sage Hillock, his healer, his savior, his angel, once again.

CHAPTER 4

Sage left the monastery, taking her horse and wagon with her. Robin's dog rode in the wagon with his paws up on the back of her seat. She figured she would have had a better chance to outrun men who might be trying to kill her if she had taken just the horse and not the wagon, but she didn't have a choice.

Now that she realized her life was in danger, she had to protect her siblings. Her plan was to load them into the cart and take them back to the monastery with her until she could decide how to permanently protect them. She only hoped her attackers hadn't already been to her home. Fear coursed through her, not wanting her brothers or sister to be in danger because of her. Her life was starting to feel like a nightmare that wouldn't end. Times like this were when she missed her mother and father the most. Sage was in charge of her family now, and also had to support her siblings by doing her healings and selling herbs. Since the death of the nobleman a fortnight ago, things were going badly. Trying to clear her name and also support and take care of her siblings was becoming more of a burden than she could bear.

"Get down, Griffin," she scolded the dog as they headed out through the gates of the monastery. Thankfully, the storm had stopped and the wind died down enough to make the trip tolerable.

Griffin barked and moved around the back of the wagon, looking over one side and then the other, as if he were keeping watch. Sage did feel safer with Robin's dog along, and was glad that Robin suggested she take Griffin with her. That showed that he cared. Mayhap he wasn't just a self-centered nobleman like the rest of the ones she'd met.

Animals were usually good judges of character when it came to people. Griffin seemed devoted to Robin and even helped fight off Sage's attackers. She hoped she wouldn't need protection again, but if so, just having the hound with her eased her mind.

Driving as fast as she dared in the snow, she approached her home quickly. Shock set in and horror filled her by what she saw. Flames leaped from the roof of her house and smoke filled the air.

"Nay!" she screamed, stopping the horse and jumping out of the wagon. Griffin leaped over the side, running along with her. "Oscar! Noel!" she called out for her brothers, stopping at the door to the small cottage, feeling the intense heat that kept her from getting closer. She pulled her hood tightly around her head and lowered her face and made her way to the burning building anyway, because she had no choice. Her siblings were inside and she had to save them.

Since Sage wore gloves, she reached out to open the door, willing to risk her life and do whatever it took to save her siblings. Just as the door started to open, she heard a loud noise and the roof collapsed, forcing her to jump back or get hit by the burning boards. To her utter shock and horror, the house fell at her feet into a pile of rubble, continuing to burn.

"Nay!" Her heart raced and lodged in her throat. This couldn't be happening. She was too late. "Amira!" she shouted, picturing her sister of twelve years being crushed to death under the weight of the fallen roof. Tears streamed down her cheeks as she attempted to enter the burning ruins anyway, her only focus on saving her sister and brothers.

Griffin shot forward, grabbing her sleeve, pulling her away and not letting her enter the burning building.

"Nay. Let go of me! Leave me be!" She tried to pry the teeth of the hound off of her sleeve, but the dog was large and very strong. She wasn't able to do it. Griffin yanked her further away from the fire. Sage was pulled along with him. She was too weak to fight off the dog. Her body trembled with fear and her knees knocked together. Sage stumbled and fell, hitting the snowy ground hard. Weeping hysterically, she hid her face in her hands, crying so much that she thought she'd retch. She had been too late to save her siblings, and now they were gone. No one could survive being inside the burning house and having it fall atop them. Her attackers had now killed off her family in their attempts to get to her.

"Nay! This isn't fair," she screamed aloud, still crying. All will to continue to live, left her. This was her fault. All she wanted to do now was to die along with her siblings, because she would never be able to live without them. Her guilt already consumed her, making her feel like a horrible person for not checking on them sooner.

Griffin started barking furiously, dragging her from her guilt and pity.

"Quiet," she shouted, sniffling, not even looking at the dog. The dog continued to bark.

She finally looked up to see the hound facing the creek,

watching something intently. Then he ran back to her, grabbing the hem of her gown in his teeth, pulling at her once again.

"Why don't you leave me alone?" she wailed, trying to push the dog away. She wiped at her tears with the back of her hand. "My life is over. I can't go on without my brothers and sister. This is horrible and I cannot believe what's happened."

The dog barked through his teeth now, as he tugged urgently at her skirt. The next time she looked up she saw two figures coming toward her from the creek. The air was smoky and she could only see shadows. At first she thought it might be her attackers returning. She jumped to her feet and yanked her dagger from her waist belt. "I'll kill you. I'll kill you all for what you did," she said, no longer caring what happened to her, but wanting revenge for the deaths of her siblings. These men would now pay with their lives.

Then, a miracle happened again that day. As the figures came closer, she realized it was three people instead of two. The tallest one was carrying someone small in his arms. Suddenly, she knew who they were, and they weren't here to kill her. Her heart sped up and hope filled her being as she called out.

"Oscar? Is that you?" she asked, coughing from the smoke.

"Sage?" came a girl's voice, as one of the figures ran toward her. The smoke cleared enough for her to see her sister, as well as her sixteen-year-old brother Oscar, carrying her youngest brother Noel, who was only six.

"Amira!" cried Sage, running to her sister, gathering her in her arms and pulling her close to her in a hug. Sage wept with tears of joy now.

"Sister, we're so glad to see you," said Oscar, coughing from the smoke as well.

Sleepy little Noel looked up and rubbed his eyes. "Is that Sage?"

"It sure is," said Oscar, shifting Noel to one arm and hugging Sage with his other.

"Thank God you are all alive!" gasped Sage. "When I saw the house on fire, I thought you three were dead." She still felt her body shaking, but now it wasn't from fear. Now it was from happiness and excitement.

"We would have died if we hadn't been out ice fishing when the house caught on fire," explained Oscar.

"What happened?" asked Sage. "Who did this?" Part of her knew the answer but she needed to be sure.

"We don't know who they were, but when we noticed the flames, we saw three men on horses by the house," her sister told her.

"I figured they started the fire," said Oscar. "That's when I knew we were in danger and had to hide rather than try to save our home."

"That was the right move," Sage assured him.

Griffin barked and Noel jerked, hugging Oscar tighter.

"I'm scared," said the little boy.

"Oh, don't be frightened, Noel," Sage told him in a calming voice. "That's just Griffin." She ran her hand over the dog's head. "He won't hurt you. He's here to protect me."

"You have a dog?" asked Oscar, looking at the beast cautiously. "Where did you get him?"

"Oh, he's not mine. Griffin is Sir Robin's dog," she tried to explain, but could see her siblings didn't understand.

"Who is Sir Robin?" Amira slowly reached out and petted the hound. Griffin licked her face and made her laugh.

"I want to pet the doggy too," said Noel, suddenly becoming brave when he saw what his sister was doing.

"All right, you can pet Griffin, but be careful." Oscar put

Noel on the ground. The dog ran over to lick the little boy's face as well. The hound standing on all four legs was as tall as Noel. The boy was knocked to the ground from the huge dog just pressing up against him.

When Sage was sure Noel would start crying, her brother surprised her and started laughing instead. It did her heart good to see and hear this.

"Oh, it is so good to see all of you." Sage scooped up Noel and kissed him on the cheek.

It was still smoky and they occasionally coughed, but being together was all that mattered right now.

"Sage, when we saw the men, Oscar made us stay by the lake and hide in the brush," said her sister.

"He told us to be quiet," added Noel.

"Well, that was a smart thing to do." Sage let out a deep sigh. "Those same men tried to kill me earlier today."

"They did? Why? Who are they? How did you escape? Are you all right? Did they hurt you?" asked Oscar, running all his questions together at once.

"I have a lot to tell you," said Sage. "But I am fine. A knight named Sir Robin was passing by with Griffin when I was attacked." She nodded at the dog. "They saved me, but then Sir Robin fell through the ice and I ended up having to save him."

"Sage, we need to talk," said Oscar in a serious tone. "I'm not sure what is going on, but I don't like it. We were all almost killed today. So were you. Why are our lives in danger?"

"I agree, we must talk and we will. In time. Right now, we need to find a safe place to go," said Sage. "I will tell you everything later, but first, we need to leave here and get to safety. There is no telling when or if those men will return."

"I'm scared," said Amira, clinging to Sage.

"Don't worry, sister. We'll protect you," Oscar told her,

always acting as the protector of the family since the death of both of their parents.

"Everything will be fine. I promise," said Sage, trying not to show her siblings how upset she really was right now, or how much she wanted to believe her own words, even if she didn't.

"Where will we live?" asked Noel, looking at the house with a pout on his face.

The rest of them turned and stared at the burning pile of rubble. The flames were dying down now, but their home was demolished and certainly nothing inside would be salvageable.

"Well, I don't suppose we can live here anymore," mumbled Oscar. "Plus, it would take too long to try to rebuild the house. Especially in winter."

"And those men might return," added Amira.

"Nay, we can't stay here," agreed Sage, staring at the house, holding Noel in one arm and smoothing back her sister's hair with the other. "We've lost everything," she said, shaking her head. "However, we still have each other, and that is all that matters. There is no sense staying here any longer. We need to leave now."

"I'm cold. And hungry," said Noel, leaning his cheek against her chest.

Oscar's eyes met Sage's in silent concern. What could she possibly say that would be of any benefit or comfort to any of them right now?

"We'll go to the monastery," she decided. "We will stay there until we find a new home."

"We will?" asked Amira.

"Will the monks and nuns let us do that?" questioned Oscar.

"Well, I don't see why not," said Sage, turning and walking to the wagon, still holding on to her brother and sister. "I mean, they take in nobles and travelers all the time. How is this any different? The nuns and monks also administer to those who have been wounded or are ill."

"But we're not noble, and neither are we wounded or ill," said Oscar under his breath.

"Nay, we're not." Sage shrugged. "But we are in need, and I'm sure Sister Alberta will not turn us away."

"We have to tell her that those bad men burned our home," said Amira.

"Nay." Sage stopped dead in her tracks and turned to look at her sister. "No one is going to say a word about this to anyone at the monastery. Do you understand?"

"Why not?" asked Oscar.

"It will only bring trouble. If anyone thinks we're the cause of danger at their door, they will turn us away for good." Sage truly hoped this wouldn't happen, but it was a possibility.

"Then what will we do?" asked Amira.

"We'll take one day at a time, and in the meantime, be quiet about what really happened," said Sage.

"Aren't they going to wonder why we're there and not at home?" asked Oscar. "We need to tell them something."

"Let me handle that." Sage took the responsibility on her own shoulders. "I'll do all the talking. Now, not a word about what really happened to anyone. Not until I figure out what to do about this. Do you all understand?"

"All right," said Noel, yawning and resting his head on Sage's shoulder. His eyes started to close.

"I understand," said Amira.

"Oscar?" Sage waited for her brother to agree, knowing that he wouldn't.

"It's not right to lie to monks and nuns," protested Oscar. "And it's not right to ask us to do it."

"We're not lying. Holding back information is not the same

as a fib." Sage wasn't so sure of this, but she needed time to think without alarm being raised at the monastery.

"I don't agree," said Oscar. "I will let you handle this. For now. But don't think I am going to cover this all up and pretend like it never happened. We need help, Sage. We're in danger."

"Everything will be fine. Leave it to me." Sage didn't want her eldest brother scaring their younger siblings. Having them crying about things would only make this worse. "Everyone, get into the back of the wagon. There is a blanket back there you can cover up with to stay warm and dry." Sage laid her sleeping brother down in the wagon. Amira climbed in and snuggled up next to him, pulling a blanket over them both. Griffin jumped in and lay down, resting his chin on Noel's chest.

"I like you, Griffin," said Noel, in a sleepy voice with his eyes still closed.

"Me too," said Amira, putting her arm around the dog.

When her siblings were secure, Sage turned to find Oscar already sitting on the bench seat of the wagon with the reins in his hand.

"Oscar? What are you doing?"

"I'll drive," he told her.

"All right," she said, not wanting to fight. She climbed up and sat next to him. As they pulled away, she looked over her shoulder, watching as the snow started to fall on the ruins of their home, helping to diminish the smoldering rubble. "I still can't believe our home and everything we own is gone," she said, shaking her head, feeling a deep sense of fear invade her body. They had no parents, and now no home. Why did life keep getting more difficult? This wasn't the way things were supposed to be.

They rode in silence for a while, then Oscar spoke in a low

voice. "What's really going on, Sage? What is it that you're not telling us?"

"What do you mean?" she asked, not sure what to say at a time like this.

"You said someone tried to kill you. Now, they tried to kill the rest of us, too. Why?"

"Let me worry about this, Oscar. You just watch over Amira and Noel."

"Nay, I will not just let this go!" Anger filled his words. "I am six-and-ten years of age now, Sister. I'm old enough for you to confide in. I want to help. So, tell me. What really happened and why do these men want us dead?" His eyes flashed over to her, half closed in suspicion and determination. "Tell me the truth. And remember, I'll know if you're lying."

Sage glanced to the back of the wagon to see the others, including the dog, fast asleep. She let out a deep sigh. "I'm sorry, Oscar. It's all my fault that we are in deadly trouble."

"How so?"

"One of my healing potions didn't work the way it should have," she told him. "I mean... I think that's what happened. The whole thing is kind of foggy to me. I don't remember giving him too much, but instead of my potion healing a nobleman, it accidentally killed him instead. And now, because of it, I have doomed my entire family. I honestly don't know how to fix my mistake."

"What herb did you use?" asked Oscar, knowing a little about healing, having helped her to collect herbs on many occasions.

"It was foxglove," she told him.

"Oh, Sage! You know mother told you to never use too much of that herb. It's too dangerous."

"It's only dangerous in large amounts. But I used only a small amount on Lord Burchard to treat his heart and his bad headaches, I swear. I've done this dozens of times and it always worked before."

"If so, then how do you know that is what killed him?"

"He had all the symptoms of an overdose of foxglove. Besides, Lord Burchard's steward dug through my healing bag when I wasn't looking and found the bottle of foxglove, nearly all gone. He made sure to show and tell everyone about it."

"Nearly gone? But you said you didn't use that much."

"I—I didn't think so." Sage brushed some stray hair from her eyes. "Now, I'm not sure. Oh, I don't know, Oscar," she said, shaking her head. "I can't think straight right now."

"I hope you weren't making any love potions, Sage. We don't want anyone accusing you of being a witch."

Sage was asked to make a love potion at Lord Burchard's castle, but thankfully she'd refused. "Nay. No worry of that, Oscar. Now, can we just focus on getting to safety and talk about all this later?"

"Of course we can." Her brother laid his hand on her arm. "I know you're a competent healer, Sage, and would never purposely do anything to harm a soul. I'm sure it was just fate that the man died and had nothing to do with your healing treatments. It was naught but an unfortunate coincidence, that's all."

"An unfortunate coincidence? A man is dead," she said, tears dripping down her cheeks. "He is gone, and I am being blamed."

"Yes, mayhap, but it wasn't your fault."

"If I was at fault, then I should be the one to die, but not you and innocent children." She looked back at her siblings once again.

"We'll get through this, Sage. "Don't be too hard on yourself."

Sage carried all the guilt of the world on her shoulders. It wasn't like her to be so careless with her potions. But then again, she had been so tired and upset after her parents died just six months ago, that she hadn't been sleeping well or making good decisions ever since then.

It was already dark when Sage arrived with her siblings back at the monastery. The gates were closed for the night. She had to make her presence known in order to get the monks to open the gates and let them enter.

"Sage? Is that you?" asked one of the monks, passing by with another monk at his side. Both of them had their hands folded in prayer. The monk cocked his head, looking at her in the dark.

"Yes, Brother Isaac, it's me. Please open the gate anon," Sage called out to him.

"Who is that with you?" asked the second monk, whose voice she recognized as Brother Francis.

"I have my siblings with me," Sage explained. "It is late and we need to get out of the cold. We need shelter for the night. Please, let us in."

"Of course," said Brother Isaac.

The two monks hurried over the snow-covered ground and slowly pulled open the heavy iron gates of St. Erasmus to give Sage passage.

"I'll take the horse and wagon to the stable," offered Brother Francis, once they were inside and the gates closed again.

"Thank you," said Sage, getting down from the bench seat of the wagon. "Can you also let the abbot know that my siblings will stay with me in the room I use while I'm here?"

"Of course," said the monk with a nod of his head.

"Oscar, you know where that room is," said Sage, since her siblings had visited her there several times when she stayed for weeks at a time to help plant or cultivate the herb garden. Sage also often stayed here for days at a time helping the nuns and monks with the injured who came to the monastery to be healed. She had a small room on the far side of the courtyard they let her use while she worked.

"Yes, I know it," said Oscar, waking up his siblings. He helped Amira to the ground and then picked up Noel who was still half-asleep. "Aren't you coming with us, Sage?"

"Nay," she said, petting the dog on the head. "I'm going to go to the kitchen to find some food for all of you to eat. But first, I need to stop by the infirmary to check on someone."

"We'll be waiting," said Oscar, heading across the courtyard with their siblings.

"Your help isn't needed in the infirmary tonight," Brother Francis told her. "Sir Robin is the only one in there right now, and he is sleeping."

"Still, I want to make certain his wound isn't still bleeding, or that he hasn't come down with a fever."

"I understand. Then, take a candle or torch with you," said the monk. "You don't want to stumble in the dark."

"Thank you," said Sage, heading for the infirmary with Griffin leading the way as if he knew where she meant to go. The dog sniffed the ground as if he were picking up Robin's scent.

Sage was concerned for her siblings, but before she tended to them, she needed to make certain Sir Robin was all right. Since the last lord's death, Sage's confidence had been shaken so badly that she no longer knew if she was even qualified to be called a healer.

The last thing she needed right now was for Sir Robin, another nobleman, to die.

CHAPTER 5

Robin stirred in his sleep, having a nightmare. He was fighting off the girl's attackers and then almost drowning all over again.

"Nay!" he cried out. His eyes snapped open. His heart raced but he found himself lying in a bed. Thankfully, it was only a dream and was over now. Falling through the ice earlier had been bad enough, but being saved by a girl made him feel worthless and weak. God's eyes, how had he ever gotten into such a situation? He only hoped word wouldn't get out about this. Hopefully, since monks had long periods each day of not talking, this secret would stay inside the walls of the monastery and go no further. If his cousin Rook ever found out, he'd tease Robin mercilessly until the day he died.

It took him a moment to realize exactly where he was. Then he remembered that he'd been brought to the monastery and his wound had been sewed up by the healer girl.

He heard a noise from the other end of the infirmary, and immediately was on alert. The room was dark, but light from the moon as well as the reflections off the snow filtered in through the window, making a slight haze around him. Once more he heard the strange tapping noise, and sprang up in bed, looking for his blade. He saw his weapon belt hanging on a nail on the wall. Slowly, he pushed up from the bed, not wanting to alert any attacker.

The stitches in his leg still felt like the jaws of death biting into his flesh, but he held in the groan lodged at the back of his throat. Creeping over to the wall, he slowly pulled his sword from the scabbard, hearing the pitter-patter of feet coming closer and closer.

Just as he turned with his blade in his hand, a strong force knocked him to the ground.

"Ooomph!" he cried out, as he lost his sword trying to catch himself to keep from falling on his hurt leg. With his back on the ground now, he felt something wet on his face. It was then that he realized it was his damned dog!

"God's teeth, Griffin, don't do that." He tried to push the huge hound away.

"Sir Robin? Is that you?" came a soft, feminine voice from behind the dog.

A slight glow spread through the room as someone lit the bedside candle that was perched atop the tall metal holder.

He sighed when he realized it was the girl. That is, the same girl who'd saved his life.

"Oh, it's you," he said, pushing up to a sitting position. "What brings you here this time of night?"

"Are you sleeping on the floor, Sir Robin?" she asked, stretching her neck to see him better. A bewildered look spread across her face. "Why don't you use the bed? After all, that is what it's here for."

"Yes, well, I happen to like the floor," he said, clearing his throat and pushing his dog away as he got up. "It's—it's better for my back."

She scrutinized him, taking a few steps closer. Her foot hit against his sword on the ground. She bent over and picked it up.

"Do you usually sleep with your sword?" she asked. "That's an odd thing to do. Especially in an infirmary inside a monastery. Do you see this place as some sort of threat?"

"Never mind that, and quit asking so many questions." Robin snatched the blade away from her, sticking it back into the scabbard hanging on the wall. "What is it you want? Why are you even here?"

The dog jumped up onto his bed and lay down.

"I came to check on your wound. I hope you haven't broken the sutures. You really should stay in the bed."

"I'm fine," he said with a shrug, sitting down on the bed and rubbing his hand through the dog's fur. "Egads, you stink."

"Pardon me?"

His head snapped around to find the girl staring at him. Her mouth turned down into a frown and her eyes were mere slits.

"Nay, not you. I was talking to the dog," he explained. "Why does he smell like—" Robin sniffed the dog and made a face. "Like a fire?"

"He does? Hmmm. That's interesting." She went over to her bag of healing herbs and opened it up, peering inside instead of looking at him when she spoke. "I guess I hadn't noticed."

He thought something seemed odd about all this. The wench acted too unconcerned and almost as if she were hiding something from him, but he couldn't be sure. Still, he didn't like that.

"How did your trip go?" he asked, digging for information.

"My trip?" She still didn't turn around.

"Yes. Your trip back home. I hope Griffin warded off any attackers you might have encountered."

"Oh, that. Nay, I didn't encounter any attackers, so the dog wasn't needed after all." She continued to dig through her bag.

"Come here," he said, still not believing a word she said.

She stopped what she was doing and slowly turned her head to look at him. "Yes? Is there something you need, Sir Robin?"

"There is. I need you to look at my leg." He pretended to rub it to get her to come closer to him.

"You did burst the stitches after all, didn't you?" she said in an accusing manner, laying her open bag of potions on the bed. "If you had slept in the bed instead of on the floor this wouldn't have happened," she scolded. When she moved nearer to inspect his leg, he reached out and grabbed her by the arm.

Her eyes shot up to his and then back down to her arm again. "What are you doing? Let go of me," she said in alarm. She had that same look of fear in her eyes as when he'd found her being attacked by the men on the road.

"Sorry," he said, quickly letting go, not meaning to frighten the girl. He leaned in closer and sniffed her. "Uh huh. Just as I thought. You smell like smoke too. Did something happen while you were gone?"

"I'd appreciate it if you stopped sniffing me, acting like an animal. Now, lie back and let me look at your wound."

"If you insist." He scooted backward. Griffin jumped off the bed.

"Have you had any side effects from the comfrey salve I used on your wound? The comfrey is good for healing skin, bruises, and even bones. However, it's not good on deep, open wounds, but yours wasn't that deep and I did sew it up, so it should be fine."

The girl talked so much that Robin couldn't get a word in even if he tried.

"Nay, no problems. Not really," he said, inspecting her bag as she peeked under the binding at his wound. "But I do have a murderous headache."

"What?" Her head snapped upward and he cursed himself inwardly for using the word murderous. He needed to be more sensitive around the girl after what she'd been through today.

"I probably got the headache from taking that plunge into the icy water. Mayhap you have something to cure it?"

"Let's focus on one thing at a time," she said, wrapping his leg back up. "To my surprise, your stitches look fine, even though I half expected to find your wound gaping open again. We'll have to watch for infection, so be sure to keep the wound wrapped up. I'll apply a poultice to it in the morning that will help with swelling. Now, I advise you to stay off the floor and sleep in the bed like everyone else so you don't injure yourself further."

"Everyone else?" he chuckled, pulling a bottle out of her bag. "And how does everyone else sleep?" he asked.

"Well, I don't suppose you'd know."

"How about some of this? Will this cure my headache?" he asked, holding up a bottle to the light of the candle. The bottle only had a little liquid left in it. "It looks like you use this one a lot. Foxglove," he said, reading the name written on the bottle.

Her eyes sprang open wide. "Nay! Don't touch that. Put that down." She grabbed it from him and stuck it back in the leather bag, pulling the entire thing over to her. "You shouldn't touch things that aren't yours and that you know nothing about." She held the damned bag to her chest as if she coveted it, or were trying to keep it from him for some reason.

"Is something upsetting you?" He could tell she was frightened and he didn't think it was because of what happened earlier with the attackers. Neither did he really think she feared him. After all, he'd saved her neck today, so why would he hurt her? But if she was truly scared, why would she have left the monastery on her own in the first place? None of this made any sense at all. She was such an odd girl. Nay, he decided. Something else was bothering her and he needed to find out what.

"Why would you ask me that?" She pulled the strings tightly on the bag, not looking at him again when she spoke. Her attitude was almost defensive.

"You were in such a hurry to get home, but yet you returned here so quickly. I am just trying to understand you, that's all."

"Since you'll most likely never see me again once you go back to Shrewsbury Castle, I see no need for you to understand me at all." She slipped the strap of her bag over her shoulder. "Now, you need rest in order to heal. And drink lots of fluids, too, to expel any toxins inside you." She nodded to a cup and decanter of water on the bedside table.

"I see," he said, a pause of silence between them. Hearing her say that he'd never see her again hit him hard. True, he was in a hurry to get home, but he wasn't in a hurry to leave Sage right now. He liked her. He wanted to get to know her better. After what they'd been through together in one day, he couldn't just leave her. Not now. He cleared his throat to get her attention and continued to speak. "Actually, I never properly thanked you for saving my life," he said, even though having a woman save his life was something he hoped never happened again.

"Oh, I quite remember you thanking me," she said, looking up at him shyly. Her long lashes curled upward, firelight dancing in the depths of her pale green eyes.

"I guess I don't remember, so I'll do it again," he told her. "I want to thank you for sewing me up and not letting me bleed to death." He nodded at his leg. Robin sat there wearing only his braies once again, never having donned the robe the monk's gave him.

"I was only doing my job," she said ever so softly. "And you should really put on the robe."

"I can't sleep in a robe. Normally, I sleep naked."

That got her attention. She stared at him for a moment and then quickly looked away as if perhaps she'd had an embarrassing thought.

"Well, there is no need to thank me again."

"But you saved my life, so just think of it as me paying back the favor."

Her cheeks as well as her lips were rosy. Her beauty was only enhanced in the play of the soft firelight against her smooth, creamy skin. Robin slowly reached out and took her hands in his. Then, before she could object, he leaned in and kissed her on the lips.

To his surprise, she didn't bite him or slap him or even push him away. She seemed to welcome his lips against hers. The kiss lingered and then ever so slowly, their lips parted. Robin felt his body warming from being so close to her. Wanting more, he leaned in for seconds, but to his dismay, she pulled her hands out of his grip and took a step back.

"Here, have some water." He saw the tip of her tongue dart out to touch her lips as she poured water for him rather than looking at him once again. Damn, he wanted to taste more of this beautiful woman. He didn't want her to leave. He had to think of some way to make her stay with him.

"Sage," he said.

"Yes?" she answered, putting down the decanter after having filled the cup.

"I-I'd like to invite you to return to Shrewsbury Castle with me."

"What?" She turned so quickly that she dropped the cup, spilling the water on the floor. "Why?"

"Well, I—I," He thought he had frightened her with his suggestion and didn't want her to think he was asking her to travel with him like a whore would a paying customer. Especially not after the kiss they'd just shared. "I don't have a healer at the castle and I'll need you to look after my wound until it's better."

Sage cocked her head and looked at him from the corner of her eye. "Why don't I believe that?" She bent over and retrieved the wooden cup.

"You don't believe that I want you to take care of me?"

"Nay, not that part." She refilled the cup with water. "The part that you don't have a healer at the castle. I mean, every castle has a healer. Don't they?"

"All right, I'll be honest with you. I don't know if I have a healer. But in case I don't, I'll need one."

"You don't know?" She squinted her eyes, looking at him as if she thought he were daft.

"Nay, I don't. I've just recently inherited the castle and haven't been there long. Since I haven't had need for a healer until now, I guess I just never thought to ask if I had one."

"Still, you are lord of the castle," said Sage, handing him the cup of water. "I thought you'd know these things. Isn't that part of your job?"

"I suppose it is." He took the cup and raised it to his mouth, swallowing down water, wishing it was whisky right now. "You see, I left for the Highlands so quickly, and I haven't been back for over a week now. Therefore, what I say is true. I don't know if I have a healer at the castle or not."

"Well, I'm not sure if I should go with you," she said, looking down and playing with her fingers the way she seemed to do whenever she was concerned. "I mean, I've never been there before and it is here where I usually work. Plus, I don't want to go somewhere if I might not really be needed because there might be another healer there already."

She was rambling again, talking more than Robin liked a woman to do when he was with them.

"Now that I think about it, I'm not sure how it will look," she continued. "Besides, I really don't even know you at all since I just met you. Nay, Sir Robin, I'm sorry. I don't think I can do that after all."

"Ah, well." He handed her the empty cup. "I guess I understand," he said, thinking mayhap he'd moved too quickly and scared her away with the kiss. "You probably don't want to leave the monastery."

"Nay, that doesn't matter," she told him putting the cup back down on the bedside table. "St. Erasmus has many monks and nuns who are quite skilled and can do exactly what I do. What I mean is, I'm not required to stay."

"You're not?"

"Nay. Of course not. I only help out here on occasion. When I'm needed. Plus, I tend to their herb garden in exchange for using the herbs to heal. This is also where I dry the herbs. And the monks don't like to go out in the cold and snow, so I fetch winter herbs for them. By that, I mean the herbs that are hardy and last through the cold and grow under the snow."

"Oh, I see," said Robin, his head hurting worse by how much of nothing important she kept going on and on about when he was not interested and neither did he care. He thought he read her body actions correctly and that she enjoyed the kiss as much as he did. So, he tried to think of any other reasons why she wouldn't want to go with him. "Mayhap it's your home you don't want to leave for long, then. I never asked you, but are you perhaps married?"

"Me, married?" Her eyes opened wide again. "Nay, I'm not." Her cheeks flushed once again and she lowered her face.

"Oh, so it's your parents then that you don't want to leave behind for long. Perhaps they are old or ailing and you need to be here for them?"

"Nay, my parents are both dead," she answered shaking her head.

"I didn't know that. I'm sorry."

"How… how long would you want me to stay with you? At Shrewsbury Castle. Just until your wound is better?"

"Well, if you're not in a hurry to get back to your all-important home, I'd like to invite you to stay at least through Christmastide."

"Christmastide?" Her eyes opened wide in surprise.

"Why, yes. We're nearly upon it."

"And it'll last for twelve days once it starts," she pointed out.

"That's right," he said with a slight nod. "Twelfth Night is when it ends. Is that too long? Or not long enough?" he asked with a grin, hoping she was at least a little attracted to him and wanted to get to know him better, too. "I'm planning a big celebration for Christmastide. All of my family will be attending. Would you like to meet my family, Sage?"

Her face blushed once more, and he felt as if mayhap he'd been too bold to ask her this when he barely even knew her.

"I'm sure you have a lovely family, Sir Robin. And I'm certain you'd like to show off your new castle to me as well."

"But, you are going to stay here because you can't leave your home, aren't you?" he asked, realizing the girl was never going to agree to go with him now. Once again, he was moving too fast with the wench.

"On the contrary—when I returned home tonight, I found my house in flames. It burnt to the ground. It's gone. There was nothing I could do to save it. So now I have nowhere to go. Nowhere to live."

"You what? You don't? What happened? Are you all right?" A thousand questions swarmed his head at once. "So, this is why I smelled smoke on you and the dog." He found it odd that she wouldn't have told him about this right away, seeming that it was so important she went back home. Plus, the girl loved to talk and it was hard to shut her up. Why in heaven's name hadn't she told him about something so very important?

"Yes. You were right, Sir Robin. You are very perceptive, it seems." Her mouth turned down into a frown and he wasn't sure she wouldn't cry. "I lost everything today," she said in a mere whisper.

"You didn't lose your life. I saw to saving that, didn't I?"

"Yes, you did. I didn't lose my life... thank you."

"All the more reason to come back to Shrewsbury with me now, Sage. You can be my castle healer. Shrewsbury Castle will be your new home from now on."

He had hoped that would please the girl and help her make her decision to go with him. Still, she seemed to hesitate for some odd reason, and he couldn't even guess why.

"What? Really?" The thought of living with him seemed to please her, but frighten her at the same time. Then, after she seemed to consider it, she nodded ever so slowly. Her face lit up into a full smile.

"You'll join me then?" he asked, seeing no reason why she'd say *no* now.

"What if you return to discover that you already have a healer at the castle?" she asked instead of giving him an answer.

He shrugged. "Then I'll have two healers, won't I?"

"Y-you can do that?"

He chuckled. "My dear Sage, I am lord of Shrewsbury

Castle. I make the decisions now and can do whatever the hell I please. So, will you be accompanying me or not?"

She bit her bottom lip, raised her chin, and nodded. It seemed suddenly that a weight had been lifted off her shoulders. "I accept," she announced. "Yes, I think I like the idea of Shrewsbury Castle being my new home. It is a perfect answer to all my many problems."

He wasn't sure what other problems the girl had besides losing her home, but neither did he care right now. He got the answer he wanted and that satisfied him. Robin would get his time alone with the girl to get to know her better after all.

"Good. Then it's settled." He smiled and lay back on the pillow with his arms under his head. The dog jumped back up on the bed and lay down next to Robin. He reached out and petted Griffin's matted fur. "We'll leave first thing in the morning."

"That soon?" she asked, a tinge of nervousness showing in her tone.

"Yes, of course. Unless you'd rather wait a day or two, but I assure you, I'm fine to travel."

"Nay, that is wonderful. No need to wait. The sooner the better. I'll meet you in the courtyard, ready to go first thing in the morning." She turned to leave.

"After the first meal," he corrected her. "I like to eat and don't want to miss out on food."

"All right," she said, her smile lighting up the room as well as his heart. "I'll see you in the morning, after the first meal." She opened the door, stopping and turning her head slightly to speak to him. "Thank you, Sir Robin."

"For what?" he asked.

"For being the answer to all of my problems."

There she was again, mentioning all her problems, although he had no idea what the hell she meant. It was probably nothing more than her herb plants dying, or mayhap the monks didn't want to share their kitchen with her. Whatever it was, he wasn't worried. He was sure it was menial and meant nothing at all.

Robin stared at her as she left the infirmary. Then again, mayhap he was misreading her words and actions. Sage was a beautiful woman, but very complicated and secretive. He would put a quick stop to that as soon as they got back to the castle.

"Yes, that'll all change," he said carelessly, still petting the dog. "You like Sage, don't you, Griffin?" The dog licked his hand and then put down his head and let out a big sigh.

That made Robin chuckle. "My, my, what is that all about?"

Griffin looked up at him with worried eyes and let out a small whine.

"You silly dog. You're acting as if this isn't a good idea that Sage moves into the castle with us. I assure you, it is. After all, how much trouble could one common girl possibly be?"

CHAPTER 6

Robin finished his meal the next morning, thanked the nuns and monks for sheltering him, and made his way to the courtyard with Griffin following at his side. Brother Francis had told him he'd have his horse waiting and ready to go.

Sure enough, when he approached the courtyard, there was Brother Francis with the reins of his horse in hand. He was also holding the reins of Sage's horse with her wagon attached.

"How is your wound, Sir Robin?" asked the monk.

"It's still a little sore but nothing that'll stop me from getting back to my castle."

Sage walked past him carrying two canvas bags.

"Oh, there you are, Sage. Are you ready to go?" he asked her.

"Just about," she answered over her shoulder, throwing her bags of medicine and herbs into the wagon. Another larger bag followed that he hoped held food.

"You don't need that wagon," he called out. "It'll only slow us down. Leave it here. We'll tie your things to the horse."

"Nay, I need it." She busied herself doing something, not looking at him as usual.

"I have plenty of wagons at the castle." He walked up behind her. "Really, taking the wagon will only slow us down. Plus, it'll only attract more thieves along the way. Leave it behind with the monks."

She finally turned to look at him. The winter sun shone down on her uncovered head, making the red tones of her blonde hair even brighter. Her green eyes seemed even clearer today than yesterday. Damn, she was comely as well as compelling.

"I lost everything yesterday, Sir Robin," she told him once more in a solemn voice, although he didn't need to be reminded. "I want the wagon. It's all I have left."

"What?" he asked, not understanding at all. "If you lost everything, why do you need an entire wagon? What possessions could you possibly have that would fill it up?"

"Not what. Who," said the monk under his breath.

Robin was about to ask what he meant when Sisters Alberta and Bernadine came from the building that housed the nuns. With them were a small boy, a girl, and a young man.

"Sage, we will miss you," said Sister Bernadine.

"Yes, your skills at the monastery were superb and well appreciated," added Sister Alberta. "Please be sure to bring your family back for a visit."

"Family?" asked Robin, very confused. He looked over at the monk. "What is she talking about?"

"Sister Alberta is speaking about Sage's siblings." The monk nodded as the young man helped the little boy into the back of the wagon and the young girl followed.

"I want Griffin to ride with us," called out the little boy waving his arm at the dog.

"Come here, Griffin," called out the girl.

Griffin looked over at Robin and whimpered. The damned dog almost seemed to know the children, and acted like he wanted to ride in the wagon with them. Unbelievable. Even his dog knew about this, yet he had no idea.

"Oh, Robin, I hope you don't mind if my siblings join us at the castle," said Sage as she climbed up onto the bench seat of the wagon along with the young man, who had features similar to hers. "After all, we don't have a home anymore, so my sister and brothers have nowhere else to go."

He didn't like this idea at all and was about to object to it when one of the nuns spoke.

"Sir Robin, it is so thoughtful and kind of you to take in these homeless orphans who are down on their luck," said Sister Bernadine.

"Yes, may God bless you on your journey. You are a good man and we will keep you in our prayers," said Sister Alberta, making the sign of the cross over his head.

Well, damned, why did the nuns have to say this? Robin didn't want all these children along, that was for sure. He only wanted to spend time with Sage and was hoping to get a lot closer to her. But now that the nuns were praising him and blessing him, how the hell could he object?

"Well... I mean I..."

"Sir Robin, my siblings would love if Griffin rode in the wagon with them. They've taken a liking to him. Would you mind?" asked Sage.

Robin looked down at the dog who was looking up at him with wide eyes, just waiting for his permission. The hound's tail swept back and forth over the ground.

"Go on, you traitor," he growled, and swished his hand through the air. Griffin barked happily and bolted over to the wagon, jumping right over the back. He put his paws up on the side and barked at Robin once more, while the two children squealed happily and hugged the dog.

"We'd better get going, don't you agree?" asked Sage, looking up at the sky. "After all, it looks like it's about to snow again. I don't fancy being in another storm. I doubt that you do either, after falling through the ice."

"Fine, fine," Robin grunted, just wanting the wench to stop talking. To stop reminding him he fell through the ice and she'd had to save him.

He pulled himself up onto his horse, feeling the pain in his leg sharper than ever now. He'd had no idea at the time when he asked Sage to come live at the castle that he was inviting her three siblings to join them. This wench was a sneaky one, and he didn't like that. He also didn't enjoy being put on the spot in front of nuns and monks, either. "If you can't keep up, I'm leaving you all behind," he threatened, heading out of the monastery fast atop his horse, not bothering to look back to see if they followed.

"Sage, aren't you going to introduce us to Sir Robin?" asked Oscar, driving the wagon and trying to keep up with the knight.

"Hard to do that when we can't even catch him," said Sage, realizing she probably should have told Robin yesterday about her siblings joining them. Or mayhap it would have been more proper to ask. She had done neither, for fear he'd say no. And if he'd denied her request, she wouldn't have been able to join him at the castle either, because she would never leave her siblings behind.

"You made him feel foolish in front of the nuns and monks," her brother pointed out.

"I couldn't tell him about you ahead of time," she protested.

"Why not? Were you afraid he'd say no?"

"Yes," she admitted, glancing back at her siblings happily playing with the dog. After everything her family had been through lately, it did her heart good to see little Noel and also Amira smiling again. "It is better this way," she told him. "Now, we'll not only have a home but we'll also be protected by knights inside the walls of Shrewsbury Castle."

"Sage, did you tell him why those men were trying to kill you?"

"Well, nay. Not yet. But then again, he didn't really ask."

"Sage," said her brother sounding severely disappointed in her.

"I will," she added quickly. "I'll tell him when the time is right."

"You'd better do it soon. It's not right to fool a nobleman. It can only bring you trouble."

"It's not that I am trying to fool anyone," she told her brother. "I am at my wit's end trying to be mother to the rest of you, as well as play father. I figured this was a perfect way to protect all of us."

"I'm the protector of the family now since I'm the eldest son. You don't need to worry about that anymore."

"You? Oscar, you don't know anything about fighting—be serious."

"I know how to hunt and how to use a knife."

"It's not the same."

"Well, neither do you. And at least I have a blade that is big enough to kill a man." He moved his cloak aside to show her the hilt of a very large dagger in a scabbard attached to his belt.

"Where did you get that?"

"I found it in Father's things. It was one of his fishing knives."

"You shouldn't have taken it."

"Why not? Father's dead, Sage. It's not like he is going to need it."

Sage didn't like talking about their parents who had died recently. It brought too much pain and discomfort to her. Pain that she'd rather forget.

"I don't like it that you have that and mean to use it, Oscar."

"Why not?"

"It only means trouble."

"No, it doesn't. Just the opposite, actually." Oscar patted the hilt of the dagger with his hand. "It means we're going to kill those bastards that came for us before they can return to kill us."

"What is going on back here?"

Sage jerked, almost falling from the seat when she noticed Robin riding next to the wagon. She'd been so deep in her conversation with her brother that she hadn't even seen him come back to meet them.

"What do you mean?" she asked, feeling her heart lodge in her throat. She hoped he hadn't been listening.

Griffin stuck his head over the side of the wagon, panting, and looking like he was actually smiling.

"Is Griffin an orphan too, just like us?" asked Noel, peeking over the back of the seat to talk to them.

"Noel, sit down before you fall out. And why would you say something like that? It's not true," scolded Sage.

"So, we're not orphans?" asked Noel.

"Nay, we're not," said Sage. "Don't say that again."

"They're not?" asked Robin, still riding next to them, raising a brow.

"Well, mayhap we are, but I don't like to hear my little brother talking that way. It upsets me," Sage told him.

"I'm Oscar, Sir Robin. It's nice to meet you," said her brother. "I'm sorry my sister is so daft that she didn't even introduce us earlier."

"Hello, Oscar," said Robin.

"In the wagon is our sister, Amira, and our little brother, Noel," continued Oscar.

"Hello," said Robin with a nod of his head to the others. He seemed as if he wasn't sure what to say.

"Sir Robin, how is your wound?" asked Sage. "Is it bleeding again?"

"I don't know, but I'm feeling more pain than before," he answered. "Mayhap you should check it."

"Oscar, pull off to the side of the road. I need to look at Sir Robin's wound and apply some more salve."

"Here? Now?" asked Oscar, his eyes darting back and forth.

"Yes," said Sage, not really thinking Robin's wound needed to be checked, but she wanted to apologize to him in private for not telling him earlier about her siblings. "Stop here, please."

"There is a river just up ahead to the left," said Robin. "It would be good to water the horses."

Once they all stopped, the dog jumped out of the wagon.

"Oscar, can you tend to both the horses?" asked Sage, helping her siblings out of the back of the wagon and collecting her bag of healing herbs. "I need a moment alone with Sir Robin."

"I will," said her brother.

Robin dismounted, handing the reins of his horse to Oscar, having overheard what she said.

"Stay close by. Don't let your siblings wander off," Robin

told Oscar. "Griffin will keep an eye on things for us but we need to stay alert."

"It's all right. I'm ready for anything," said Oscar, tapping his hand on the hilt of his dagger before turning and heading for the river.

"And stay off the ice if the water looks frozen," Robin called out after them.

As soon as they were alone, Sage turned to Robin. "Let me see that wound."

"To do that, I'd have to remove my breeches, and I assure you it wasn't easy to put them on in the first place with my thigh wrapped," he told her. "I don't think that would be a good idea, do you?"

"Well, I suppose not. But what if the wound is infected?" She reached out to touch his leg but his hand shot out to grab her wrist.

"The wound is fine and we both know it. Now, tell me why you wanted to be alone with me."

"I-I'm sorry," she said, slowly looking up into his bright blue eyes.

"Sorry for what?" he asked. "For lying to me, tricking me, or putting me in a horrible position?"

"All of them," she said with a sigh.

"Sage, why didn't you tell me you had siblings?"

"I was afraid you wouldn't want them, and I couldn't leave them behind."

"What kind of a man do you think I am?"

"I-I'm not sure." She really felt bad now. Especially since she still wasn't telling him about everything. He had no idea men were out to kill her and her family.

"I think you'd better ride with me for the rest of the trip."

"Ride with you? On your horse?" This thought surprised her and scared her as well. To ride with him, she'd have to be pressed up against him. She'd have to hold on to him or he'd hold on to her. Either way, this would be more intimacy with a man than she'd ever had in her life. And Sir Robin wasn't just any man. He was a noble. A very handsome one. Being pressed up close to him would only make her want to kiss him again.

"Bring the horses, we're going," Robin shouted.

"Already?" asked Oscar. "But they've just started to drink."

"They'll be fine. It's going to snow," he said, peering up at the gray sky. "I want to be safely inside my castle, sitting in front of a warm hearth with my feet up before that happens again."

"Is it far to your castle?" asked Sage, following Robin as he collected his horse from Oscar.

"Not really. Only a few more hours away."

"A few more hours?" she asked, feeling like that was eternity. Riding with Sir Robin's arms around her for that long was going to affect her more than the ride here. He turned to help her mount his horse.

"Up you go," he said, placing her in the saddle and climbing up after her, settling himself behind her. He held the reins, but wrapped his arms around her waist and held her close to him.

Sage's body began to heat up quickly. She swore she felt her insides trembling with excitement. Why did this feel so good? Why did being in Robin's arms feel so right? Part of her wanted it to stop right now, and another part of her never wanted it to end.

"We're going to pick up the pace a little," said Robin, his deep voice right in her ear. "Can you keep up, Oscar?"

"Oh, yes I can, my lord. You can count on me," said her brother, always up for a challenge.

"Make sure Amira and Noel lie down so they don't fall out," Sage called over her shoulder. "Noel is going to want to play with the dog. He is going to stand up and lose his balance. It's not safe."

"Stop worrying, Sage," said Oscar. "I can take care of the others."

"Griffin, watch the children," Robin called out to the dog. That was all he had to say. The dog lay down at the feet of the children, looking around and protecting them from his prone position in the wagon.

"That dog is priceless," said Sage in awe. "How did you ever train him to listen like that?"

"I didn't," Robin answered. "Griffin was a Highland stray who wandered into the tavern. He takes orders well, so I am guessing he belonged to a Scot at one time. The dog took a liking to me. We seem to know what each other is thinking without even using words."

"Do you mean you can read minds then?"

"Nay," he answered with a soft chuckle. "Although I wish it were true."

"Why is that?"

"If I could read minds, I'd know more about you than you've told me. And that isn't much at all."

"I suppose I have kept to myself and I'm sorry. I'm just not used to anyone wanting to know things about me, I guess."

"Well, I'm interested," he told her. "Will you tell me?"

Her heart swelled when he said this. No one ever expressed interest in her life. All people ever talked about was what she could do for them. Robin was not like all the other noblemen. He was different and really seemed to care. Mayhap she should open up with him just a little more. "What is it you want to know?"

"Well, for starters, how and when did your parents die?"

"Oh, that." Of all the questions to ask, why did he want her to talk about her parents? This was very hard for her.

"Unless you'd rather not tell me."

She felt that if she denied him his answers, it would make things awkward between them. She'd already kept things from him, and didn't want him to think she was harboring more secrets. Even if she was.

"Their death was an accident," she told him, feeling emotional already. "I wasn't able to save them, because I was too shocked and didn't know what to do." The tears came now, and Sage couldn't stop them, even though she tried.

"I didn't mean to make you cry. I'm sorry if I'm asking things that make you uncomfortable. I was just curious, that's all."

"It's all right." She wiped away her tears with the back of her hand. "My family is poor. My father was a fisherman and my mother a healer."

"So that's where you learned your skill."

"Yes. I traveled to towns with my mother and assisted her. I helped her grow and pick herbs and to make potions. She taught me everything she knew and all she'd learned from her mother."

"And your brother, Oscar? Is he going to be a fisherman someday like your father?"

"I hope not." She felt a knot in her stomach thinking about this.

"Why not? It's a good trade," he told her. "I'm sure your father must have taught him all about it, no?"

"I hate the water and don't even like my siblings being near it," she said, looking straight ahead at the road, trying to brush away her memories of that horrible day six months ago.

"Why? What is it that frightens you about water?"

"My parents died in the sea six months ago."

"Oh, I didn't know."

"My father worked on a fishing boat. He lived near the

shore but we lived here because this is where my mother's healing skills were needed. We went to meet Father, and were considering moving to a town on the coast. My mother wanted the whole family together again."

"That's understandable."

"Well, to have some time alone, my parents went out in my father's fishing boat while the rest of us stayed on shore. A storm blew in from nowhere. Before I knew what happened, they were knocked overboard and the storm smashed my father's boat against the rocks. The waves were too high. Although they tried to swim to shore, they didn't make it. They were too far out in the water. They were both—they both drowned."

"That is a sad story."

"It gets worse," she told him. "While I watched it all happen from the shore, I was too frightened by the storm and the waves to even move or to find my brother for help. I never learned to swim. I was too scared to go after them to try to save them. The sea swallowed them up in front of me as I stood helpless and unable to think of any way to save them."

"There was no one else around who could help them?"

"Nay. Not where we were. It was a secluded area. I'm sorry, but I just don't want to talk about it anymore. Can I please go back to my wagon?"

"Nay, stay here," said Robin, holding her even closer. "I promise I won't ask any more questions for the rest of the trip. I just want you to relax and to know that now that I'm here with you, Sage, you can release all your worries."

Sage only wished it were that easy to do. But her troubles were too many and it was too hard to let go. Not even someone as strong as the knight trying to comfort her right now could soothe her and make her feel safe and happy again.

CHAPTER 7

Robin rode through the gates of Shrewsbury Castle with his arms around Sage who sat in front of him. A feeling of relief, excitement, and pride filled his heart. It was damned good to be home. Behind them, Sage's brother drove the horse and wagon with the younger siblings and his dog in the back.

"Sir Robin. You've returned." His squire, Tobias, was the first to greet him, running over to take the reins of his horse. His steward, Ferdinand, was right behind him.

"My lord, we were wondering when you'd return," said Ferdinand, a shorter, older man who was steward to the last Lord Shrewsbury. "They've been waiting for two days now and I was getting concerned and wasn't sure what to tell them." He shifted his weight from foot to foot the way Robin noticed he did when he was worried.

"Ferdinand, you'll have to be more specific, I'm afraid. I have no idea what you are talking about." Robin slid off his horse. Before he could even reach up to help Sage dismount, she had her feet on the ground and was standing right next to him.

"My lord, he's speaking of the fact that you have visitors," said Tobias, looking a little sheepish as well. "Who is the girl?" asked his squire behind his hand.

Robin suddenly realized why they were both acting so oddly. He hadn't introduced Sage to them.

"I am Sage Hillock," said Sage, not bothering to wait for him to answer. "And who might you two be?"

Both the men looked up at Robin with wide eyes, not saying a word. The girl had been so bold as to overstep a lord... a knight... and he didn't like it at all.

"This is my squire, Tobias, and my steward, Ferdinand," said Robin, brushing the snow off his cloak. "Sage is my new healer," he added, feeling as if he needed to explain.

"My lord, pardon me for being so bold as to remind you, but we already have a castle healer," said Ferdinand, shifting faster from foot to foot now. "He is away with his family at the moment in a neighboring village, but will be returning soon."

"Well, then we'll have two healers, won't we?" Robin answered with a shrug.

"Cousin, you've finally returned."

Robin looked up to see his cousin, Lord Rook Blake, who recently married his gardener girl. His twin sister Raven married the armorer. They were the children of Lady Devon and Lord Corbett Blake. Walking with Rook was their cousin, Lord Edgar Blackmore, or Gar as he liked to be called. Gar's sister Eleanor just married a scribe.

"Rook and Gar. What brings you two here? My Christmastide celebration doesn't start for another week yet," said Robin. "You are much too early."

"I agree with you. Believe me, Cousin, I'd rather be back at Rookrose Manor with my lovely wife, Rose," complained Rook. "However, Father insisted I come help you with the preparations at the castle since this is all new to you."

"I'm only here because I happened to be visiting Rook and he dragged me along with him." Gar shrugged. He was the eldest of the cousins at four-and-twenty years. Robin didn't see him much anymore, since Gar had been made a sea captain by King Edward III and was away at sea a good amount of time on secret missions. Robin thought it seemed a fitting job for Gar, since he'd more or less been raised by pirates. His mother, Echo, along with Robin's father, Madoc, were twins and both stolen as babies. Echo grew up on a pirate ship thinking she was the daughter of the late infamous pirate, Captain Powell ap Llyr. Robin's father was raised by the pirate's late wife.

"I'm the new castle healer. My name is Sage Hillock," said Sage, once again speaking when she needed to stay quiet. Bid the devil, didn't the girl have any manners at all?

"It looks like you've been picking up strays, Robin. Do you really think you should being doing that?" asked Rook.

"I'm not a stray!" spat Sage, not liking being spoken about that way. "I'll have you know, right after Sir Robin saved my life, I saved his. He was wounded by one of my attackers and he fell through the ice and nearly drowned."

"Oh, my," said Ferdinand with a hand to his mouth, looking as if he wanted to be anywhere but here at the moment.

"I was speaking about the hound," said Rook, nodding at the ground.

Sage looked over to see Griffin sitting silently at Robin's side.

"Oh, of course. I misunderstood. Please forgive me." Sage never felt so embarrassed in all her life. "Sir Robin, I'll wait in the wagon for you, along with my siblings."

"Siblings? You brought the wench's entire family with you?" asked Gar. "That's an odd thing to do."

Sage's gaze flew over to Robin. She hoped he wouldn't tell them they were orphans and homeless as well. Part of her wanted him to keep that quiet. It would only raise more questions that she wasn't willing to answer. It was better not to let the nobles know.

"They're here because I've hired them as well," Robin told him.

Sage let out a deep breath of relief. She didn't know what he meant, but supposed he said that just to keep her from being embarrassed.

Oscar walked up with Amira, who held on to the hand of little Noel.

"You hired them? Really, now," said Rook, sounding as if he didn't believe it and could see right through the lie. "What is it, pray tell, that they will be doing?"

Robin cleared his throat. "Well, Oscar is going to... work in the stable," he said.

"I am?" Oscar glanced at Sage and she nodded slightly, hoping he'd understand to stay quiet for now.

"And Amira here, she will be a... kitchen maid," Robin continued, sounding to Sage as if he hadn't thought any of this through and was only making it up as he went along.

"Oh, I think I'd like that," said Amira. "After all, I do know how to cook." Sage's sister seemed pleased by the suggestion.

"Amira makes good food," said Noel.

"What about the little one?" asked Rook. "Now, don't tell me he's going to train as a page because you know as well as I that he isn't a noble. And I don't know what the hell a common child is going to be able to do for you."

"Nay, not a page. Of course not," said Robin. "He's just a commoner, that's right. Noel will... I mean..."

"My little brother will be assisting me in preparing my potions and herbal remedies," said Sage, trying to help Robin out. However, it only seemed as if her plan backfired.

Rook and Gar burst out laughing.

"Next, you'll tell me that the hound has been hired as a nursemaid to tend to the noble children," said Rook, still laughing. "So, is she?"

Robin answered through gritted teeth. "First of all, my hound's name is Griffin. He is a he, not a she. And for the record, he's a better protector than any squire."

"My lord!" said Tobias, obviously insulted.

"Tobias, you know I didn't mean you. Now, please show Oscar to the stables and introduce him to the stablemaster at once," instructed Robin. "Ferdinand, I'd like you to take Amira to the kitchens so she can help prepare the next meal."

"What about me? Don't forget about me." Noel tugged at Robin's tunic as well as yawned. Griffin licked the little boy's hand and Noel reached over to pet the dog on his head.

"You'll stay with me for now, Noel," Sage said before any crude suggestions could be given by Robin's cousins. She quickly grabbed her younger brother's hand. "Sir Robin, if you'd be kind enough to show me where I'll be staying, I'd like to get settled now."

"Of course. Ferdinand, show Sage and her siblings to a chamber in the castle that they can all share," Robin told his steward, who was already walking away.

Ferdinand stopped abruptly and turned on his heel. "A chamber in the castle? Did I hear you correctly, my lord?"

"You heard me."

"Won't they be sleeping in the great hall like the rest of the servants?"

Sage held her breath, waiting for Robin to answer. She didn't want to sleep on the floor with drunkards and rats, and neither did she want herself or her siblings being exposed to men with less than respectable intentions.

"Nay. I want them in a room. But they'll all share the same one," said Robin. "Now go."

"Really, Robin, what are you thinking?" asked Gar, shaking his head.

"You act as if there's a problem," said Robin. "Well, there's not."

"Nay, I agree with him," said Rook, watching Sage walk away. "I'm not sure my father, or for that matter, yours, is going to like to hear you rode up with some common wench who claims she saved your life. And that you're taking in her siblings and giving them all a room reserved for a noble."

"It's not what you think. Don't say it that way," said Robin, squirming, hoping no one overheard them. "It'll sound ridiculous to the other nobles."

"It is ridiculous," mumbled Gar.

"Shouldn't you be out pillaging ships, Gar?"

"That's not what I do, and you know it," said Gar. "And quit trying to take the focus off of you."

"You do seem to be trying to do that," agreed Rook.

"Why should either of you even care what I do?" asked Robin.

"I don't care, but our fathers will," Rook answered.

"By the time my parents or yours get here for the Christmastide celebration, she'll be gone, so stop it." Robin never liked being told what to do. Especially not now, when he was a lord of a castle, something that Rook and Gar were not.

"Don't count on that," said Rook. "But it's your decision, Lord Shrewsbury."

"Well, I did tell Sage she could live here since she and her siblings don't really have anywhere to go, but what does it really matter?" asked Robin.

"Robin, my father as well as your parents are already here," Rook informed him.

"What? Where?" Robin looked around, not wanting to hear this. He needed to make a good impression on the other nobles. But dragging a common wench and her siblings to his new castle wasn't going to paint him in a good light at all. Any fool could see that.

"Your father is with Uncle Corbett in the mews," Gar told him. "Uncle Madoc's brought along some of his birds. He says he's going to train them as homing pigeons for you. Now that you have a castle, he said you need a way to communicate with the others in the family."

"God's eyes, nay," groaned Robin, knowing his father was getting carried away with the pigeons again. True, he did race them and win money at one time. But that was before he discovered he was a noble. It was when he was naught more than a petty thief. "I don't want him doing that. With him, it's always about his silly pigeons. What about Mother? Where is she?"

"She's in the kitchen with your sister," said Gar. "They're planning the Christmas feast with the cooks."

"Sister? Which sister?" asked Robin, feeling his anxiety growing. His younger sisters, Regina and Dorothy, were no problem at all. However his oldest sister, Martine, was more than a challenge at times.

"It's Martine," Rook answered.

"Bloody hell," mumbled Robin, knowing that nothing was ever good enough for the girl. She was very judgmental. And in the kitchen right now. Right where his steward was taking Sage and two of her siblings. "Let's go inside out of the cold, shall we?" said Robin.

"Oh, you need to warm your bones at the fire," said Rook.

"Nay. What I really need right now to warm myself is some of the MacKeefe's Mountain Magic."

After having drunk so much of the potent spirits with his Uncle Storm in the Highlands, Robin didn't think he'd ever want any again. But with the way Sage spoke so boldly, and the fact his dominant Uncle Corbett as well as Robin's parents and his opinionated sister were here, it made him realize now why the hell the Highlanders always drank so much!

CHAPTER 8

"Who are they?" asked a woman in the kitchen when Sage entered with the steward and her siblings.

"My lady, this one is here to work in the kitchen," said the steward, pushing Amira forward.

"Well? What's your name?" asked the woman with the dark hair.

"I'm Amira," said Sage's sister softly.

"What about this one?" The woman looked over at Sage next. "We could use someone a little older to help prepare the food for Christmastide."

"I am Sage Hillock, a healer, not a kitchen maid," Sage answered before the steward could say a word. "And who would you be?"

By the look on the woman's face, Sage realized she had spoken too freely once again. It was obvious the woman standing before her was a titled lady. Still, Sage didn't care. She didn't like the way the nobles acted so haughty.

"Mother, Martine," said Robin, rushing into the kitchen, followed by the Lords Rook and Gar. "I can explain."

"Please do." The younger of the two women crossed her arms over her chest and scowled. "I have never had a commoner speak to me this way before. She needs to be punished."

"Martine, please." The older woman who Robin called his mother, put her hand on the girl's arm. "Let Robin explain."

"Thank you, Mother." Robin reached over and kissed the older woman on the cheek. "And thank you for assisting with the Christmastide celebrations."

"Robin?" Martine raised a brow and nodded at Sage.

"I'm afraid I spoke out of line, my lady. I didn't realize who you were." Sage noticed Robin's tenseness dissipate as Sage made a big show of curtsying to the women, trying to make things right.

"Mother and Martine, this is Sage and her siblings, Amira and Noel." He looked at Sage. "This is my mother, Lady Abigail, and my opinionated sister, Lady Martine."

"Robin!" scolded Martine, not happy with her introduction.

"We have another brother too," said little Noel. "His name is Oscar. He was sent to shovel horse poop."

"Well, hello. It's nice to meet all of you," said Lady Abigail.

"Where did my brother find the likes of you?" asked Martine.

"He saved the girl's life from bandits," Lord Rook spoke up.

"And then she saved Robin's life when he fell through the ice," answered Lord Gar with a chuckle.

"Don't you two have better things to do?" asked Robin in a huff.

"Nay." Gar shrugged. "I'm not required back on my ship until after Christmastide."

"Not really," said Rook. "I've got my manor under control."

"Then go to the great hall and I'll find something for you two to do." Robin jerked his head toward the door.

"I get the feeling he's not happy with us," said Gar, as he and Rook headed out of the kitchen.

"Maybe the girl can make him happy," Sage heard Rook say as they left, chuckling under their breath.

"Well, get to work then, Amira," said Martine. "But the boy will have to go."

"I want my brother to stay here with me," said Amira. Sage could see how upset her sister was, being in an unfamiliar place.

"I want to stay with Amira," said Noel, tugging on Sage's skirt.

"Lord Robin, isn't there something my brother can help out with in the kitchen?" asked Sage. "My siblings have been through so much lately, that it would be better for them if they could stay together."

"I'm sure we can find something for him to do here. Martine?" Robin passed it off to his sister.

"Nay. He's just a child," said Martine. "He'll only get in the way."

"I promise I won't." Noel looked as if he were about to cry.

"Now, Martine, I'm sure Noel could help with fetching ingredients or bringing the dirty dishes to the scullery," said Robin's kind mother. "Follow me you two." Lady Abigail held out her hand. "Are you hungry? We can also find you something to eat."

Noel and Amira both looked up at Sage, waiting for her permission.

"Go on," said Sage. "We need to help out at the castle in return for Lord Robin inviting us to live here."

"Live here? As in permanently?" asked Martine, as Robin's mother walked away, talking to Sage's siblings. "Why are you inviting entire families to live at your castle, Robin? That's not the way nobles do things. You are acting irresponsible and compulsive. Just like you always do."

"For your information, Sister, their home burned down and they have nowhere to live. Neither do they have parents," explained Robin.

"Burned down? How? That seems odd to me." Martine scrutinized Sage. This entire conversation was making Sage uncomfortable.

"Lord Robin, I really need to change the dressing on your wound now," said Sage, changing the subject as quickly as possible. "Is there somewhere we can go to do so?"

"That sounds as if you want to be alone with my brother," said Martine, stirring up trouble. Thankfully, Robin helped Sage out of this awkward position.

"This way," said Robin, taking Sage by the arm and escorting her from the kitchen.

"I get the distinct feeling your sister doesn't like me," said Sage, as soon as they were out of earshot.

"Martine doesn't like anything I do, nor does she approve of any of my friends. I'm used to it by now. Don't let it bother you."

"Friends?" Sage's heart jumped. Was he calling her a friend? That couldn't possibly be what he meant. Could it?

"We'll go to my solar for now. Later, my steward will show you where you and your siblings will be staying. For now."

"For now?" she asked, thinking that it sounded as if he was changing his mind about letting them live here.

"I'm giving you a chamber for now," Robin explained. "But of course, you and your siblings won't be able to stay there forever."

"Why not?" she asked, as they walked up the stairs and

down a long corridor. "I thought you said we could live here, since we no longer have a home."

"Yes, but we'll need to find you a cottage in the village," he told her, stopping outside his closed door.

"In the village?" Anxiety coursed through her. If she lived there, it would be too easy for her attackers to find her. Plus, she would have no protection for herself or her siblings. They needed more than anything to stay inside the castle walls. "I thought we'd be living here. Inside the castle walls. With you."

"Nay," he said, opening the door and walking into the room. She followed. "Some of my servants sleep in the great hall, but it's not safe for young women like you and your sister. There are too many drunkards and lusty men. It's not safe. I'm going to find you a nice cottage in the village where you will be well-protected."

"How kind of you," she mumbled, knowing that this wouldn't be safe for her or her siblings at all. The only true safe place would be at the castle. She would have to do something—anything at all to try to change his mind. Perhaps she could kiss him. That might work. Then, he'd want to keep her closer to him. Of course, it might mean he'd have other intentions too. Well, she wouldn't warm any man's bed.

"Where should we do this? On the bed?" he asked, startling her, making her think he'd read her mind. "Close the door. I don't want anyone watching us." He unclasped his weapon belt and laid it down. Then he removed his boots. His long fingers tugged at the string holding up his breeches.

"What are you doing?" she gasped, her mind now racing just as fast as her heart. She turned her head the other way so as not to see him as he undressed, planning to bed her right in the middle of the day.

"You said you wanted to tend to my wound. Now close the door and get over here."

"Oh. Your wound. On your leg. Yes. Of course." Feeling suddenly foolish by her own thoughts, she walked over and closed the door. When she turned back around, she saw him removing his tunic as well.

Her eyes settled on his naked, broad chest. He had muscles in his upper arms that were impressive. Her gaze scanned down his enticing chest, past his flat nipples, and down to his taut stomach. Dark blond circles of hair trailed downward, disappearing under the band of his scanty braies. His long, bare legs looked ever so sturdy.

Her mouth felt dry and she could barely swallow. She'd seen him half-naked in the monastery, but there were monks or nuns around them then. Now she was in a room with the door closed, about to administer healing to a very handsome man. A man who wore nothing but a small pair of braies that seemed to be getting tighter and tighter each moment she stared at him.

"Sage?" he asked, plopping down on the bed and lying back. He propped himself up with one elbow and patted the mattress next to him "Come here. What's the matter? You look as if you're afraid I might bite you."

"I-I don't think that," she said, making her way over to him. She laid her medicine bag down on the bed next to his legs.

His hand shot out and his long fingers clasped around her wrist. "Unless you *want* me to bite you, then, I could," he said in a deep, lazy voice.

"What?" Her head snapped upward and her eyes popped open.

"Relaaaax. I'm just jesting," he said with a chuckle, releasing her wrist and lying back on the bed. "What is the matter with you? You are so tense that you are going to snap."

"Yes, I'll try to relax," she said, reaching out with shaky

hands to unwrap his leg. Her fingers grazed against his other thigh, sending a delicious shiver up her spine. Damn, why did she feel so hot? Normally, when she administered her healing to men, she was focused on her job. Now, all she could think about was if he would try to kiss her again, the way he did in the infirmary. Part of her wanted him to do just that.

"Do you like what you see?" he asked, making her jolt. She dropped the bindings and stood up straight.

"What do you mean?" Her heart pounded so rapidly that she was sure he could hear it pounding in her chest as well.

"My wound. The stitches," he said. "How does it look? Is it infected?"

"Oh, that." Her gaze swept downward and she let out a deep breath. "The stitches are holding, but it is too soon to tell if it's infected. I'm going to apply a poultice made from sage for now, and wrap it back up. The sage will help heal the wound, repair the skin, and hopefully keep you from any infection."

"Whatever you think."

"Just to be sure to keep your wound clean and dry so it doesn't get infected, I'd like to make up a mixture that includes garlic and honey. That would help prevent it. However, I don't have any with me. Since my home burned down, I lost a lot of my herbs and supplies. Would you have the things I need for me to use here at the castle?"

"Yes, I'm sure we do. Just ask the cook in the kitchen for anything you need."

"All right. We're done here," she said, wrapping his wound back up and wiping her hands on a clean cloth.

"Are we?" He sat up, coming much closer to her.

"My lord?" she asked, seeing the lustful look in his hooded eyes.

"Sage, I really want to thank you for everything." His arms

closed around her waist and he pulled her closer, making her drop the cloth.

"I don't know what you mean, my lord."

"I think you do."

If she had been thinking clearly, she would have moved away. But when he reached up and kissed her gently on her neck, she lost all common sense.

"Wh-what are you doing?" she asked in a breathy whisper, her eyes closing and her head falling back as his kisses trailed closer and closer to her cleavage.

She gasped when he pulled her bodice apart and licked her skin at the top of her breasts. Immediately she felt excitement swelling inside her as her body heated up.

"After that kiss we shared, I haven't been able to stop thinking about you." He reached up and put his hand around the back of her head, pulling her closer. His lips met hers again and she felt her legs becoming weak. And when his tongue entered her mouth, she felt a tingling between her thighs, as she imagined another part of him entering her instead.

"I have been thinking about it too," she admitted, watching as he boldly pulled her bodice apart further. Her breasts rose and fell with her deep breathing.

"Mmmm," he said with a satisfied groan, looking down at her chest. His fingers slid into her bodice and around one breast as he lifted it completely out from her clothing. "Oh, my," he said, staring at her nakedness. Then his thumb flicked across her nipple and it felt so good that she nearly cried out. But that was nothing compared to what she experienced next. He opened his mouth and closed his lips over her nipple, suckling at her while he fondled her bottom end with his other hand.

Then he fell back on the bed, pulling her along with him.

She lay on top of him while he buried his face in both her bare breasts now, helping himself to seconds. And she didn't mind.

"Oooh, oooh," she moaned in delight as he suckled one nipple and then the other. Her back arched on its own, and she felt a vibration between her thighs, bringing her to life. All she could think about now was bedding Lord Robin. She wanted to feel his engorged form inside her, and she wanted him to take her in every way possible. She'd dreamed of making love with a handsome man, and now it was going to happen.

"You like this?" he asked, his hands squeezing her buttocks right through her clothes. Then, he pulled up her gown, spreading her legs and pulling her higher.

"I-I-I think so," she said, feeling so excited that she wasn't sure she wouldn't explode.

"I do, too," he said, reaching under him and pulling down his braies. When he moved her to the side to do it, she looked down to see his full erection—bigger than she ever thought it could be. She wasn't even sure she could take him in completely. That thought started to scare her, and she realized that there was no turning back now.

"What are you going to do?" she asked, having never made love with a man before, and being nervous. Still, she wanted to experience it.

"I'm going to couple with you. What do you think?"

"Is it going to hurt?" she asked, not able to look away from his erection.

"Oh, are you a virgin?" he asked.

She bit her bottom lip and nodded, not able to say a word. Her focus was on his manly form. She had to know how it felt. Slowly, she reached out to touch him, but at the last moment, pulled back her hand.

He chuckled. "You can touch me. Go ahead," he gave her permission.

"You are so-so big, my lord."

"That isn't the first time I've heard that from a woman, and I'm sure it won't be the last. But I assure you, it makes all the girls scream out their pleasure even louder."

With his words, he brought her back to her senses. She realized that to him, a nobleman, she was naught more than a form of quick release. A mere commoner to use as he would. Nothing but a blatant folly. To him, she was not more than a means to scratch his lustful, noble itch. He mentioned *all the girls*, which told her he must bed women often. Lots of them. Well, she decided she didn't want to be just another one of these women. Nay. She wouldn't be just another one of his whores, no matter who he was. When she made love to a man, she wanted it to mean something to both of them. She could see now that she'd made a terrible mistake and she couldn't continue with this. And she would never let him do it again.

Sage pulled away from him and jumped off the bed, hurriedly pulling her clothes back into place.

"Wait. What are you doing? We're not done yet," he told her.

"Oh, yes, we are," she retorted, too ashamed of herself to even look him in the eye. "I am not one of your strumpets, so don't even think you can treat me that way." She tied her bodice as she spoke.

"I don't know what you mean. I was only thanking you properly." He pulled up his braies and sat up on the edge of the bed.

"Thanking me? Properly?" she repeated. "Are you sure that's what you were doing?"

"Why are you in such a huff, Sage?" He dangled his long legs off the side of the bed.

"God's eyes, I saved your blasted life," she spat. "It seems the least you can do is to treat me with a little respect."

"Now, wait a minute," he said, standing up. She reached around him to collect her herbs and ointments, pushing them back into her medicine bag. "I'm a noble. You can't speak to me that way."

"And I am your healer, in case you've forgotten. I should be treated with more thought and care than one of your castle whores."

"Oh, I understand," he said, standing up, towering over her. "You're just scared since you're a virgin. Don't worry, it'll be better next time when you're not so frightened of me."

She reached out and slapped him hard across the cheek. That shut him up, as well as seemed to shock him.

"What the hell did you just do?" His voice sounded mean and angry. "Must I remind you that I'm a nobleman and you are just a commoner?"

"I'm quite aware of that, since you can't seem to stop reminding me."

"You can't do that!" His hand went to his cheek.

"You told me that you are lord of the castle and can do whatever you please."

"Yes. That's right." He rubbed his cheek, still staring at her as if he thought her action outrageous.

"Well, Lord Robin, I don't care if you are lord of a castle or king of the land, you have no right to treat women so poorly."

"I'm confused," he said, squinting his eyes at her. "Are you saying you don't want to make love to me? Because most wenches are knocking each other over for a chance to be bedded by a nobleman."

"I'm not most wenches!" She slipped the long strap of her pouch over her shoulder. "And I advise you to remember that, my lord."

"Sage, for heaven's sake, you're naught but a commoner. Why are you getting so upset about this?"

"Would you treat a lady that way you just did me?"

"I don't know," he answered with a shrug. "Ladies never couple with a man before they're married, so I haven't tried. But I'm sure if I wanted one, I could get one."

"You are such a pompous ass, Sir Robin." Sage spoke freely now, and she didn't care if he liked it or not.

"If you hadn't saved my life, I'd throw you out of here right now and tell you to never return," he said as she headed for the door.

"Don't bother. I'll leave here myself. And don't expect to see me again."

She stormed to the door, pulling it open, but stopped as soon as she remembered she had people trying to kill her and that she had nowhere to go.

"Well, I guess I'm glad I have another healer who will return soon, since you're leaving me when my wound isn't yet healed." He hurriedly dressed.

"I-I didn't say I'm leaving," she said, feeling like crying now.

"Didn't you?" he ground out. "If not, what was that big act all about?"

"I'm sorry," she said in a mere whisper, closing her eyes, not able to look at him. Neither could she leave him. If so, she would be putting not only herself, but also her siblings' lives at risk.

"You confuse me, wench," he spat, pushing his feet into his boots. "Are you staying at the castle or leaving? I'd like to know your intent."

"I'm...I'm staying," she said, wanting more than anything to leave him just to prove her point. Instead, she had to bite her tongue and let him feel as if he'd won this battle.

"Good," he said, sounding pleased by the thought. "And I promise you, next time you won't be so scared. You'll like it if you just give it a chance."

"Nay!" she said, her head whipping around to face him. "I will stay as your healer only. But never will I warm your bed, so don't even bother trying." With that, she left the room and slammed the door, running down the hall, knocking right into Lord Gar.

"Whoa there, sweetheart," said Gar, catching her before she fell. "Where are you going in such a hurry?"

"Mayhap ask her where she's been and leaving in such a hurry." Rook, who was with him, nodded at the door to Robin's solar just as he opened it and stepped out into the corridor.

"Bloody hell," she heard Robin mumble. When she looked back at him he was running his hand through his long hair.

"Oh, I see," said Gar with a chuckle. "You've been to Lord Robin's solar. Yes, I'm sure that's enough to scare any wench away."

"Let her be," Robin called out from down the hallway.

As soon as Gar released her, Sage ran, wanting to be anywhere right now but in the presence of Sir Robin. The reason was more than the fact she was disgusted by the way he'd treated her and that he'd almost bedded her. The real reason she needed to get away from him was because deep down, she liked him kissing her. She also liked the way he'd made her feel with his exciting foreplay.

Damn it, if she wasn't so angry with the man right now, she'd say she was even starting to have feelings for the fool. That scared her more than everything else combined.

CHAPTER 9

"So how was she?" Gar asked as he, Rook, and Robin sat together in the great hall having a tankard of ale.

"What the hell are you talking about?" Robin downed a big swig of ale, frustrated with Sage, and still feeling his need for release.

"The wench. You bedded her. How was it?" Gar leaned back on his chair at the dais and propped his feet up on the table.

"That's none of your concern," growled Robin. "Now get your damned feet off my table. Show a little respect."

"All right. Calm down." Gar slid his feet off the table.

"He didn't bed the girl." Rook studied Robin's face, tapping his fingers on the table.

"What?" Robin looked up, placing his tankard down after having had another swig.

"You heard me," said Rook. "And I'll bet it's because Sage—that's her name, isn't it?"

"Yes. So what of it?" Robin motioned for a serving girl to bring more ale.

"She probably demanded you respect her and so you had to let her go."

Gar laughed heartily. "Nay, Rook. Our cousin would never do such a fool thing. After all, the girl is only a commoner. If he wanted her, he'd take her."

"And my wife Rose was a commoner too," said Rook. "I'm telling you, I know that look on Robin's face because I had it myself when I wanted a girl I couldn't have."

"I can have any girl I want," spat Robin. "Just like Gar said. Now, damn it, wench, bring my ale. What is taking so long?" he shouted to the serving girl.

"Mmm hmm," said Rook into his tankard.

"I'm sorry, my lord." A serving wench hurried across the hall headed in their direction.

"Prove it," Gar challenged him. "Get that serving girl to meet you up in your room right now."

"Fine," said Robin, knowing that might take the edge off his frustration. After all, Sage did leave him in a very uncompromising way.

"Your ale, my lord." The wench poured his ale. "Will there be anything else?" She looked up at him and smiled. "Anything at all?"

"Go on," Gar whispered. "Now's your big chance. Show us."

"He won't," said Rook into his cup.

"Yes, there will be something else," Robin told the girl. Just as he said it, he looked up to see Sage enter the great hall with his sister. Sage looked over at him, but when they caught each other's eye, they both quickly looked away.

"My lord?" asked the comely wench. "What is it I can do for you?"

Damn it, Robin couldn't go upstairs with the wench now. Not after seeing Sage. He wouldn't want Sage to know how lusty he was still feeling after she'd turned him down. Plus, it wouldn't do him any good to have his sister watching him and asking questions later. He looked at the serving wench once more. He'd noticed her when he first got to the castle and had planned on having her. But now, after being with Sage, the wench did nothing to arouse him. Instead, he kept thinking of Sage and what almost happened abovestairs. What he wanted to happen, that is. Damn it, why was it so hard to push Sage from his mind?

Mayhap it was because he liked her. And even though she didn't think he respected her or needed to, he supposed in a way, she made a good point. After all, if it weren't for her, he'd be dead right now. She risked her life to save him. He supposed that did demand a bit of respect after all.

Gar cleared his throat, getting Robin's attention. "She's waiting, Robin."

Robin looked back over to the serving girl who stood next to him. "Yes," he said, feeling so pressured. "Be sure to fill Lord Rook and Lord Gar's tankards before you leave." He picked up his tankard and chugged ale rather than to look at the disappointment on the girl's face. He knew she wanted him to require more of her than just ale. Just like any wench would. Any wench but Sage, that is.

As soon as the girl left, Rook spoke up.

"Just like I said. He's fallen for the commoner and doesn't even want the usual lightskirts anymore."

"Stop it. I have not," said Robin. His gaze shot over to Sage again. There was a group of men around her, some of them being his knights. He didn't like it. "If you two really want to help with the preparations for Christmastide, do something besides analyzing my every word or action." He drank the rest of his ale, slammed down the tankard and got up.

"Well, what is it you want us to do?" asked Gar.

"I don't know. You two think you know everything about running a castle, so figure it out."

"Where are you going?" asked Rook.

"To the mews. To greet my father." Robin left the dais, walking right past the crowd of knights and men gathered around Sage. "What's going on here?" he asked. The men parted and left him staring right at the healer girl.

"I was meeting the other knights of the castle. Your sister was kind enough to introduce them to me. Is something wrong?" asked Sage. "Are your stitches pinching you? Or is there something else that is causing you discomfort?"

Dammit, she knew what she was doing and exactly what she meant. He didn't fancy her little games at all.

"Mayhap he needs saving again from the wench," sniggered one of the men.

"That's enough," Robin ground out. "Everyone, go about your business. Sage, meet me in the mews anon."

"Me? Whatever for?" she asked. "If one of your birds is ill, I don't know anything about curing it."

"Never mind. Just do as I say." He took off at a near run, wanting to get out of here and into the fresh air to clear his head.

"Well, my brother seems perturbed for some reason." Martine walked with Sage as she headed out of the great hall. "Did you do something to anger him, commoner?"

Sage stopped in her tracks, not liking the way the girl spoke to her.

"Lady Martine, I appreciate you introducing me to the knights, but somehow I feel as if you are only doing it to somehow spite your brother. Also, I don't like being called a commoner."

"Well, I can't say it isn't enjoyable to make Robin feel uncomfortable, but I can't take all the credit. He seems perturbed with you, if I'm not mistaken."

"Well, for your information, he was the one who did something to anger me," said Sage, turning and continuing to walk. She wasn't sure why Martine was following her. The girl was about Sage's age, but didn't even seem to like her. Still, the girl wouldn't leave her alone ever since she left Robin's room.

"Really? What did Robin do?" asked Martine, hurrying to catch up with her. Sage stopped once again.

"Does it really matter?"

"It does to me."

"Fine," she said, knowing if she didn't get her answer, Martine would keep asking. "Your brother tried to bed me."

"What?" Martine's eyes opened wide.

"He thought he could treat me like he does his whores, but I didn't like it."

"No. I don't suppose you would."

"I almost got drawn into believing he really cared for me. Then, I realized it wasn't that at all. So I stopped him cold in his tracks. And I swear if he tries anything with me again, I'll make him sorry he did."

Martine stood there with her eyes wide and her mouth open. Then all of a sudden, she started laughing, taking Sage by surprise. She wasn't sure why the girl reacted this way to her story. She was sure she was about to get reprimanded, but just the opposite happened.

"Why are you laughing? It's not funny," said Sage, putting her hands on her hips.

"Nay, it's not funny for you. I'm laughing because my brother deserved that! I know you're only a commoner, Sage, but I rather think I like you after all. You're someone who is not afraid to stand up to curs like my brother. No woman has ever put him in his place before." She looked around to make sure no one was listening. Then she leaned in closer and spoke softly. "Good for you, Sage. I'll never admit this to anyone, but I like a strong woman who speaks her mind and stands up for herself, even if she is only a commoner."

"You do?"

"I do." Martine winked. "But that is our little secret between us. Now, let's go see what my arrogant brother is doing in the mews."

"All right," said Sage, no longer wanting Martine to leave. She supposed she had gotten the wrong impression of the woman at first. Sage liked having someone who understood her. Yes, mayhap she wasn't so alone here after all. If Martine truly had these feelings and opinions, then perhaps she could be an asset to Sage in the long run. Mayhap, even a friend.

And Sage didn't have friends.

Sage opened the door to the mews and walked in to find Robin talking to two men. He held a pigeon on his finger.

"Hello? I'm here," she said.

"Who is this with Martine?" asked the older man with the long hair, who looked a lot like Robin.

"Father. Uncle Corbett," said Martine, pushing past Sage to give her father a hug.

"Sage, this is my father, Lord Madoc, and my Uncle Corbett," said Robin, nodding to the men in turn. "They are brothers."

"My lords," said Sage, lowering her head and curtsying. "So nice to meet you."

"Sage is my healer," Robin told the men, giving the bird back to his father.

"She saved Robin's life," Martine blurted out, getting a scolding look from her brother.

"Really?" asked the man named Corbett. "Robin, you are a knight. Shouldn't you be the one doing the saving?"

"I did save her life from three men who attacked her. I was wounded and thrown from my horse in the process, and that's how I ended up breaking through the ice," explained Robin.

"Well, it's a good thing she was there then. So, who were these men who attacked her?" asked Madoc.

"I don't know," said Robin.

"Were they bandits?" asked Corbett.

"I don't think so." Robin looked over at Sage. "They had swords. And horses."

"No, bandits wouldn't have swords," said Madoc. "I'd know."

"My father was a thief before he discovered he was a noble," said Martine, getting scolding looks from all three men now.

"What did they look like? Did they have crests on their tunics?" asked Corbett.

Sage had to stop this conversation from going any further. She didn't want anyone to find out she was responsible for another lord's death.

"It all happened so fast, that it was hard to tell," said Sage. "What are you doing with all the birds, Lord Madoc?"

"Our father raises homing pigeons, and used to race them to win money," said Martine. "I think they're dirty birds, but Father has taken a liking to them."

"They are not dirty," said Madoc, putting the pigeon back into a cage. "They are messengers. Between the homes of those in my family."

"Oh, I would love to hear more about it," said Sage, not really that interested in birds, but wanting to veer the conversation away from herself.

"Mayhap some other time." Robin took her by the arm.

"Right now, I need to show my new healer my castle and where she'll be working."

"Don't you already have a healer here?" asked Madoc.

"My healer is away right now," said Robin. "Sage is only here temporarily. Until my wound heals."

Sage didn't like Robin saying she was temporary, but decided now was not the time to speak up about it.

"Uncle Corbett, Mother wants to send out the invitations for the Christmastide celebration and needs you both to tell her which lords to invite," said Martine.

"Shouldn't that be my job?" asked Robin. "I am lord of Shrewsbury, not them."

"You don't really know any lords near here to invite," said Martine. "Uncle Corbett knows everyone."

"Why don't you join me?" asked Corbett. "I agree that you should be the one sending out the invitations."

"Well, all right," said Robin, looking over at Sage. "I'll join you in my solar as soon as I get the healer situated." He pulled Sage out the door of the mews and over the snow-covered courtyard.

"Slow down," complained Sage. "I'm going to fall on the ice if you keep up this speed."

"I need to talk to you. In private," he said, taking her into the keep.

"Where are we going?" she asked as he all but dragged her up the stairs. "To your solar again?"

"Nay," he said, stopping in front of another room and opening the door to enter. "This will be where you and your siblings will stay. For now," he added, entering the room.

Sage followed behind him, taking in her surroundings. It was a chamber fit for a noble. A massive bed sat up on a dais, with red velvet curtains surrounding it. There were shutters over the windows, but light peeked in through the cracks.

Ornamental wall hangings depicted jousts and hunts, and there was even one with the king on horseback.

"This is too beautiful. And so spacious," she said, looking around in awe. "Several families could live in here and never feel crowded." It was dark and cold in here, and she wrapped her arms around her to keep warm.

"The bed is big enough for you and your sister to share." Robin went over and lit a fire on the hearth. "I'll have pallets sent up for your brothers to sleep on."

Firelight lit up the room, giving her an even better look at her new living quarters. Several trunks were pushed against the wall and a wooden table with two stools were across the room. There was even a wardrobe—a second small room attached, used for changing.

"But this is the room of a noble," said Sage in awe. "Are you sure you want us to stay here?"

"Yes," he said. "For now. You are close to my own solar, so you'll be able to come if I call for you."

"Don't you mean I am close enough for you to keep an eye on me? So I won't say or do anything wrong?"

"There you go again, thinking the worst of me."

"Am I wrong?"

"I am not the ogre you think me to be, Sage. If only you could see past your clouded opinions."

"Martine seems to agree with me."

"Martine will do whatever she can to make me look bad. She's always been a thorn in my side."

"I think you are wrong. You just need to get to know your sister better."

"I don't need a commoner telling me what to do. Now, you'll do any healing for others in the small room just off the kitchen. The cooks are always getting cut from the sharp knives, so I think it's best you stay near them."

"I understand," she said, wondering when Robin was going to mention what happened between them. "Is there anything else you'd like to talk about?"

"I'll let you know when there is, but for now, I need to help in preparing the invitations."

"I thought you said you were going to show me around your castle."

"That will have to wait." He made his way to the door, stopping to speak to her without turning to face her. "I don't want you mingling with the rest of the knights anymore. Or the male servants either."

"What? You cannot be serious."

"There is no need," he said over his shoulder.

"And if they are hurt and I need to heal them?"

"If one of them is hurt or ill, then of course you'll need to tend to their malady. But otherwise, stay away from them. Do you hear me?" He actually turned to look at her this time.

"Oh, I hear you loud and clear, my lord."

"Good. Sage, I don't want you disobeying me. I don't want trouble."

"Of course not, my lord. You'll get no trouble from me."

Sage wasn't sure if Robin was jealous of the other men talking with her, or if this was some sort of game he played. Perhaps it was naught but a form of punishing her for walking away from him when he'd planned on bedding her.

Well, let him play his games, because Sage had games of her own. And the first thing she was going to do was to figure out a way to spend time with each and every man in the castle, only because she knew it would bother Robin to no end.

CHAPTER 10

Christmastide was approaching fast, and Sage had finally started to feel comfortable at the castle. Three days had passed since she'd arrived in Shrewsbury, but already she had started making friends. Even her siblings were starting to get used to their new home. Life at a castle, even being there as servants, was so much better than living in a secluded hut in the woods or staying at the monastery. The best part was that Sage didn't have to constantly be looking over her shoulder, thinking someone was out to kill her—which she was sure they still were.

"Sage," called out her brother, heading across the kitchen to where Sage had been preparing herbal remedies to use for healing. Her sister was plucking a chicken. Noel sat on a stool helping Sage to pull dried sage leaves off the stems.

"Oscar, how are things in the stable?" Sage looked up to realize that her brother had brought not one, but two boys with him.

"Sage, Berthar and Firmin are brothers. They're stable boys, just like me. They wanted to meet you," said her brother.

"Oh," said Sage, looking up and smiling. They were both a little younger than her own age. She could tell by the smitten looks on their faces that they liked her. "I'm sorry, but I'm not allowed to talk to any boys or men. It's Sir Robin's orders."

"What?" asked Oscar, picking up a currant from a bowl nearby. "That's silly. They just want to meet you." He popped the currant into his mouth.

Sage was about to agree when she noticed Robin enter the kitchen. He stopped to talk to the cook about something. As much as she wanted to irk the man by talking with these boys, she did promise Robin that she wouldn't cause trouble.

"Nay, I'd better not. Sir Robin won't like it. I'm sorry. I can only speak to males if they are hurt or ailing."

"Well, I cut my finger on a nail in the stable today," said one of the two boys, coming forward and holding out his hand. "Can you take a look at it for me?"

"I suppose so. Let me see it." Sage took the boy's hand in hers and inspected his cut. It already was healed over. "You say you got this today?" She looked up at him suspiciously, knowing better. That cut was at least three days old.

"Mayhap it was yesterday, I can't remember. Hello, Sage, my name is Firmin." A wide smile spread across the boy's face.

"My shoulder hurts," said his brother, pushing Firmin aside. "I was kicked by a horse."

"Oh, my! That could be deadly. Let me see it right away." Sage stood up and walked over and put her hands on the boy's shoulder. "I don't feel any broken bones. Is it bruised at all?"

"Why don't you check?" The boy eagerly pulled his tunic off his shoulder. "I'm Berthar, by the way. And you sure are pretty."

Sage realized quickly what was going on here. There were no bruises at all on the boy's skin.

"So you say you got kicked by a horse?" she asked, knowing it was a lie.

"Licked by a horse is more like it," snorted Firmin. "Can you look at my knee next, Sage?" He held up one leg.

"What's going on here?" asked Robin, making Sage jump, since she didn't know he was standing right behind her. "Sage, didn't I tell you not to talk to males?"

"These boys had ailments," Sage told him. "However, I think they'll be fine now."

"Get back to work. All of you," commanded Robin, sending Oscar and his friends running from the kitchen.

"You really don't need to rule with fear." Sage went back to the table and bagged up the herbs.

"I don't do that," protested Robin, leaning one leg in a half-sit resting on the table. It didn't look as if he planned on leaving anytime soon.

"Thank you for the help, Noel," said Sage, kissing her younger brother on the cheek. "Why don't you take these dirty bowls to the scullery so they can wash them."

"All right," said Noel, jumping off the stool.

The plump woman who baked the chickens started screaming. Sage's head snapped up. She saw Griffin with a cooked chicken in his mouth that the cook had just removed from the spit over the fire. The dog lay down right there, devouring the poultry as if he ruled the place.

"Give me that, you filthy beast!" The woman picked up a broom and started to swat the dog with it.

"Nay! Leave Griffin alone, he's my friend," cried Noel, running over to the dog and wrapping his arms around the dog's neck. The cook continued swinging the broom.

"Robin, do something!" cried Sage. "The cook is going to hit Noel with the broom if she's not careful. Plus, she means to hurt Griffin."

"That's enough," said Robin, heading over and taking the broom from the woman. "This is my hound. He can eat whatever he wants. He has my permission."

"Of course, my lord. But dogs belong in the kennels, not the kitchen," said the old woman grabbing back her broom.

"This is my castle hound. He's allowed inside the keep."

"Then why don't you wash the smelly thing? And teach it some manners?" The old woman made a face, showing her broken and blackened teeth.

"Get back to work," Robin told the woman, sending her back to the fire and spit. "Griffin, that's not nice to steal food." Robin took the remains of the chicken and threw it on a wooden table.

"Griffin is just hungry," said Noel, still holding onto the dog around his neck.

"You like the dog, don't you, Noel?" asked Robin.

"I do."

"Then take him over to the scullery with you and give him a bath. Have the other boys help you."

Sage giggled as the dog followed Noel over to the area where the dishes were washed.

"You know Griffin won't like that," said Sage.

"You're right. I'd better help hold him down. He's too much for any boy to handle." Robin rolled up his sleeves and hurried over to the scullery. Sage followed, not wanting to miss this.

By the time Robin had managed to give the dog a bath with the help of half a dozen boys, all chaos had broken out. Griffin got away from Robin and shook the water off his coat. With the dog's long, matted fur, the spray of water went everywhere, soaking anyone who was standing nearby. The girls in the kitchen screamed and ran the other way with Griffin chasing them and barking. Then the dog headed out into the great hall, his paws slipping on the wet floor as he tried to run.

"Aren't you going to go after him?" asked Sage.

"Why bother?" Robin stood up, soaking wet, pulling his long hair back and tying it with a band of leather.

"Lord Corbett as well as your parents and sister are in the great hall, aren't they? I thought they were inspecting the work of the servants. I believe the servants are in the process of hanging up the kissing boughs and stringing up evergreen branches and dried berries for the upcoming celebration."

"Bloody hell, that's right." Robin slipped on the wet floor and almost fell, trying to make his way out of the kitchen to stop the dog before he caused any more chaos. Noel ran after him, followed by Sage.

Robin stopped abruptly at the entrance to the great hall, groaning when he saw the looks on everyone's faces as well as all the Christmastide decorations hanging askew and half-trampled.

"Nay, Griffin," he shouted. "Bad dog."

"Robin, what is this all about?" asked his father, standing there with a parchment in his hand talking with Corbett.

"I gave the dog a bath and he got away from me."

"I'll get him," said Noel, running after the dog, chasing him. Griffin barked and ran in circles, thinking Noel wanted to play.

"The decorations are all ruined," whined his sister Martine.

"I'm sorry. I didn't know the dog would run." This wasn't how Robin wanted his position as lord of the castle to begin.

"Robin, you need to take control of your castle," said Martine.

"She's right," agreed his mother. "Something needs to be done to maintain order, now that you are Lord of Shrewsbury."

It surprised Robin to hear his mother say this, since she was usually the only one who supported anything he did.

"It's my fault," said Sage, rushing over and grabbing the dog by the scruff of his neck. "I never should have suggested he give the dog a bath. I'm sorry."

"Sage, you didn't—"

"I'll remove the hound at once," said Sage, walking with the dog and her little brother, heading for the door.

"It figures." Gar walked up to Robin, shaking his head. "You take in a stray commoner and her family and this is what happens. Mayhap you need to be a little more selective about who you bring home, Cousin."

"But I..."

"Robin, you are doing nothing at all to help plan this Christmastide celebration," complained Martine. "Now, are you going to stand there all day with your mouth open, dripping water all over the floor, or are you going to start taking charge of things, like you should be doing?"

"I—yes. Of course," said Robin, looking over his shoulder to see Sage leaving the great hall with his wet dog. Damn, he wanted to speak to her. That was the whole reason he went to the kitchen in the first place. He hadn't seen much of her in the past few days. And while Martine accused him of not doing a damned thing to help plan the Christmastide activities, it wasn't true. He'd not only organized a mock battle with his knights that would happen, but hired minstrels to play music, and even selected the group of mummers he wanted who would be entertaining his guests. He took inventory of the undercroft and larder, and spoke to the woodward about patrolling the forest on his property since he was worried about poachers. He'd had to go over the ledgers with his steward, collect rent from the villagers, and settle a dispute with neighboring serfs involving a pig and two goats. That is why he hadn't had a free moment to look for Sage until now. There was plenty to do, being lord of a castle.

It was late in the day before things calmed down and everyone stopped pestering Robin with one question after another. He hadn't even seen Sage at the meal, and wondered to where she'd disappeared. Griffin hadn't been there either, but for that he was glad. It had taken longer than he'd hoped to help the women fix the decorations and replace the ones that were ruined by the dog. This wasn't man's work in the least, but he'd offered to help, trying to smooth things over, since he was at fault here.

"Robin, how about a game of dice up on the battlements with the guards?" asked Gar. "I hear they're no good at it and that it's easy to win their coins." He laughed.

"Nay, I don't think so." Robin pushed up from the table and yawned. It had been a long day and all he wanted was to get some sleep.

"My father brought some Mountain Magic from Blake Castle," said Rook. "He said it is for the Christmastide celebration, but there is lots of it. I'm sure I can sneak out some for us ahead of time."

"Nay. No Mountain Magic." Robin ran a weary hand through his hair, remembering the last time he had some with the MacKeefes. His head hurt just thinking about it. "I think I'm going to bed."

He walked past his father and uncle. Madoc stopped him.

"Robin, Corbett and your mother and I are leaving for Devonshire first thing in the morning."

"Why?" asked Robin with another yawn. "I thought you were going to stay for the Christmastide celebrations."

"We'll be back before Twelfth Night. We have things to attend to, but we'll bring more of the family with us when we return. You seem to have this under control here and don't need us anymore."

"All right. I'll look forward to the whole family being together for the holiday. But right now, I need to get some sleep, so excuse me."

Robin headed up to his solar, wondering about Sage as he passed by the door to her chamber. He had really wanted to talk to her. To apologize for the way he'd acted. He raised his hand to knock on her door, but then lowered it slowly. Her siblings were in there with her. He wanted to be alone with her and couldn't do it this way. He'd just have to wait until morning.

He made his way into his room, lighting a fire on the hearth. Then he stripped off his clothes and got into bed, knowing he would be dreaming of Sage tonight, just like he had for the past few nights. If she wanted to keep her distance from him in waking life, at least he could be with her, if only in his dreams.

CHAPTER 11

Sage lay on the floor in her chamber with Griffin, trying to dry him off by keeping him close to the fire on the hearth. Her siblings were already sleeping, and she fell asleep with her arm over the dog to keep him from running off.

With her eyes closed, Robin filled her thoughts. No lord of a castle would even consider bathing their own dog. Robin did. Plus, she heard he'd helped the women and servants fix all the decorations that Griffin ruined. No nobleman would do anything so beneath his status. Robin was different. While he was indeed a noble, he still did things that commoners would be expected to do.

She liked that about him. She also liked the way he'd been kind to her siblings, especially little Noel where Griffin was concerned. Being close to Robin made her smile. Seeing him slip on the wet floor made her laugh. Robin wasn't like the other nobles after all, she decided. He did care about people, but in his own way. Even if she thought he'd only wanted her like he did the rest of the girls who came to his bed, mayhap she was wrong. Perhaps she'd stop avoiding him tomorrow and find out for sure. After all, he did say he wanted to talk to her. Mayhap she should give him another chance.

The dog moved and woke her up. Then Griffin ran across the room and scratched at the door and started to whine.

"Shhh," she said to the dog, not wanting Griffin to wake her siblings. She got up, wearing only her night rail, padding to the door with bare feet. "Do you need to go out?" she asked, realizing he might need to relieve himself since it had been a while since they went outdoors.

Griffin pawed at the door and whined some more.

"Oh, all right," she said, grabbing her cloak from a hook on the wall. She decided she'd take the dog out to the courtyard herself. It was the middle of the night and no one would see her in her night clothes so she wasn't worried about that. She just wanted to make sure Griffin didn't run off and cause trouble by stealing another chicken. Plus, she didn't want the dog to get dirty again when they'd worked so hard to make him clean.

She opened the door and Griffin bolted out, running down the corridor, not down the steps to go out into the courtyard. Instead, he was heading right toward the chambers of the nobles.

"Nay," she whispered hoarsely, running after the dog. Before she could stop him, Griffin jumped up on one of the doors, scratching at it and looking as if he were trying to get in. "Get back here. You're going to wake up the nobles," she scolded softly.

Being still half-asleep, she wasn't fast enough. Griffin's large body pushed against one of the doors and it opened and the dog disappeared into the dark room.

All Sage could think about was that the dog was going to wake and scare a noblewoman, and she'd be in more trouble with Robin tomorrow than the hound would. She needed to get Griffin and leave before the noble awoke.

"Griffin, come back here," she whispered, peering into the darkened room. There was a little bit of a fire on the hearth yet and by the scant light she could see the dog. He was lying in front of the fire. "God's eyes, why me?" she mumbled, knowing she needed to remove the dog from the chamber. The sound of two guards talking echoed along with their footsteps as they headed down the corridor toward her. Her heart jumped. She couldn't be found inside the room of a sleeping noble. She'd be thrown in the dungeon for sure just from looking into their room. Plus, there was no telling how the men would act to find her in her nightclothes.

Sage slipped into the room and closed the door, listening for the guards to pass. But instead, she heard a deep voice from the dark, coming from the bed.

"How did you get in here?"

She swallowed deeply. That was Robin's voice. She'd know it anywhere. In her haste to catch the dog she'd been careless and hadn't noticed that she was walking right into the den of the lion.

Sage stood motionless in the dark, hearing her heart drumming in her ears. There was a swishing noise that sounded like blankets, and then she saw Robin's shadow as he crossed the room, heading for Griffin.

"Griffin, how did you get in? Did I leave the door open? You look dry," he said to the dog, petting the dog's fur. "Did Sage do that? She's nice, isn't she? I really like her. I just wish she liked me, but she doesn't."

He moved into the light of the dying fire, still hunkered down and petting the dog. It was then that she realized he was stark naked! She gasped, quickly clamping her hand over her mouth but it was too late. He shot up to a standing position, grapping his sword from the table, spinning around and holding it out with two hands.

"Who goes there?" he commanded. "Speak up before I lop off your head."

"N-nay. It's me, Robin. Lord Robin. Sir Robin," she said, afraid he might kill her if he thought she was an intruder there to harm him. She couldn't let him make that mistake. She rather liked her head.

"Announce yourself," he commanded, cocking his head and narrowing his eyes, trying to see in the dark. It was hard for him to see her in the shadows, but she saw him perfectly. The fire danced and the light kissed his skin, lighting up his entire nakedness for her to see. She would have closed her eyes to be polite if she hadn't been so scared of possibly losing her head. Nay, she needed to make her presence known.

"It's Sage. Please don't hurt me, my lord." She slowly walked forward into the glow of the firelight, letting him see that it was really she.

"Sage?" he asked, shaking his head, seeming very confused. "What are you doing here in my room? In the middle of the night?"

"I—I was chasing after Griffin and he ran in here," she said. "I didn't realize it was your room. Not at first. I just wanted to collect him and leave, but then they came down the hallway and Griffin lay down by the fire. I had to make a decision quickly. Since you warned me that men are not to be trusted and I was only in my nightclothes, I came into the room to hide from them."

"You're rambling with your words again, making no sense at all." He turned and put his sword down on the table. "So, why are you really here?" He yawned and rubbed his face.

"My lord," she said, feeling extremely uncomfortable. "You said you wanted to speak with me."

She thought by now he'd put on some clothes, but he didn't seem as if being naked in front of her bothered him in the least. If she wasn't so tongue-tied right now by his mere presence, mayhap she would have mentioned it. Then again, mayhap that would only point out that she'd noticed his state.

"Yes, Sage, I did. Come closer to the fire where I can see you better."

"I would but..."

"If you show up here in the middle of the night, you must really want to talk. So why are you being so shy?"

"I-I—" She figured actions were louder than words. So, she removed her cloak and handed it to him with her head turned. "Please. Put this on."

"Why would I—" He stopped in midsentence and she heard him swear under his breath. "I'm sorry," he said, yanking the cloak away from her and holding it in front of his groin. "I was very tired and this is how I sleep. Naked. I told you that at the monastery. I didn't know you'd show up here or that I'd forget I wasn't wearing anything. I mean I—"

"Now, it is you, my lord, whose words are rambling."

"Yes. Yes. I suppose so." He cleared his throat. "Won't you have a seat?" He turned to pull over a bench for her and when he did, she got a glorious view of his naked backside. Quickly, he pulled her cloak around him before turning back around.

"Thank you." Sage sat down in front of the fire. The flames were burning out and the room held a chill to it. She wrapped her arms around herself.

"You're cold," he said.

"Nay. I'm fine," she answered, afraid he was about to give her back the cloak. If she saw him naked once more, she was going to do something she might regret. All she could think of now was letting him warm her up.

"I see you are cold. Don't lie," he said, his gaze settling on her chest. "Unless you are just happy to see me."

When her eyes followed his, she realized with the thin shift and in the firelight, her naked body beneath the cloth was visible. And her nipples were taut. His words made her embarrassed.

"Mayhap I should leave." She stood up but his hand clamped around her wrist, keeping her from going.

"Nay. Please stay. I'll stoke the fire. You'll be warmer soon, I promise."

His eyes interlocked with hers. In the light of the fire she could see his sincerity shining in his bright blue orbs. She also noticed a hint of longing mixed with sadness. She didn't want to disappoint him. She'd already caused him problems with his family, but she didn't mean to do it. Nay, she wanted to please him, to impress him, and to make him smile, not frown.

"Just for a few minutes," she said, sitting back down. He stoked the fire and turned around. When he did, she saw the skin of his upper thigh. It only made her wonder about his wound.

"How is your wound?" she asked.

"Did you want to see?" He started to pull aside the cloak but she raised a hand to stop him.

"Nay. Not now. Mayhap in the daylight would be better. When we are both dressed."

"Yes," he said with a nod. His tongue darted out to lick his lips, which only made her want to kiss him now. "Perhaps that would be better." He pulled the cloak tighter around him and sat down on the bench next to her. "Thank you for drying off my dog. I didn't think giving Griffin a bath would wreak so much havoc."

"Is everything back in order?"

"Yes. Everything is fine. Besides, Christmas isn't for another four days yet. We have plenty of time."

"Yes. Plenty," she repeated. They sat there in silence, and Sage's heart began to beat quickly one again. "Did all the invitations to the surrounding castles go out then?"

"They did." He nodded. "It should be a huge celebration."

"That's nice," she said, not knowing what else to say. This wasn't usual for her, since she usually had no trouble making conversation, even if she didn't have any real friends. Then again, they were in the dark, alone, and half-naked, so she supposed she had every right to feel nervous.

"Robin, I—"

"Sage, I—"

They both started speaking at the same time and then stopped and laughed.

"Go ahead," he said, holding out his hand.

"Nay, you go first," she insisted.

"All right," he said, blowing out a breath and then leaning his elbows on his knees, staring at the blazing fire. "Are you getting warmer?"

"I am. But I don't think that was what you wanted to say." She planned on telling him that she was wrong in pushing him away when he wanted to be intimate. That she perhaps judged him too quickly. While it seemed detrimental at the time, now she felt as if she'd over-reacted. Sage wanted to make love to him, but she didn't know how to tell him that she'd just been furious at the time, thinking of all the girls he'd had in his bed. She'd also been scared, and really did want him to respect her, since she saved his life.

"I'm sorry, Sage."

"Sorry? Whatever for?"

"I was acting like a pig, and you don't deserve that."

She giggled at his analogy. "I think you mean cur, but it doesn't matter. I forgive you."

"Yes, you are a commoner, but you are also a bright, amazing woman." He continued talking, still staring at the fire. "I suppose I was only thinking of myself when I tried to bed you, but I know now that it made you feel like one of the castle whores."

"Robin," she said, but he kept on talking.

"I'm not used to women turning me away, and I have to admit that I felt hurt and insulted by it. Still, you didn't deserve to be treated poorly."

"Robin," she said again.

"I mean, I suppose I deserved the slap, but then again, you are a commoner and I am a noble and that only confused me more. I am new to this position, and things aren't as easy as I thought they'd be."

"Robin, for heaven's sake, stop it," she said louder.

"Huh?" He finally turned to face her.

"I said I forgive you."

"You do? I mean, Sage, I really like you. I want you to know that."

"I do know. I heard you tell the dog." That made them both smile.

"I guess I just needed someone to confide in," he said with a shrug.

"And Griffin seemed like the logical choice for that?"

"Well, yes," he said, looking down at the hound. Griffin looked over at them, panting. Sage swore the dog was smiling. "I mean, at least he doesn't give me a hard time the way my cousins do. He doesn't talk back or question my choices either. As I said, he's a perfect one to confide in." He reached down and rubbed the dog's head.

"I suppose you have a point there." Sage bravely reached

out and touched Robin's arm. Then she pulled herself closer to him and laid her head on his shoulder.

"Sage?" he said, sounding cautious. "What are you doing?"

"I'm... just getting warmer," she told him, wetting her dry lips with her tongue.

"I promised you I wouldn't touch you intimately again."

"I know you did. And I appreciate that. That shows me that you respect me."

"You're not making it easy."

"That's because I think I've had a change of mind."

"You did?" His eyebrows arched. "Please, don't say it if you don't mean it."

"I do mean it, Robin. I hope you don't mind if I call you Robin."

"My title only needs to be used when others are around. You can call me Robin if we are alone."

"Thank you."

"Why don't you tell me what you wanted to say now." He got up, breaking their connection. Her heart dropped. He turned his back to her and once again stoked the fire.

"I wanted to say that I misjudged you and for that I am sorry."

"What do you mean?" He looked over his shoulder with the poker in his grip.

"You saved my life on the road. You risked your own life for me, even though you didn't know me. Even though I was only a simple commoner."

"You were a lady in distress. I am a knight. Saving you was my job. My duty."

"I'm not sure I like to be called a duty."

"You know what I mean."

"I am not a lady. Not a noblewoman, and I have no title. It

would have been just as easy for you to keep on going and never even stop to help me."

"What kind of an ogre do you take me to be?" He shoved the poker into the iron stand. "I never would have left you alone with those men who might have robbed you and raped you. Or by the looks of it, kill you."

"No. No, I don't suppose you would."

"You never did tell me why you think those men were after you or what they wanted." He sat back down next to her, his face so close to hers that she could feel his breath on her cheek.

"I suppose they wanted what any attackers do."

"Nay. I don't believe that. They didn't seem as if they were trying to rape you," he surmised. "They weren't even attempting to steal any of your belongings. Not really."

"I didn't have much for them to take." Her gaze fell to the floor.

"I think they were mercenaries. Working for someone. Otherwise, they'd have daggers, not swords."

"I suppose that's possible."

"If so, that means they were sent to kill you, Sage. Someone paid them to hunt you down."

"It... did seem as if they were trying to kill me, I agree."

"And yet you don't wonder why?"

"Who can ever know what is in the mind of those who harbor evil intentions?" Once again, she snuggled up to him, sliding her hand under the cloak, wrapping her fingers around the muscles of his upper arm. "Kiss me, Robin."

That got his mind off the attackers. He looked at her first in surprise. Then, his gaze traveled down to her mouth and settled there. "I want you so bad that it's not even funny," he said softly, still staring at her mouth.

"Then what are you waiting for? I told you that I now want it too."

"Are you sure about this?" he asked, his mouth coming closer to hers. "I wouldn't want to be called a goat again."

She laughed. "I think you mean a cur."

"Nay, I mean a goat. With a horn and all." He pulled aside the cloak and looked downward. Her attention followed. She saw what he meant. His manhood stood up, straight and hard.

"Oh, yes. A goat," she said, just as his lips covered hers.

Sage wasn't sure what kind of power this man held over her, but it was making the want she felt for him so strong that she couldn't pull away now, even if she tried. His hand went to the back of her head and he pulled her even closer, letting the kiss deepen. His hot tongue filled her mouth, and she matched his actions with her own. Then his hands slipped downward and he slid her night rail off her shoulders, leaving them bare.

"Are you sure about this, Sage?" he asked. She could hear the longing in his voice. "Because, I don't want you telling me I'm treating you like a whore when this is over."

"I'm sure," she said.

"This is going to be done in lust only, I'm afraid. What I mean is, I am very attracted to you, but we don't know each other well. It is not love, if that's what you are hoping or looking for. I want to be clear about that."

"I know. I understand and feel the same way. I agree," she said, reaching beneath the cloak and flipping it off his shoulders. "Robin, you make something in me come alive and I need to find out more."

"More? You mean completion. Surely, you've felt that before?"

"Nay. Never."

"Then I shall make certain I am not satisfied until you are completely sated. Over and over again." As he spoke, he slowly trailed his fingers downward, lowering her bodice, cupping her breasts with his large palms. "There are many ways to pleasure a woman," he said into her ear, nibbling on her lobe, letting his tongue flick out as he spoke.

"Oh, is there?"

"More than you think," he said, pushing her gown down to her waist. The cool air kissed her hot flesh, making her feel lusty.

"How many... ways are there?" she asked, her head going back as he trailed kisses down her neck while he rolled her nipples with his fingertips causing them to become taut.

"Would you like to find out?" Before she could answer, he'd taken her breast into his mouth, once again using that talented tongue of his to make her feel euphoric.

"Yesssss," she said, breathing harder and faster as his kisses trailed down her stomach. He stopped only for a moment to let his tongue swirl around her navel. The action almost made her shoot right off the bench in anticipation.

Before she knew it, Robin was on his knees in front of her, pulling her nightgown all the way off and laying it at her feet. The dog rolled over the other way, as if he didn't want to look.

"Open your legs for me, sweetheart."

"My-my legs?" she asked, feeling a little scared.

"I'm going to show you pleasure, I swear. You don't need to be frightened." With his big hands he parted her legs, his eyes interlocked with hers. His fingers worked magic, making her feel excited. And when he did something she never expected, using his mouth, she squealed in passion, her body tingling with a new life she'd never felt before.

"Ooh, ooh," she said, her eyes wide and her legs parting more on their own. She grabbed his head and pulled it closer, loving every minute of this. It was something new and exciting. She was making love with a handsome man in a way she had never dreamed of before. "Do it, Robin. Make love to me the normal way now. I need to know how it feels."

"Not yet. I want to make sure you are really ready."

"Oh, I am, I am," she said, feeling her body trembling. Heat swelled within her. Her body started to vibrate.

"Something is happening," she said, feeling so naughty and loving the way it felt. "I want you, Robin. I need you. I need you right now."

He picked her up, carrying her to the bed. Then he put her flat on her back and straddled his legs around her.

"Now, you're ready," he said, kissing her while he slid his manly length inside her, little by little but pulled back out until she could stand the teasing no longer.

"I want you, Robin. Please stop teasing me. I want you inside me now."

"Now, how can I deny a lady her request?" he asked, holding himself up, looking down at her with such dangerous and lust-filled eyes that it made her feel wanton and needy. And the fact that he'd purposely called her a lady when he knew damned well she wasn't one, made her feel like a queen at this moment. She didn't think it could get better than this, but she was wrong.

His thrusts started slowly, but when she rocked her hips to meet his, he turned into an animal of the finest kind. They became one, and she reached up with her legs, wrapping them around his waist, holding on to his shoulders as he took her for the ride of her life.

Colors. Vibrant colors of blue and pink exploded behind her closed lids as she let loose with any inhibitions, living for the moment, enjoying the time she shared with this talented, sexy man. He brought her to peaks she'd never known. She squealed and moaned and then to her surprise, she cried out with joy when she found her release.

He found his too. And when his life seed filled her, she squealed and cried out again.

Both of them breathing hard, he flipped on to his back next to her, and she knew it was over. That thought upset her and frightened her. Yes, she'd found her release, but now she only wanted to find it again.

"I'm not done yet," she said, causing his eyes to pop open.

"What?" he asked in surprise. "But I thought you were sated."

"Oh, I am. I was," she assured him, climbing atop him. "But I want to be sated again and again just like you said."

"Oh, Sage, I'm sorry," he said, looking downward. "I think it's going to be a little while before I can sate you again."

She looked down to see what he meant. Her heart dropped in her chest. She was still feeling randy.

"I can't help it," she told him. "I feel as if I could do it again." She mounted his leg and used that to satisfy herself, once again finding that feeling of euphoric completion, even if he wasn't inside her.

Then she fell onto her back next to him with a smile on her face. She tried to slow her rapid breathing. "Now I'm done," she told him.

"And you called *me* the goat?" He laughed, and she laughed too. Never had she thought someone like Robin could bring her to life and make her feel so aroused, so excited, and so sated over and over again.

CHAPTER 12

Robin awoke the next morning, surprised to see Sage already dressed and standing at the side of the bed. The shutter was open. Scant first rays of daylight as well as a cold winter breeze blew into the room.

"Sage?" He sat up, rubbing his eyes. "Why is it so cold in here?"

"I thought some fresh air in the room would do us both some good." She walked over and closed the shutter. "Plus, I admit, I knew it would wake you up."

"Yes, it certainly did that," he grumbled, pulling the blanket up to his chin and rolling over, closing his eyes again. He wasn't used to getting up this early.

All of a sudden the blanket was torn away from him and the cold air bit at his bare skin.

"What the hell are you doing?" He rolled over and looked up to see Sage looking down at him.

"I wanted to check your wound before I go. I hope we didn't break open the stitches with our... our vigorous activities last night." She smiled coyly.

"Oh, yes. That," he said. Just thinking of coupling with Sage was starting to make him lusty again. "I enjoyed it. Did you?"

"I don't think you need to ask." Her cheeks blushed as she tended to his wound. "I'm going to put on another compound and wrap it up again. Your wound looks like it is healing nicely. I'm impressed. I thought for sure it would have broken open."

"Sage." He touched her hand. Her gaze flickered over to him. "I wouldn't object to a repeat of last night."

She almost seemed to be considering it for a moment. But then her smile faded and she pulled her arm away from him and finished wrapping his wound. "After today, I don't think your wound will need to be wrapped anymore. Then again, you'll still need to be careful. And of course I'll have to watch for infection. We don't want it to get infected, because that wouldn't be good." She busied herself putting things into a bag that wasn't there last night. As a matter of fact, she had been wearing a night rail last night, but now she was fully dressed.

"How did you get your clothes and healing bag?" he asked.

"I returned to my chamber earlier. However, I must leave now. We wouldn't want anyone to know I was here with you last night." She turned to go but he sat upright, pulling her over to him in a hug.

"What's your hurry?" He kissed her neck. She looked the other way. "You're not enjoying this like you did last night. Why?"

"Of course, I am," she said, pulling out of his embrace. "I just have a lot to do today, that's all. I promised your sister I'd help finish planning the feast for the Christmastide celebration."

"You did? She asked you?"

"Yes. We're friends now, I'll have you know. Besides, your

parents and Lord Corbett left already and she said she could use my help."

"They left?" His head snapped around and he looked back at the window and then over to her. "It's only sunup."

"Not everyone sleeps as late as you do."

"Bid the devil, I wanted to see them off. Now they'll wonder what I was doing that I wasn't there to say goodbye."

"Don't worry. I was there to see them off so they won't know we were together."

He grabbed his clothes and started dressing quickly. "Sage, I don't understand. Why are you so afraid anyone will know that we've coupled? What difference does it make?"

A shadow of sadness darkened her face. "I'm afraid I acted compulsively last night."

"You mean impulsively."

"That too. I must admit that this morning I am embarrassed by my actions."

"Why?" This all seemed so ridiculous to him. "Coupling is a natural thing," he told her, pulling up his breeches. "Who cares if we spent the night together?"

"I do," she said softly, clinging to her herbal bag like a lifeline.

"Are you saying you regret what we did?" He sat on the bench to put on his boots.

"I don't regret it, but I don't think we should do it again."

"What? Why not?" God's eyes, this girl was confusing him. She also seemed hot and cold more constantly than even the weather.

"Robin, you are a noble. I am a commoner."

"So, tell me something I don't know." He stood up and stretched and yawned.

"Nothing can ever come from what happened."

"Huh? I don't understand what you're trying to say." He

walked over and grabbed a boar's bristle brush and ran it through his long hair.

"Your sister told me that Lord Corbett and your father expect you to marry a noblewoman. That they invited all the eligible ladies to the Christmastide celebration and that you are expected to choose one to marry."

"Oh, that. Yes, the King made me Lord of Shrewsbury, but I am to marry a noblewoman in return. "I will do what's expected, but none of that matters right now."

"Doesn't it?" Her mouth became a hard line and her eyes narrowed. He felt as if mayhap he'd said the wrong thing.

"Sage, if you have something to say then do so. I don't fancy playing such silly games so early in the morning when I'm barely awake."

"Silly games?" She glared at him. "Is that all our love-making was to you?"

Damn, he said something wrong again. He really needed some ale to wake up. Nay, what he needed was whisky to deal with the likes of her.

"We had a good time last night, yes. I made it clear that it was done in lust only and you agreed to it."

"I did, but it bothers me now that you said that."

"It was a bedding. You knew that. So what is the problem?"

"Bedding? Is that what we're calling it now? Not even coupling? Or, God forbid, you might think of it as lovemaking, the way I considered it."

"Stop it," he commanded, holding his hand out and looking the other way. "If you're looking for something more than just a good bedding, I'm afraid you've come to the wrong place."

"Well," she said with a huff. "I guess so. I'm sorry I bothered you, my high and mighty lord. I will not consume your precious time with silly games again." She turned and stormed out the door.

"Sage! Wait," he said, starting to go after her just as Rook and Gar walked into the room.

"What was she doing in here?" asked Gar with a smile, looking down the hallway after Sage.

"I think we can all guess," said Rook in a knowing manner.

"Sage was tending to my wound." Robin let out a deep sigh and collapsed atop the bed.

"Is that what you're telling people?" asked Gar with a chuckle, closing the door. "So, tell us. How was she?" He pulled over a chair and sat down backwards on it, leaning his arms on the back. "And don't leave out any of the details."

"Gar, what's the matter with you?" asked Rook.

"What?" Gar shrugged. "You don't want to know?"

"It's none of our business." Rook went over and stoked the fire.

"Rook, since you've married that gardener girl, you really have changed," complained Gar. "I swear I don't even know who you are anymore."

"Yes, we coupled," said Robin, lying back on the bed with his arm over his face. "First she didn't want it, and then she did —she really, really did. Now, she doesn't want it anymore."

"What the hell does that mean?" asked Gar.

"It means that Sage isn't just another common serving wench willing to spread her legs for the lord of the castle and think it was a privilege to do so." Rook stuck the poker back into the iron holder. "Am I right, Robin?"

Robin removed his arm from his face and sat up. "I'm not sure. The girl confuses me."

"You have feelings for her, don't you?" asked Rook, leaning against the bedpost with his arms crossed.

"Sure he does. Feelings of lust," said Gar. "Who wouldn't?

Did you get a good look at the wench? She's not bad on the eyes."

"Gar, please," said Rook, shaking his head. "I'm trying to have a serious conversation with Robin."

"I don't like serious conversations." Gar got up and headed for the door. "I'll be in the practice yard if you want to blow off any steam, Robin. Mayhap more time spent with your weapons and less with indecisive wenches is what you really need right now."

"I'll join you shortly," said Robin as Gar left the room. Robin walked over and closed the door after him, looking back at Rook. "I know it's odd to even say this, but I think I might have feelings for Sage. I mean, besides lust, that is."

"And you don't want those feelings because you are a noble and you know you're required to marry someone of your status," Rook said for him.

"Not so." Robin walked back to the bed. "I never said I wanted to marry the girl. Besides, that is out of the question."

"Is it?" Rook bit at a hangnail. "Unless you are forgetting, I married a commoner. So did Raven, Lark, and Eleanor. It wouldn't be the first time it happened in this family."

"Lark and Eleanor's husbands were really nobles. Or at least half-noble," Robin corrected him. "That doesn't count."

"Robin, if you like the girl, then do something about it."

"What? What the hell am I supposed to do? I'm expected to marry a noble to make up for the rest of you fools who fell in love with someone from below the salt. I am not going to let down my father, and I am especially not going to get on Uncle Corbett's bad side. And even if I wanted to marry a commoner, I can't. I've been ordered by the King himself to marry someone of my own status."

"Well, then. I guess there is nothing else I can say." Rook got up and headed to the door. He stopped before leaving, looking back over his shoulder. "Just do yourself a favor, Robin."

"What's that?"

"Don't let someone you really care for be disappointed in you because you didn't have the courage to be true to your own heart."

With that, he left the room, leaving Robin standing by himself wondering what the hell was happening to him. His only concern was duty and keeping up his image. He had his own castle now, and by rights, he needed to marry someone of his own status. He needed heirs. Noble heirs. He didn't need a commoner confusing and clouding his mind. Nay, he didn't need Sage or anything she could give him. Robin didn't need to feel her in his arms or feel as if they completed each other, the way he felt last night. He was done with all this. He didn't want or need Sage Hillock ever again.

Or did he?

"Sage? Sage, did you hear me?" Martine leaned over the wooden table in the kitchen, looking at Sage. "I said we'll have the stuffed pheasant with brown sage gravy as one of the main dishes for Christmastide. So, do we have enough sage to make the gravy or not?"

"I—I think so." Sage was torn from her thoughts of Robin, not able to get her mind off of him. "I filled up a large jar of dried sage yesterday, and I noticed there was still some growing under the snow of the castle's herb garden if we need more."

"You seem as if you've got something on your mind this morning. Care to share?"

"I'm fine."

"We have to go over all the ingredients for the menu and make certain we have enough of what we need."

"Enough of what we need," she mumbled, thinking she'd had exactly what she'd needed last night with Robin, but now she'd never have it again.

"What's wrong with you?" snapped Martine.

"Why do you want my help?" asked Sage.

"What?" Martine's brows dipped. "I told Mother I'd handle the menu for the celebration."

"But I'm just a commoner. You don't need me to assist you. Mayhap you'd better ask another of the noblewomen in the castle instead." She stood up, feeling like she was in a daze.

"Oh, I see what this is about." Martine crossed her arms over her chest.

"What?" Sage didn't know what she meant.

"This has to do with my pig-headed brother, doesn't it?"

"I—I don't know what you mean." Sage was surprised that Martine could see right through her.

"Did he do something to hurt you?"

"Nay! Robin wouldn't hurt me. He's gentle and—" She stopped in midsentence and her eyes raised to see Martine smiling now.

"He bedded you, didn't he? Just admit it."

There was that word, bedded again. It made her feel like one of the lightskirts. Sage hurried out of the kitchen with Martine right behind her.

"If you don't tell me, I'm going to ask him myself."

"Nay!" Sage stopped and spun around on her heel. "Please, don't do that."

"You *did* couple with him. I knew it!" Martine was too wise for her own good.

"Please, don't say anything to anyone. Especially not Robin."

"Why not?"

"Because, it's never going to happen again, that's why." She turned and continued to walk.

"That bad, was it? I figured my brother was no good in bed." Martine chuckled.

Sage stopped and let out a deep sigh. Then she turned and looked at Martine, knowing if she didn't tell someone how she felt, she was going to burst.

"I'll tell you whatever you want to know, but not here."

"We'll go to my chamber," said Martine.

"Nay. Someone might see us and wonder why you have a commoner in your chamber. Let's go to the mews. I heard the falconer saying he was going to be away for a while this morning, so there shouldn't be anyone in there right now."

"All right," agreed Martine.

The two women hurried out to the mews, ducking inside the building and stopping just inside the door. Sage scanned the area first to make sure it was empty. The doves in the pen cooed and the falcons squawked, probably wanting to eat them. Thank goodness the doves and pigeons were locked up in a cage.

"Tell me everything," said Martine.

"Oh, Martine, this is hard for me to talk to you about Robin. After all, he is your brother."

Robin stopped scooping up the bird seed he'd kicked over, having come to check on the new homing pigeons before he made his way out to the practice yard. Hunkered down at the far end of the mews and behind the cage, he stayed quiet, hearing Sage say his name.

"I made love with Robin, but now I wish that I hadn't," said Sage.

Robin's heart fell in his chest. He knew he should make his presence known, but he wanted to find out what was on Sage's mind and how she really felt about him. If he'd hurt her in any way, he'd never forgive himself. He thought Sage wanted their intimate time together just as much as he had, but now he wasn't sure.

"My brother is a cur," spat Martine. "He used you just like he uses any pretty servant girl who catches his eye. Now that he's lord of a castle, I'm sure it's only going to get worse."

"Do you really think so?" asked Sage.

"Yes, I do. He's a male and a noble. They all act that way."

"But Robin seemed so different. He acted like he really cared about me."

"He didn't. Trust me. You are nothing to him but a way to satisfy his carnal urges. That's all."

Robin was about to stand up and tell Sage that his sister was wrong, but something made him stay down. Perhaps it was because deep inside he knew that what his sister said was partially true, and he was disgusted with himself.

"I gave myself to Robin freely and it was a wonderful night," said Sage.

Robin leaned forward to hear more.

"He didn't force himself on you, did he?"

"Nay. Not at all. I knew it was being done in lust, but I agreed to it."

"Why would you agree to couple with my brother at all? There have to be many other men out there who would be better choices for you."

"I know," said Sage softly. "I mean, I have deep feelings for Robin, but I know he doesn't feel the same way for me. I was a fool, Martine. I let my heart guide me when I should have listened to my head."

"He has to marry a noblewoman. It's crucial," explained

Martine. "Uncle Corbett wants to bring back honor to the family name, and my cousins are all marrying from below the salt, making things worse instead of better."

"I understand," said Sage. "I suppose it is best to stay away from Robin. I'm not right for him and I don't want to get in the way. He deserves a lady. Someone who is noble and who can bring much to the alliance. I am an orphan with no home. I have nothing at all to offer. If Robin didn't let me and my siblings stay here, I don't know what I'd do."

"Good idea to keep away from him. Now, show me what herbs this castle has that can be used for the feast."

Robin slowly stood up with a handful of seed and watched the women hurrying back to the keep. His heart had been full last night when he held Sage in his arms. Now he felt so empty. This wasn't what he had planned at all.

He was expected to marry well, and being the dutiful knight he was, and a new lord of a castle, he would do just that. But in doing that, what would happen to Sage and her siblings? He supposed it shouldn't matter to him, but somehow it did.

He felt something for Sage that he'd never felt for any woman before. She was kind and a good healer. She cared about people. About him. She was also the bravest woman he'd ever met. No other woman would risk her life to save his, the way she did when he'd fallen through the ice. Part of him felt like he owed her something. But what Sage wanted, he could not give.

She didn't need to say aloud that she wanted his love. Not just his physical love, but the devotion that two people share when they find true love—something that is not easy to attain.

Two white doves were mixed amongst the pigeons in the cage. Robin's father had raised these birds his entire life and knew a lot about them. He had told Robin that some doves mate for life. And if one of the pair dies, the other will mourn its loss forever.

He felt just like one of these doves right now, because his heart was breaking. Without Sage in his life, he would feel empty and lonely. But how could he ever give her what she needed? And when he married a noblewoman as was required of him, how could he ever let Sage stay living at the castle? It would be too hard for both of them. Then again, how could he ever send her away? The girl had no home now. She had no parents. All he wanted to do was to nurture her and protect her.

But he couldn't.

He was a noble. She was a commoner.

And as much as Robin's heart ached right now, he knew what he had to do, and sadly, it didn't include Sage Hillock.

CHAPTER 13

Robin busied himself practicing sword fighting with his cousins, as well as getting to know his staff at the castle. He'd spent the last two days managing his estate and settling disputes. He never realized how much time things like this consumed. And since his guests would be arriving for the celebration on Christmas in two days' time, he'd planned a hunt for some of his men to supply more food for the nobles. His hunting party would only be gone overnight. The weather had become much warmer, and he hoped to bag a deer or two to add to the table on Christmas to feed the many extra mouths.

"Where's Rook?" Robin asked his squire, Tobias. "We're ready to leave on the hunt and I don't see him." He bent over and petted Griffin, whom he'd planned on bringing along on the hunt. He hoped the dog had some tracking skills and was planning on finding out.

"He went to see the healer," said Tobias.

"He what?" Robin was surprised at hearing this. "Sage?"

"Yes, I believe that's her name," said Tobias. "The healer girl."

"What does he think he's doing? We've no time for this. Go get him. Nay, never mind. I'll fetch him myself."

Robin figured Rook was interfering once again where he and Sage were concerned. He didn't want his cousin filling the girl's head with ideas that commoners could marry nobles, even if Rook had done just that. After all, it was a mistake and anyone could see it. It was best if he just forgot all about the girl.

"Rook, we're leaving," he called out, walking toward the little room at the edge of the kitchen that he'd told Sage she could use to administer healing to others. He wasn't even close to it yet but stopped in his tracks.

There was a line of men coming out of the healer's room, wrapping halfway around the kitchen and trailing out to the great hall.

"What the hell is going on here?" he demanded to know.

He noticed some of his knights, as well as servants, his kennel groom, and of course those pesky stableboys, all waiting in line to see Sage.

"My lord," said his kennel groom, Dominic. "By all means, go to the front of the line." He smiled and stretched out his arm.

"Dominic? You too? You're supposed to be readying the hounds for the hunt."

"I'm sorry, my lord. It's just that one of the hounds is biting his tail and I wanted to ask the healer to give me a salve to make him stop."

"That is absurd. All dogs bite their tails. It is nothing to see a healer about. Now, get back out there and prepare to leave on the hunt anon."

"Yes, my lord." The man stepped out of line and stopped.

"Will you ask Sage about it for me? That is, if you're going to see her?"

"Go!" he shouted, sending the kennel groom away.

"Why are you all here?" He asked the men as he walked by.

"I've got a bad headache," said one of the servants, rubbing his head.

"My father's knee is bothering him and I want to ask Sage for a potion," said another man.

"Back to work! All of you," Robin shouted, sending the men running. He stormed into the small room, stopping in his tracks when he saw Rook sitting half-on and half-off a table. Sage closed up her bag and started to don her long cloak.

"What's going on here?" he asked Rook. "You're holding up the hunting party from leaving."

"I'm sorry. I'm ready now," said Sage, her back to him as she tied her cloak. "I've been very busy the past few days and just wanted to take care of some more patients before leaving."

"You're going somewhere?" asked Robin.

"She's coming with us on the hunt." Rook stood up and smiled.

"Rook," said Robin in a warning voice. "I don't think this is a good idea."

"Rook told me that I was needed," said Sage.

"Did he, now?" Robin glared at his cousin.

"I've never been on a hunt before, but Rook said that men are always getting hurt and that it would be advantageous to have a healer along."

"Always getting hurt? Rook? Really?"

"It does happen," said Rook with a shrug, standing. "Plus, the hounds will be along and might need her, too."

"Oh, that reminds me." Sage spun around. "I thought I saw Dominic out there. What did he need?"

"Nothing important, I assure you," said Robin. "It was some silly nonsense about one of the hounds biting its tail."

"Biting its tail?" Sage seemed to be in thought, and turned and started packing up another bag. "It could be fleas or mayhap a tick. Or perhaps something bit him. Either way, I have remedies I will bring along to cure it."

Robin let out a deep sigh and glared at Rook again who just shrugged.

"Women are not allowed on the hunt." He tried a different approach.

"Rook tells me that women go along on the hunt all the time," said Sage.

"It's true," said Rook. "You know you can't keep my sister Raven from joining us on a hunt."

"That's different," said Robin.

"Really?" Sage turned to face him. "How so? Because she is a noblewoman and I'm only a simple commoner?"

"Yes, Robin. Is that what you mean?" asked Rook, his insolence grating on Robin's nerves.

"I'm going to kill you," Robin told his cousin under his breath.

"I'm all packed and ready to go," came a voice from behind him.

Robin spun around to see his sister Martine in traveling clothes, wearing riding boots, and yanking her gloves into place. He groaned.

"Nay. You're not coming with us," he told his sister.

"Why not?" asked Martine. "Sage is going."

"I never said she could."

"Are you going to let Martine go on the hunt because she's noble, but I can't because I'm not titled?" asked Sage.

"Nay, I didn't say that either."

"Good, then we'll all go," said Martine, sounding as if the decision were final.

"I didn't agree to any of this," Robin spoke through gritted teeth. Rook looked thoroughly amused by all this, and Robin was ready to belt him.

"So, I'm confused. Are we going or staying?" asked Sage.

"Yes, Cousin. What will it be?" asked Rook.

"Brother?" Martine stared daggers from her eyes.

Robin knew it was senseless to argue about this anymore. It was only eating up precious time and not worth it. "Fine," he said, releasing a puff of air from his mouth. "Get your horses, and hurry it up. But if you two can't keep up, I swear we'll leave you in the dust."

"Come on, Sage," said Martine, holding out her hand. "My brother is all talk. He wouldn't really leave us behind in the dust."

"Just try me," Robin shouted after them, as the women walked out the door.

"Well, we'd better get moving," said Rook, starting to walk away.

"Hold it right there," Robin warned him, stopping his cousin from going. "Why are you doing this to me?"

"Doing what?" Rook purposely acted stupid.

"You know what I mean. It's bad enough having to take Sage along, but did you really have to ask Martine on the hunt as well?"

"In my defense, Martine overheard me talking with Sage and invited herself," said Rook. "But, had I thought of it first, I would have been sure to invite her." His dung-eating grin was back.

"Just to spite me."

"Now, why would I want to do that?" asked Rook.

"Because I gave you a hard time when you inherited your manor. Now that I have a castle, you're jealous, just admit it."

"Robin, you're an ass," said Rook. "And I could never be jealous of someone like you."

"Then why go through all this trouble to upset me?"

"Did you ever think I'm not doing it to upset you, but to bring you to your senses instead?"

"Bring me to my senses? By having two girls along on the hunt? Have you gone mad?"

"Mayhap it's not me who has gone mad," Rook told him. "Now, please don't make things worse between you and Sage, because it took a hell of a lot of convincing to get her to agree to go anywhere with a pompous ass like you!" Rook turned and left the room.

"Who needs friends when they have family like this?" Robin muttered. "I agreed to let both the wenches come, didn't I? I'm not an ass, so don't call me that."

Robin hurried out to the courtyard, wondering how many others thought he was an ass as well? Even if there were more, none of it bothered him as much as thinking that this is what Sage thought of him.

He didn't want her to think he was an ass, a dog, a goat, or any other animal for that matter. Nay, he wanted Sage to see him as her true knight in shining armor, even if his armor was a bit rusted at the moment.

Thankfully, the day was sunny and the traveling wasn't as cold as Sage thought it might be. She hadn't believed in the least that she was being brought along on the hunt because the men would need her healing abilities. Rook had told her right before Robin walked into her healing room that Robin really liked her and that he wanted to be with her, but was too stubborn to admit it aloud. She wasn't sure if she really believed him, but when she saw how upset Robin had become once again that she had a line of men waiting to see her, she knew he was jealous.

Jealousy rearing its ugly head wasn't usually an admirable trait. But in this case, it did her heart good to hear him sending the line of men away. That meant he truly didn't want other men talking to her. And if he didn't want them speaking with her, he certainly didn't want them doing anything else with her either.

Martine was only there because Sage had convinced her to join them. She felt uncomfortable being the only girl along on the hunt. Martine, on the other hand, was a busybody and wanted to be privy to anything that might happen between Sage and the girl's brother.

"I've had the squire pack a tent for the two of us," Martine informed her from atop her horse as they rode. "Unless you are planning on sleeping in the same tent as my brother."

"Nay! Of course not. And thank you for accompanying us," Sage told her.

"I would have had my handmaid along as well, but I knew my brother would seethe with one more girl joining the hunt."

"I can tend to your needs, my lady," Sage offered.

"Thank you." Martine looked one way and then the other and leaned over on her horse, speaking in a soft voice. "You can just call me Martine, but use my title around the others."

"Of course, my lady," said Sage. "I mean, Martine."

"What does my brother tell you to call him?" Martine was curious to know.

"She'll call me her lord, as is proper. Commoners need to use our titles." Robin rode up behind them overhearing his sister's question. Sage noticed how handsome he looked in his riding attire. He wore the Blake family's coat of arms on his tunic. An argent eagle with wings spread covered an azure field —silver and blue.

"Martine, why don't you catch up with Rook and Gar at the front of the line?" asked Robin.

"Why would I want to ride with them? I'm talking with Sage."

"I'd like to speak to her now. Alone."

"Fine," she said, rolling her eyes. "But don't think this means you can order me around from now on." She directed her horse, catching up to her cousins.

"You and Martine don't get along well, do you?" asked Sage.

"It's only because my sister is stubborn. I think it's a family trait, actually. Any women from the Blake family line tend to have a mind of their own."

"I like that," said Sage with a smile.

"I somehow thought you would." He smiled back.

"Robin, I mean, Lord Robin, why did you allow me to join you on the hunt?"

"Would you rather that I had made you stay back at the castle?"

"Is that what you really wanted?" She answered his question with one of her own.

"You're here, aren't you?" He returned the favor and stared at her. Sage saw his attention roam down to her mouth. He must want to kiss her, she guessed. She wanted that too.

"I am here. For now," she answered, watching his spine stiffen.

"For now. What does that mean? Why would you say that?"

"It means, I will be leaving with my siblings soon, my lord."

"Why? Do you not like it at Shrewsbury Castle?"

"Oh, yes, I do. It's the best place I've ever lived."

"Then why would you want to leave?" he asked her, seeming totally confused.

"Because, my lord." She looked down to her horse as she spoke. "I cannot live at Shrewsbury once you are married."

"And... why not?"

She slowly raised her face, turning her eyes toward him. "I fear a lot of things in life, but none is as frightening as thinking that no man will ever make me feel the way you did the night we spent together. And that, my lord, is why I will not put myself through the misery of watching another woman find that same happiness with you. A happiness I thought I had found with you but is now lost again. I can never live up to what you require in a lover. A wife."

With that, she kicked her heels into her horse and caught up with Martine so she wouldn't have to listen to any lies Robin might tell her, just to make her feel like she had any chance at all with him, when she knew it was the furthest thing from the truth.

CHAPTER 14

While the hunt had been successful, Robin felt like a failure because he couldn't get Sage to say two words to him for the rest of the day. It was dark now. The tents had been erected and the fires were blazing. The winter cold usually bothered him, but tonight a fire burned in his heart. The flames only grew higher each time he looked at Sage.

She sat around the fire talking with Martine and Rook. Dominic, the kennel groom, couldn't seem to keep away from her since Sage had taken care of the hound biting its tail. Robin wasn't sure what the problem had been and neither did he care. Sage seemed to take the attention of each and every man there. They liked her for some reason, even though she was a commoner. She seemed to make friends quickly here, although when he first met her he had the impression that she didn't have a friend at all.

Nay, he just couldn't figure the girl out.

Even Griffin, that furry traitor, had been cozying up to Sage all night instead of being at Robin's side. The dog almost seemed to be hers instead of his.

The smell of woodsmoke and roasting rabbit on the fire filled the air. Still, the only scents that filled Robin's senses were lavender and roses. The scent of Sage. Her contagious, sweet laughter filled the air, only making him want to hear her laughing with him instead of the others.

The firelight danced on her soft skin as she leaned forward, poking a long stick at the flames. That only reminded him of their naked bodies entwined together, becoming one in the firelight of his solar the night they made love.

Damn, why couldn't he push thoughts of Sage from his mind? They didn't belong there. He was supposed to be thinking of alliances now that he was Lord of Shrewsbury. He'd have many beautiful noblewomen to choose from during the Christmastide celebration. He had until Twelfth Night to find a wife and make an alliance with another nobleman. This is the way nobles married. They married for wealth, status, and the promise of safety and not going to battle. No man worth his salt married a woman who had nothing to offer.

Not even a nobleman was allowed to marry for no other reason than that the woman made him happy and he wanted to give her everything... including his heart.

"God's eyes, Robin, you really are smitten with the healer, aren't you?" asked Gar, shaking Robin out of the trance he was in.

"What are you saying?" He turned to look at his cousin who staggered back and forth gripping a tankard of whisky. "Gar, you've had too much to drink."

"I didn't want to believe that you could possibly be as stupid as Rook, but you are proving me wrong, Cousin."

"What does that mean?"

"It means, you are falling for a commoner, just like he did."

"Nay. I'm not. I don't care about her. You don't know what you're saying." Robin thought if he said this aloud enough, mayhap he'd start to eventually believe it. Sadly, it didn't change the way he felt about Sage.

"I know the look of a man being consumed by a woman, and you've got all the signs." He raised the tankard to his mouth.

"I am not consumed with anyone."

"You're going to disgrace the family once again, marrying a wench from below the salt," Gar warned him.

"You are soused, Gar, and don't know what you're saying. Go get some sleep." He yanked the tankard out of his cousin's hand. "Everyone, get to sleep," he said to his men. "We will be leaving early in the morning. There is a lot to be done before the guests start arriving for Christmastide."

Several grunts and groans went up from his hunting party, but one by one they got up and headed to their tents as instructed. When Robin saw Sage following Martine to the women's tent, he called out.

"Healer, I need your services before you retire."

"Healer?" Sage repeated, not afraid to let him know by her tone that she didn't appreciate being addressed by her occupation.

"Services?" asked one of the men, who looked like he was well in his cups. "What kind of services, my lord?"

"My wound," he explained. "I need her to check it before she retires."

The soused man opened his mouth to say something undoubtedly rude. But with one nasty stare from Robin, he shut his mouth and hurried into his tent.

"Of course, my lord," said Sage. "Let me get my bag of herbs and ointments."

"Fine. Fine," he said. "Meet me in my tent."

She looked up for a second and their eyes met.

"To clean and check my wound. That's all."

With a slight nod, she entered her own tent to get her things.

Nervously, Robin chugged down the contents of the tankard he'd taken away from Gar, almost choking when he realized it was Mountain Magic.

"Where the hell did he get that?" he asked, feeling the burning of the potent whisky all the way down to his stomach. He'd only brought ale and wine on the hunt, so Gar must have sneaked this out of the undercroft.

"My lord, I am ready." Sage stood at the entrance of his tent.

"Of course." Robin threw down the tankard, kicked a little dirt at the fire, and made his way to his tent. "Go ahead," he said with a nod, holding the tent flap open for her to enter first. She gave him an odd look, seeming reluctant to do so since nobles always entered first and commoners or servants held the door for them. "It's all right, Sage. Go on in."

She didn't argue. She entered his tent. Since the tents weren't high enough to stand in, they both sat shoulder to shoulder atop a blanket on the ground.

"Let me light a lantern," he said, doing so, lighting up the tent.

"Let me see your wound." She was emotionless and straight to the point.

"I'll have to remove my trews to do so," he said softly.

"Then so be it," she told him, looking him straight in the eye.

"It won't... bother you?"

"Nay. Why should it?" She turned and opened her bag, pulling out clean, soft strips used for bandages. "I am a healer. I see all parts of bodies, and I assure you, seeing you without your trews isn't going to affect me in the least."

"Of course not." He cleared his throat and lay back, shimmying out of his trews.

"Let me take a look." Her nimble fingers unwrapped the bandages on his leg. Her hand brushed up against his thigh and it took all Robin's restraint not to be affected just from her gentle touch against his skin. "It is healing nicely," she told him. "I'll put an herbal ointment on it, but will re-wrap it since you are on a hunt. It will help protect it for now."

"Whatever you say," he told her, almost moaning aloud when she rubbed the herbal ointment in small circles over his leg and replaced the bandages.

"Leave your trews off until morning," she told him. "That way, your clothes won't pull on the wrappings. "Cover up with a blanket to keep warm."

She quickly packed up her things.

"Sage," he said, no longer able to hold back his emotions. "Stay the night with me. Here in my tent. To keep me warm." He reached out and caressed the side of her face, watching as her eyes closed and she leaned in to his touch. He could see that she didn't loathe him as much as she pretended to.

"I can't." Her eyes snapped open and she moved back.

"Can't? Or won't?" he asked, reaching out once more. This time, he leaned forward and gently pressed his lips to hers.

It might have been the middle of winter, but to Robin it felt as hot as summer right now. Kissing Sage warmed his belly twice as much as the Highlanders' Mountain Magic.

"Oh, Robin," she whispered with her eyes closed. Her breathing became heavier, only amplifying the rise and fall of her breasts. He wanted more than anything to slide his hand down and cup one of the tempting rounds, but he didn't. The last thing he wanted was to scare her away or for her to feel used or disrespected.

"I miss you, Sage." He kissed her again. Not in a lustful

manner, but still filled with passion. This time, he wanted her to know he had feelings for her that weren't always primal and animalistic.

"I haven't gone anywhere, Robin. How could you possibly miss me? That makes no sense," she whispered against his lips.

"You are here, but yet you're so far away. I feel as if sometimes you are so close and at the same time so far away."

"I am only trying to protect myself. You need to understand that."

"I can protect you, Sage, if you'll give me a chance."

She reached out and touched his lips ever so gently with the tips of her fingers. "You don't understand. You are the one from whom I am trying to protect myself."

He blinked several times in succession without saying a word. Did she think he'd hurt her? Had he done so unknowingly? God, he hoped not.

"Tell me how to make you trust me again."

"I do trust you, Robin." She got up, taking her bag with her. "The one I cannot trust is me. Goodnight, my lord."

The flap of the tent opened, sending in a cold breeze that made him shiver. Was this her way of saying goodbye? Was she saying they really would never be together again? Of course, that's what it was, he decided. She knew he was to choose a noblewoman to marry soon. She'd also made it clear that she'd never be just a mistress to him.

Then again, someone as wonderful as Sage shouldn't need to be just a mistress. Sage needed a man who would only have eyes for her and who would treat her like a queen. She deserved a husband and many children who were so close as a family that no one could ever pull them apart. Yes, Sage deserved to be treated like a noble even if she was only a girl from below the salt. But what man would be willing to do all those things?

God's eyes, Robin wanted to be that man. The only problem being that he had a family name, a title, a castle to uphold. Everyone was counting on Robin to marry a noblewoman, to make a strong alliance, to do the right thing.

Everyone, that is, except for the only person who mattered to Robin. Everyone but Sage Hillock, the woman with whom Robin was hopelessly falling in love even though every fiber of his being told him it was wrong to feel this way about a woman from below the salt.

Sage lay on the blanket next to Robin's sister, crying softly, hoping Martine was asleep. She had wanted more than anything to stay the night with Robin, snuggled up tightly in his arms. Even if they didn't couple, she wanted to feel his warm body pressed closely to hers one last time before he was married to a noblewoman. But as much as she wanted that, she knew it would only make things more difficult between them.

"Sage? Are you crying?" came Martine's groggy voice from next to her.

Sage bit the inside of her cheek and remained quiet. Right now, she didn't want to talk to anyone. All she wanted was to be left alone.

Alone with her thoughts and dreams of Robin. A man she wanted and couldn't have. A man who was from above the salt, but who filled her heart and warmed her soul. She'd have to leave soon to find another home for her and her siblings, she decided. Because she could no longer be around Lord Robin Blake without wanting to give herself to him, heart and soul.

CHAPTER 15

Christmas Day had arrived, and with it, so did many nobles, most of them being from Robin's family. Everyone had attended mass this morning, and now Sage helped out in the kitchen, preparing the feast along with her sister and her little brother.

"Sage, Cook says we need more herbs for the roasted goose," Amira told her.

"I'll go to the garden and try to find some," Sage told her, grabbing an empty basket and her cloak. She headed out the door to the herb garden that was severely unkempt. Not many herbs were still alive this time of year, but she was sure she could find a little fresh parsley, thyme, and even some sage under the dead leaves and snow. Down on her knees, she dug through the snow and quickly filled her basket with semi-frozen herbs.

She got up to leave, and bumped into someone standing directly behind her.

"Oh!" She almost dropped the basket, but two strong hands shot out to catch it, keeping the herbs from spilling.

"I'm sorry. I didn't mean to startle you." Robin stood there, holding the basket out to her like an offering of some sort.

"Thank you," she said with a nod, taking the basket of herbs from him.

"I didn't see you yesterday at the celebration of Adam and Eve Day. Neither did I see you at the passion play."

"Nay," she said, looking over at apples hanging from strings on a leaf-barren tree. Christmas Eve was the time when Adam and Eve Day happened, praising the first man and woman. Apples were hung from the boughs of a tree to symbolize the first fruit depicting good and evil. "I was tired from the hunt and went to sleep early."

She was telling the truth. However, she didn't mention the fact she'd been avoiding Robin. Since Christmastide had started and would be celebrated until Twelfth Night, she would see Robin with many noblewomen, and this was unsettling to her. Especially since she knew he was expected to choose one to marry by the end of the festivities.

"Like I told you, I miss you," he said, reaching out to push a stray lock of hair from her eyes.

"Please, Robin, don't." She stepped back and away from him. "I think it would be better if we weren't alone from now on."

"Why not?" he asked with a raised brow. "Are you afraid of idle gossip if it should start about us?"

"I'm afraid you're going to ruin your chances of marrying a noblewoman. I won't be the cause of that."

"I don't think you should concern yourself with my affairs." He frowned and looked down, digging something out of his pouch.

"If you'll excuse me, my lord, I need to bring these herbs to the cook anon."

"Wait," he said, as she started to walk away. "I—I wanted

to give you a present."

"A present?" This surprised her. No one had ever given her a present in her life. Her family was too poor to afford gifts, and even her siblings had never had the pleasure of receiving one. "If anyone should get a gift for Christmas, it should be my little brother. It's his birthday, and while birthdays are not celebrated, I'd like him to feel special."

"It's Noel's birthday?" he asked in surprise. "On Christmas day?"

"Yes," she answered, looking at the ground rather than into his alluring eyes that would only draw her in and make her want him. "My brother was born on Christmas, so my parents named him appropriately."

"I didn't know that. I'll make sure to acknowledge his birthday when I see him."

"There is really no need. We are not noble, and commoners don't celebrate birthdays. I should get back to work now."

"Sage," he said, reaching out and touching her arm. She felt the heat exchange between them even though they were out in the cold. "You don't need to work in the kitchen. You are not a serving wench. You're my healer."

"Well, there hasn't been much to heal in the past few days, so I am helping out where I am needed."

"This is for you," he said holding out his closed hand. He slowly opened his fingers to reveal a beautiful, small flower made from silk cloth and adorned with colorful ribbons. The petals of the flower were stuffed and stitched around the edges with colorful thread. "There was an old woman selling these outside the church this morning. The flower reminded me of you."

Before she could object, he reached up and took the end of her long braid and tied the flower onto it.

"I-I remind you of a flower?" she asked, not sure what

to say.

"Yes. You remind me of a beautiful flower, opening to the sun on a warm spring day." His fingers grazed the side of her cheek and she wasn't sure he wouldn't try to kiss her again. As much as she longed for his touch and even more for the press of his lips upon hers, she couldn't let that happen. Not anymore. He was about to choose a noble bride, and her heart already hurt, knowing she'd never be anything to Robin but a memory before long.

"Thank you for the flower, but I must go now, my lord."

Sage spun around and ran back to the kitchen, her heart breaking. She didn't stop until she handed the herbs to the head cook and took her place next to her sister, who was chopping leeks to be used in a sauce that would be poured over fish.

"Why are your cheeks so rosy?" asked Amira.

"It's cold outside." Sage took the knife from her sister and vigorously chopped the leeks.

"Do let me do that instead," begged Amira. "The leeks will make you cry from the fumes."

"I don't care," said Sage, brushing away a tear. Of course, it wasn't from the leeks but she didn't want anyone to know.

"Sage, where did you get this pretty flower adorned with ribbons? It is beautiful!" Amira picked up the end of Sage's braid that hung down her back, looking at the flower she'd gotten as a gift from Robin.

"Do you like it?" she asked, still chopping leeks.

"I do! I've never seen anything so pretty in my life."

"Then you shall have it as your own." Sage put down the knife and removed the flower from her hair, tying it on the end of Amira's braid instead. The girl smiled more than Sage ever remembered seeing her do before. It felt good to make her sister happy, even if she had to give up her gift from Robin to do it.

"Sage, come quickly! You're needed." Oscar came to a sliding halt, putting his hands on the wooden table and leaning forward to speak to her. "Someone is hurt." Urgency echoed in his voice.

"Hurt? Who? What happened?" Sage quickly wiped her hands on a rag.

"One of the noblewomen slipped on the ice in the courtyard just after she arrived. Lady Martine has taken her to your healing room. You'd better hurry."

"Of course," she told her brother, taking off at a half-run. She didn't stop until she'd entered her healing room. "I am Sage, the healer. What happened?"

A noblewoman who looked a few years older than Sage sat on a chair, wailing and sounding as if she were going to die. Martine had her hand on the woman's shoulder.

"Sage, this is one of the guests, Lady Jocasta," Martine introduced her. "She has fallen on the ice and hurt her elbow.

"Hello, my lady. Please, if I may?" Sage nodded at the woman's arm.

"I'm injured! It was horrible," she cried. "I'm lucky I wasn't killed in the fall. If the lord of the castle had been escorting me, it never would have happened."

Sage slowly pulled up the girl's sleeve, expecting to see a gaping wide gash covered in blood, from the way the woman was carrying on. Instead, she only saw a slight red mark and no cut at all.

"Are you sure this is the arm you hurt?" asked Sage, thinking mayhap the woman was too distraught to think straight.

"Of course, I am sure, you simpleton. Now quit asking stupid questions and dress my wound immediately. Do it, or I'll see to it that you are dismissed from your position."

Sage's eyes met Martine's but no words were exchanged.

There were so many things that Sage wanted to say right now, but the slow shake of Martine's head kept her quiet.

"Of course, my lady. I will tend to your wound at once."

Sage cleaned the girl's elbow and applied a salve, even though neither was needed. "There. You should be fine by tomorrow," said Sage.

"No, I won't! I'm drastically hurt," insisted the titled lady. "Aren't you going to even wrap up my wound? What kind of a healer are you? I will have to talk to Lord Robin about you. As soon as we're married, we'll be looking for a new healer. One who is more competent than you."

"Married?" questioned Sage, feeling a knot forming in her stomach.

"Yes. I plan on being Lady Shrewsbury soon. I promise you, I will be betrothed to that handsome Lord Robin by the end of Twelfth Night."

"Lord Robin is the one to choose his bride, not you." Sage spoke too freely as usual, and could feel the anger emanating from the shrew of a woman sitting before her.

"What did you say?" Lady Jocasta glared at Sage.

"Lady Jocasta," Martine interrupted. "I am sure that what Sage meant is that my brother will be considering all the eligible noblewomen over the next twelve days. Only one lucky lady can be his bride."

"That will be me," the haughty lady insisted. "I'll see to it. My cousin is my ward. He comes from money, and he will offer the lord of the castle the largest dowry out of anyone. Lord Robin won't be able to turn it down."

"I'm sure a large dowry is something to be admired," said Martine. "But then again, the choice is up to Lord Robin. Sage, please wrap Lady Jocasta's wound."

"But it's not—"

"Quickly," Martine stopped her from saying more. "Lady Jocasta, I am sure, is in a hurry to meet my brother."

"Yes. Of course, my lady," said Sage, feeling angrier than ever now. If the shrew thought she was so wounded, then Sage would make certain she got the proper treatment. She not only bandaged the girl's arm so much that she could barely bend it, but on top of that, Sage put Lady Jocasta's arm in a sling. "There, you go. All finished." It looked ridiculous, and Sage laughed silently to herself.

"Is all this really necessary?" Jocasta grimaced and stood up, patting her wrapped arm. "I can barely move my arm, and I look atrocious."

"I'm sure the healer would not do anything that wasn't necessary," said Martine, flashing Sage a quick smile.

"Well, how long does my arm need to be in this sling?"

"At least for a fortnight," said Sage, not wanting this to end until Twelfth Night was over.

"That long?" Jocasta's eyes opened wide. "But I need to look my best for Lord Robin. Twelfth Night will be finished by then. I demand you remove all this at once."

"Lady Jocasta, I'm not sure it is a good idea to go against the healer," said Martine.

"It's all right. I can remove it," said Sage with a shrug. "But if your arm is deformed from not being wrapped and tended to for your wound, know it was not my choice to do so, but your command."

"Deformed?" The stupid woman believed what Sage said, although Sage was only jesting. Still, she didn't like Lady Jocasta and was in no hurry to tell her otherwise. The woman carried on about being wounded and then insisted Sage wrap her arm. She'd only been giving her what she wanted. Or mayhap what she deserved.

The worse she looked in front of Robin, the better, as far as

Sage was concerned. Even though Sage didn't want to see Robin married to anyone but herself, he didn't deserve someone as haughty as Lady Jocasta either. No matter how much money was involved.

Martine looked back and winked as she and Lady Jocasta left the room.

Sage smiled and sat down on a chair, reaching for her flower that Robin gave her. Of course, she only held her hair since she'd given the gift to her sister. Her heart felt empty. She'd wanted to keep the gift from Robin, but her sister had liked it so much and she wanted Amira to be happy. Her siblings' happiness meant more to Sage than her own.

Letting out a deep sigh, Sage realized she and her siblings could not stay living here at the castle forever. If they did, Sage would live in misery each day she saw Robin with his new wife. And it would be torture for her to see someone like Lady Jocasta on his arm.

Then again, Sage and her siblings were safe here. Living at the castle, she didn't need to worry for their protection, or possibly that their home might be burned down again. Still, she knew it would never work. But her feelings about Robin should not have to affect her siblings. There was only one solution.

When Twelfth Night was over, Sage decided she'd go back to live at the monastery if the abbot would let her. She would leave her siblings here, and not have to worry about their safety or even their happiness anymore. Yes, that is what she'd do. She would miss them dearly, but it would be the best solution for all of them. This way, she'd be away from Robin, and at the same time have tended to the needs of Oscar, Amira, and Noel.

Now, all she needed to do was to find the courage to tell Lord Robin her decision.

CHAPTER 16

Robin sat at the dais with his cousins Gar and Rook on one side, as well as his sister Martine. On the other side sat his parents and some of the visiting nobles. Many of Robin's family members hadn't returned or arrived yet, but would soon.

Already, there was a huge crowd which included nobles from neighboring castles, and even the villagers, who were always invited to the Christmas dinner. As the commoners arrived, they brought with them offerings to their new lord, in the form of a cow, a pig, or one of their best fowls.

The servers brought course after course of delectable dishes, starting with a broth made from vegetables with chunks of seafood cooked into it. Those below the salt did not eat the same food as the nobles, but being Christmas, Robin made sure there was plenty of food for everyone. He even gave the cooks permission to let those below the salt feast on venison today, since his hunt had been successful and he brought back two fallow deer, as well as plenty of pheasant and hare.

Robin met many nobles today, and each of them brought with them one of their daughters whom they hoped Robin would choose to marry. So far, the biggest dowry offered came from Lord Leeds, who had yet to arrive, but was Lady Jocasta's ward and cousin. Lady Jocasta had her arm wrapped and in a sling, and looked unsightly. It wasn't the best situation for her at all.

The sound of the straight trumpet brought everyone's attention to a procession of servers emerging from the kitchen. Then the herald made an announcement.

"The boar's head and brawn pudding will now be presented to the lord of the castle, Sir Robin Blake."

Everyone clapped and cheered, watching the sumptuous feast paraded through the room. Robin never felt as important as he did right now. He looked over to his father and smiled. His father nodded in return.

The head cook led the procession, carrying a huge platter with a pickled boar's head, stuffed and roasted, with an apple wedged in the boar's mouth. Around the head of the beast were stewed pears and figs ,as well as an array of sugar-dipped, fried stalks of a variety of herbs. The boar's head was gilded in gold leaf to make it shine.

Musicians played a royal tune, while the castle bard sang out a ridiculous song worshipping the boar, as the line of servers stopped at the front of the dais.

"My lord," said the cook with a nod, placing the platter in front of Robin. Then the carver stepped forward with a large knife and spoon in his hands. He carved and served a good-sized portion to Robin before any other of the nobles.

"My lord, would you care for mushroom and onion gravy?" came a voice from the front of the dais. He looked up to see Sage holding a bowl and ladle.

"Yes. Thank you, Sage," he said, reaching out with his plate for the gravy, purposely brushing the side of his hand against hers. An immediate sense of elation washed through him. He then noticed something and leaned forward and spoke to her in a hushed voice. "Where is the flower I gave you? It's not in your hair. Didn't you like it?"

"Yes. Yes, I did. My lord," she quickly added, nervously stroking the end of her braid with one hand. "However, my sister admired it dearly, so I gave it to her."

"You did?" he asked, feeling a little disappointed that she gave it away. He set down his plate and picked up his goblet, which was filled to the rim with wine. "So, you didn't like my gift, then?" He took a sip of wine, nodding to the cook, sending him to serve the other nobles.

"On the contrary, I liked it very much, my lord," she told him. "It's just that my sister has never had a gift before. Especially not anything as pretty as the cloth flower. I wanted to make her happy."

"And I'm sure you did." He took a sip of wine and lowered his goblet. "That's what I admire about you, Sage. You are always thinking of others and want to make them happy. Never once do you think about yourself first."

He saw Sage's eyes dart over to Lady Jocasta. Then, the woman spoke from three people down at the table.

"Lord Robin, why are you talking to that healer so long?" Lady Jocasta leaned forward, looking down the table at him. "I'd like some boar's head, if you please."

"The carver will bring you some," said Robin.

"Nay. I cannot cut the meat since my arm is injured. I need you to do it for me." She pointed to her arm in the sling and pouted.

He was about to send Sage over to help her, but when he looked back, she was gone.

"Lady Jocasta's cousin and ward has offered a large dowry for her betrothal," said his father, Madoc.

"Yes, I know."

"Have you found a girl who catches your eye yet?" His mother spoke to him next, ever so gently dabbing her mouth with a square of cloth.

"I... not yet," he said, once again grabbing for his wine. "It is still too early to make that decision."

"Oh, he's found a girl who catches his eye, all right," mumbled Gar from next to him, reaching over Robin and grabbing a piece of meat from the platter with the boar's head, not waiting to be served.

"Really? Who is it, Robin?" asked Lady Jocasta's mother, who was sitting next to Robin's mother, Abigail. "I do hope you'll choose my daughter, Lady Jocasta. I believe she will make a perfect bride for you. And if the dowry isn't sufficient, my nephew will add to it as soon as he arrives, of course. He is tied up, since his brother has been murdered and he's taken the position of Lord Leeds now. There is so much to do."

"Murdered?" asked Robin in surprise. "I hope they caught and punished whoever did it."

"Not yet. But my nephew has his suspicions."

"Well, Godspeed to him to make sure justice is served," mumbled Robin, not really having his mind in this conversation.

Robin downed more wine. He didn't like this part of being noble and with a castle. Before, it wasn't so detrimental to marry a noblewoman, or at least not so quickly. Now, it was all anyone thought of, and required by the King. Since Robin hadn't been King Edward's first choice as Lord of Shrewsbury, the deal was that he'd take his father's offered place of lord, but only if he married a noblewoman. He had until the end of

Twelfth Night to choose his bride, or the king would choose her for him. He could not go against the king's wishes.

"Robin, that is so generous of the new Lord Leeds to offer to add to Lady Jocasta's dowry," said his mother.

"Of course, it is," he said, raising a hand in the air. "I just need time to decide, that's all. I don't like to be rushed."

"He means he needs time to break it to my father and Uncle Madoc whom he *really* has his eye on." Rook quickly picked up his goblet and drank.

"Oh, here comes the swan," said Robin, clinking his spoon against his goblet to get everyone's attention. He was glad for the distraction. The servers brought out a cooked swan with the feathers reattached. It was standing upright on the platter with its wings spread, looking as if it were about to take off in flight.

"The salt cellar, my lord."

He was surprised but pleased to see that Sage had returned. This time, she held a silver dish shaped like a castle. It was filled to the top with precious salt.

"Thank you, Sage. Just put it down," he said, nodding to the table.

"Lord Robin, I am much too far away to talk with you, so I moved closer." He felt a hand on his shoulder and looked back to see that Lady Jocasta had gotten out of her chair and walked over to him. A bold move on her part.

"We'll talk later. After the meal," he told her, wanting to talk to Sage instead.

"It seems you have plenty of time to talk to that commoner, but no time for me." Jocasta glared at Sage. "Have you bedded the girl? Is that why you can't keep your eyes off of her?"

Sage's head jerked upward at hearing this. She moved so quickly that she spilled the salt.

"I'm sorry, my lord." Sage brushed the spilled salt into her hand and dumped it back into the salt cellar.

"Lady Jocasta, I hardly think that is an appropriate thing for you or anyone to be asking," spoke up Robin's father. "Perhaps you should have a seat now."

"Hrmph," sniffed the girl, looking down her nose at Sage. "Perhaps that commoner should stay below the salt where she belongs, instead of spilling salt everywhere with her clumsy actions." The woman strolled back to her seat.

"Robin," mumbled Madoc, leaning over to Robin, speaking to him from behind his hand. "She's right, you know. You are paying too much attention to that healer girl. It is not befitting for lord of the castle to be acting this way. Especially not during the Yuletide feast."

"I'm sorry, Father," he said, once more looking back to see that Sage was gone. Suddenly, so was Robin's appetite. He wanted to run after Sage and tell her not to let any of this bother her.

But he couldn't.

He was a noble, a lord of a castle now, and had to act accordingly. And as much as he only wanted to be with Sage, he knew by the end of Twelfth Night he would have to choose a woman to be his wife, and it wouldn't be Sage.

Sage slowly climbed the stairs later that night, so tired from helping to clean up the kitchen after the first day of the feast that she could barely keep her eyes open. She'd taken over her sister's share of the work, sending Amira with Noel up to their room earlier.

In her pouch were a few sweetmeats that were left over from the noble's table. She'd removed them from their dirty plates, hoping no one saw her take them. Noel loved the dried fruit, although servants weren't often allowed to eat it. Hopefully, this would make Noel happy. She wanted him to feel special.

She pushed open the door to the room, expecting to see her siblings fast asleep. Instead, they were dressed in their nightclothes, but running around the room with Griffin chasing after them, his tail wagging.

"What on earth is going on here?" she asked, thinking she was dreaming at first.

"Sister, we're having fun. Come and join us." Oscar sat on a chair by the fire, his feet propped up on the table. He cradled a tankard in his hands. He looked like a man who was well in his cups, and Sage didn't like it.

Before she had a chance to even ask what he was drinking, Noel skipped by riding what looked like a hobbyhorse.

The little boy straddled a long wooden pole with a wooden horse's head attached. It had a small wheel on the bottom part that touched the floor. The entire thing was painted in bright colors. It was even adorned with a fake bridle made out of ribbons, with small bells attached that jingled when he moved.

"Noel, stop," she said, grabbing him the next time he passed by. The dog knocked into him and started barking.

"No! Quiet," she told Griffin with a wag of her finger. To her surprise, the dog actually listened to her and lay down at Noel's feet. "Noel, where did you get that toy?" she asked her little brother.

"Lord Robin came to our door a little while ago. He brought me a toy for Christmas. This is the best Christmas ever!" Noel jumped up in the air and took off on his horse once again.

Too tired to care, Sage walked over to the bed and plopped down next to her sister. Amira was stroking the silk flower between her fingers and smiling at it.

"I really like my flower," said Amira. "Oh, Lord Robin brought one for you, too, Sage." She jumped off the bed and ran over to the table, returning with a silk flower for Sage.

"He did? Lord Robin brought this? For me?" Her heart ached. She realized that Robin must have really wanted her to keep the flower, since he brought her another one as a gift after finding out that she gave the first one away.

"He also said Griffin can stay here all night long."

She heard a loud bang and realized Oscar had fallen asleep and fell off the chair. He got up, still holding on to the tankard.

"I think you need to lie down before you fall down again, Brother," she told him. She walked over and took the tankard from him. Oscar fell flat on his face on his pallet at the other side of the room. "How much ale did he drink?" she asked.

"That's not ale," said Amira, holding one silk flower in each hand and running around the room with Noel. She let the ribbons trail behind her.

"It's not? Well what is it?"

"I don't know. It's some kind of magic drink. That's what Lord Robin called it when he gave it to Oscar."

"A magic drink?" She took a sip of the liquid and coughed as a burning sensation made her throat feel as if it were on fire. "Mountain Magic," she said, knowing exactly what it was. It was the very strong whisky that the MacKeefes distilled up in the Scottish Highlands. "All right, time for bed. Both of you," she said, already feeling her head spinning just from one sip. Of course, being so tired only added to it.

"Can I sleep with my hobbyhorse tonight, and Griffin too?" asked Noel, so excited with his new toy as well as with the dog's company that she couldn't deny him his request.

"Of course, you can," she told him. "And tonight, you can share the bed with Amira and I'll sleep on the floor."

"Thank you, Sage." Noel gave her a kiss and jumped up on

the bed, bringing his new toy and the dog with him. Griffin lay down with his legs spread out over the bed behind him.

"You'd better put the flowers on the bedside table so they don't get smashed, Amira," said Sage with a yawn. "Noel is a restless sleeper, and there is no telling if Griffin will eat them."

"I will, Sage. Goodnight." Amira yawned and lay down, after covering up her brother.

"Goodnight," Sage told her siblings, blowing out the candle. Now, only the light of the fire on the hearth lit the room. She picked up the chair her brother had been using and sat down on it, taking off her shoes. She realized the sweet-meats were still in her pouch, and took them out and laid them atop the table. Yawning, she picked up the tankard Oscar had been drinking from, taking another sip of the potent whisky and cradling the mug in her hands. The Mountain Magic was relaxing her, and it was just what she needed.

She finished off what little was left, and laid her head on the table, using her arms as a pillow. Too relaxed to worry about anything now and too tired to care, Sage closed her eyes, hoping to escape to a world where she had no troubles and everyone was treated as an equal. There were no commoners and there were no nobles. There were no daises, and most of all, there was no such thing as above and below the salt.

CHAPTER 17

"Sage, come here," said Martine the next day, as Sage was helping to move away the trestle tables in the great hall, preparing for dancing that would take place as part of the Twelfth Night celebrations.

"Lady Martine?" asked Sage, joining her, noticing Martine was standing with a group of noblewomen. Already, Sage felt uncomfortable.

"I wanted you to meet my cousins," she said.

"I'd be honored, my ladies," said Sage with a curtsy.

"Everyone, this is Sage, the castle's healer. She saved Robin's life," announced Martine, making Sage cringe. She knew Robin didn't want this story going around the castle, even if it was true.

"She saved his life?" asked the Scottish blonde.

"I only repaid the favor after he saved my life, of course. He was so brave and fought off three men to help me," Sage told them, trying to paint Robin in a brighter light.

"Sage, this is my Scottish cousin, Lady Lark," said Martine, nodding to a beautiful blonde woman dressed in a gown constructed of purple plaid. “She is here with her husband, Lord Dustin, as well as her parents, Storm and Wren MacKeefe.”

“Lord Dustan was her scribe,” said the woman with red hair standing next to Lark.

“He’s a noble, Eleanor. Don’t forget that part, please,” Lark told her.

“You’re a Highlander,” said Sage, seeing the plaid and hearing the name MacKeefe. “Your clan makes that Mountain Magic.”

“Aye, that is right,” said Lark with a giggle. “But I wouldna suggest drinkin’ it if ye are no’ used to it.”

“I understand,” said Sage, having had a headache all day from the potent whisky. She had to use an herbal remedy in order to feel well enough to help out in the kitchen today. Thank goodness, she’d only had a little. Her brother, on the other hand, was still sleeping when it was already late in the day. She’d told the stablemaster that Oscar wasn’t feeling well, and her brother was excused from his duties.

“This is my cousin, Eleanor,” continued Martine, nodding to the redhead. “She just married Lord Connor Wyland.”

“He was a hangman,” Lark eagerly pointed out, getting back at Eleanor for pointing out her husband had been a scribe.

“He was a noble first, and is again,” Eleanor quickly corrected her.

“Hello,” said Sage with another curtsy.

“I’m Lady Raven,” the girl with long, dark hair introduced herself. “I married the armorer, Lord Jonathon, and my twin brother Lord Rook Blake married Rose, the gardener.” She put her hand on the last girl’s shoulder.

“My, you all seem to have married from below the salt,” Sage said in surprise. “Is that a normal thing for a noble to do?”

"Nay, not at all," said Martine. "And it makes my Uncle Corbett furious." She giggled as if she thought that were funny.

"We may be nobles, but love doesn't have a status attached," said Raven. "We all fell in love."

All the women smiled.

"Well, I'm not married yet, but hopefully I'll fall in love someday too," said Martine. "And when I do, it'll be with a noble, I assure you. After all, one of us has to make Uncle Corbett proud."

"Mayhap it'll be Robin who makes him proud," said Eleanor. "He's lord of a castle now, and the King commands him to marry someone of his own status."

"Yes, I'm sure Robin will do what the King and Uncle Corbett want," said Lark.

"Oh, I'm not so sure about that." Martine looked over at Sage and winked. "Are you, Sage?"

"Me?" Sage felt her heart jump into her throat. She had no business standing here talking to so many beautiful, honorable noblewomen. And she certainly didn't want to give her opinion on Robin, because they'd just told her it was the King's command that he marry someone of his own status. "I—I'm sure Robin will do the right thing. Now, if you'll excuse me, my help is needed in the kitchen."

"I thought you're a healer," said Raven. "Why are you working as a kitchen maid?"

"My sister and brother work there, and they are young so I help them out. Besides, there hasn't been much need of a healer since I got here."

"We'll let you go then," said Eleanor.

"It was nice meeting you," said Rose, the only one of the women who hadn't been born a noble. Sage liked her already, and wanted to talk with her more in private at a later date. After all, if these women all married someone from a different walk of life, mayhap there was still hope for her and Robin after all.

Then again, it was the King's command that Robin marry well. Going against the King's word could be considered treason. Nay, she didn't have a shred of hope after all.

Sage walked into the kitchen to see Oscar staggering in the other door.

"Brother. You're finally awake. Glad you could manage to stir before it was time to sleep for the night," said Sage, handing a pile of dirty bowls to Noel. "Take these to the scullery, Noel. And tell Amira that she is needed to serve the bean cake now."

"All right," said the little boy, walking slowly with the tall pile of dirty dishes, not wanting to drop them.

"It's night already?" Oscar yawned, scratched his head, and sat down on a tall stool. "I don't know what happened."

"Mountain Magic is what happened," she scolded. "You never should have drunk it."

"Well, I wanted to know what it was. Lord Robin asked if I wanted to try it, and I couldn't say no."

"When I see Sir Robin, I'll give him a piece of my mind for that! You missed an entire day's duty in the stable."

"Did I hear my name mentioned?"

Sage spun around to see Robin standing there with a smile. Griffin was at his side. The man seemed to show up from nowhere every time Sage started talking about him. "I see you got the flower I sent." He reached out and touched the silk flower she wore with the colorful ribbons woven into her hair.

"Yes. Thank you," she said, feeling tongue-tied around him.

"How did you like the Mountain Magic, Oscar?"

"Mmmmph," Oscar moaned and touched his head.

"Lord Robin, thank you for Noel's gift. He really enjoys it. However, you really shouldn't have given Oscar Mountain

Magic," Sage finally managed to say. "It is so strong that it burns on the way down and makes one's head dizzy and the eyes sleepy."

"You speak as if you know that from experience," said Robin with a raised brow. "Is it true?"

"Well, I might have tasted what was left of Oscar's drink," she admitted. Sage looked down to the table and ran her finger through flour dust, making a jagged trail of thought.

Robin chuckled. "I'm glad you had some, Sage. You seemed so upset yesterday, and I think you needed to relax."

"Thank you, but I'll worry about myself." Sage didn't like the fact that Robin knew she'd been upset. And she certainly didn't want him telling her what she needed.

The straight trumpet sounded from the other room. The herald called out that the bean cake was about to be served and the Lord of Misrule would be chosen.

"What is a Lord of Misrule?" asked Noel, joining them, reaching over to pet Griffin.

"Well," said Robin, reaching down and picking up the little boy. Noel giggled when Robin tickled him on the stomach and held him in his arms. "Lord of Misrule, my little friend, is determined by whoever finds a bean in their cake."

"I don't think I like bean cake." Noel made a face.

"No, no," said Robin, his deep chuckle as well as the fact he was holding her little brother, warming Sage's heart. "The cake is made from fruit... and a little brandy, I think. A bean is thrown in for good measure. Whoever happens to find the bean in their cake, gets to rule over all the others until the end of Twelfth Night."

"Really?" asked Oscar, perking up. "Is this a game for just the nobles, or can commoners play too?"

"Actually, only non-nobles eat the cake. It's devised to give a commoner a chance to feel noble for a few days."

"I want to be noble," said Noel with wide eyes.

"Then you'd better get out there and get a piece of cake before it's all gone." Robin put him down.

"Oscar, will you come with me?" asked Noel.

"I am starving since I slept through the meals. I want a really big piece of cake. Mayhap two or three. Come on, Noel," said Oscar, taking his brother's hand. "We'll push our way to the front of the line. Griffin can help us."

"Don't be rude!" Sage called after them as they left the kitchen.

"Well? Aren't you going to go get a piece of bean cake too?" Robin asked her.

"Nay," she said. "I have no desire to be noble, even if it is just pretend and only for a few days."

"The way you say that, it sounds as if you think being noble is a bad thing." He leaned on the table to talk with her.

"Isn't it?" she asked. "After all, your life is not your own."

"That's not true," said Robin.

Gar stuck his head into the kitchen. "Robin, you have a line of noblewomen waiting to dance with you. Your father is looking for you and he doesn't sound happy. You'd better hurry up and get out here. All the women are hoping you'll choose them for your bride."

"My point proven," Sage told him. "Go on, then." She nodded to the great hall and turned away from him.

"Sage, I really want to spend some time with you."

"I think we both know that is not going to happen during these festivities. You have too many people you need to talk to or dance with. Not to mention, you are required to choose a lady for your bride."

"Mayhap after Twelfth Night is over, we can—"

"Nay, Robin," she told him, spinning around to face him.

"By then you'll be betrothed, and I'm sure your bride-to-be won't like you spending time with your castle's healer."

"Lord Robin, we're all waiting for you. What on earth can you possibly find interesting in the kitchen?" Lady Jocasta walked in with several other very pretty noblewomen right behind her. "Oh, I see. Why are you talking to the likes of her?" Jocasta threw her nose in the air. "I get the first dance, and I don't want it to be shortened because you are socializing with those below the salt. I hear the musicians warming up. Please, we need to go." She held out her hand for him to take it.

"Can you even dance with your arm in a sling?" Robin asked her. "Mayhap you should have Sage take a look at it."

"The healer has already done that. Isn't it obvious?" she asked in a snide manner.

"Lady Jocasta is right," said Sage, just wanting these nobles gone. "You need to dance with the nobles, Lord Robin. It is required of you. Besides, I have things to do." She walked away before he could respond.

Robin begrudgingly took Lady Jocasta's hand and led her out to the great hall, not liking the woman but doing his duty by dancing with her. Sage's words kept echoing in his brain. He was a noble and she was right. His life was far from his own.

The music stopped and Jocasta looked up. "Oh, my. We are standing under the kissing bough, my lord. You know what that means." A sly smile spread across her face. Robin had no doubt she'd made certain they ended up beneath it.

"I don't think—"

Lady Jocasta pulled him to her and kissed him on the mouth before he could get away. When their lips parted, he noticed Sage watching him from the door to the kitchen. Her arms were crossed over her chest. She looked hurt. Robin didn't want Sage to think he was the one to initiate the kiss, but before he could even try to tell Sage, someone shouted out for everyone to hear.

"Whoohoo! I did it. I found the bean. I've got the bean!" Oscar ran around the room holding a bean above his head. He held on to five plates, and talked with his mouth filled with cake.

"He's the Lord of Misrule," called out one of his friends from the stables.

"What is your first order?" asked another commoner. "Remember, as Lord of Misrule, you can even make the nobles do things they don't usually do."

"Really?" asked Oscar, stopping to think. He put his empty plates down on the table.

Robin wasn't sure it was fair to have eaten so much cake just to find the bean, but since Oscar was Sage's brother, he didn't protest it.

"Well," continued Oscar. "I think my first order is for the steward to bring me a plate of food that only the nobles eat. I want to try swan and boar's head. Oh, and white bread, too."

"Oscar. Nay," said Sage, emerging from the kitchen. Everyone was suddenly quiet.

"And I also want Mountain Magic given to every servant here," he said with a wave of his hand through the air. "Lots of it. Keep it coming all night long."

"Lord Robin, excuse me," said Sage, suddenly right next to him. "May I speak to you in private?"

"Of course. Pardon me, Lady Jocasta," said Robin, tactfully slipping away. "What is it, Sage?" He thought she was going to say something about kissing the noblewoman, but instead she was only concerned about her brother.

"I'm afraid my brother will abuse this Lord of Misrule thing. You've got to stop him before he creates havoc with all the nobles. He has already commanded outrageous things to be done."

Robin laughed. "Sage, it's all right. The Lord of Misrule is supposed to do and say absurd things. The nobles expect it and accept it. It's just good fun."

"Really?" she asked, blinking several times in succession.

"Yes," he assured her. "No matter what the Lord of Misrule says, it has to be done."

"How long will this nonsense continue?"

"Through Twelfth Night."

Her eyes opened wide. "That long?"

"Yes, that long."

"But if my brother drinks Mountain Magic that for that amount of time—"

"He'll be passed out and you won't need to worry about him doing anything else stupid, now will you?"

"I don't know, Robin. I don't like this. Oscar isn't used to having this kind of power. He is sure to abuse it."

Sage looked so worried about her brother that Robin knew he needed to say something to calm her.

"It is really no problem at all. He's done nothing wrong. However, I'll have a little talk with Oscar, if you'd like."

"Would you do that? For me? Oh that would be great. Thank you so much."

"I'd do anything for you, Sage. Please know that I mean that." He quickly reached out and held her hand when he said it.

She bit her bottom lip, looked down to her hand, and then pulled away. "Please, my lord. This isn't proper," she told him, aggravating Robin that she didn't seem to want to be with him anymore, even though he wanted to be with her more than ever.

"Let me worry about what is proper and what is not." He

headed over to talk with Oscar, but was interrupted by Rook and Gar.

"Where are you going?" asked Gar.

"Sage is worried that her brother will mistreat his power of being Lord of Misrule," Robin told his cousins. "To ease her mind, I promised her I'd have a talk with him and warn him to behave."

"Robin, this is Christmastide." Rook snatched up two tankards off the tray of a passing servant. He kept one and handed the other to Robin. Gar stood there with his open hand, waiting for his but not getting one. "You are Lord of Shrewsbury now, Robin. You shouldn't have to deal with such petty issues as this."

"That's right," agreed Gar, looking around for the serving wench with the tankards of ale. "Rook and I will talk to the boy. You just go back to dancing with the ladies."

"Well, I don't know. I promised Sage I'd do it."

"Relax, Cousin. We'll handle everything for you," said Gar, snitching the tankard of ale away from Robin before walking away with Rook to talk to Oscar.

"Robin? What's going on?" asked Robin's father, walking up behind him.

"I just sent two fools to stop another fool, and I already feel like the biggest fool of them all," said Robin.

"Well, I'm not sure what that means but the minstrels are starting another song and there is still a line of ladies waiting to dance with you," Madoc told him.

"Aye, of course." Robin turned and walked back to the ladies, not wanting to dance with any of them, but knowing it was required of him since he was lord of the castle. But then he heard Oscar call out.

"Stop the music, I have another demand."

"Command," Rook corrected the boy. "Not demand."

"All right. Command," said Oscar, standing on a bench so everyone could see him. "This command is for the lord of the castle himself."

"What?" Robin spun around to face him. That's when he noticed Rook and Gar laughing. He knew right then and there that this couldn't be good. He should have spoken with Oscar himself. "What the hell did they tell him?" he said to himself, expecting the worst. He wasn't looking forward to shoveling dung in the stables and hoped he wasn't going to be told to run around the great hall in just his braies or anything embarrassing like that. He'd seen both of these things in the past and thought it was funny. However, now he was at the receiving end, he started to agree with Sage that her brother might not be best suited for Lord of Misrule after all.

"I command that Lord Robin only dances with my sister Sage for the rest of the night," Oscar shouted.

"What? Oscar, nay!" Sage emerged at the door from the kitchen with her mouth hanging open. Her gaze shot over to Robin and he shrugged. Mayhap this would all work out in his favor after all.

"Come on out, Sage, and dance with Lord Robin," yelled Oscar.

"No. No, I won't do it. Choose someone else," she said, her eyes darting back and forth and her face becoming flushed.

"I am Lord of Misrule and you need to listen to me." Oscar crossed his arms over his chest and his chin jutted up in the air. The boy seemed to like having power.

"Nay. This isn't right," Sage protested, as several of the kitchen maids brought her out to the dance floor.

"It *is* right, Sage," said Robin, holding out his hand, actually pleased to be dancing with Sage instead of all the other stuffy noblewomen. "Come, my dear. You heard the Lord of Misrule. My dances are only with you for the rest of the evening."

"That's not fair," whined Lady Jocasta. "We are supposed to dance with the lord of the castle. We are noble. She is not!"

Many of the other ladies waiting to dance with Robin protested as well.

"Quiet!" shouted Robin. "This is the command of the Lord of Misrule and it needs to be followed and respected. Now come, Sage. We must dance. That is the rule."

Slowly, Sage reached out and took Robin's hand. And when he pulled her closer to him, no one else in the room mattered anymore. "Play music," he yelled to the minstrels. "And I want to see everyone dancing."

The music started a cheery tune with nakers, or drums, keeping the rhythm. Several minstrels played flutes, one had a lyre, or harp, and there was even a man playing a lute. The mood changed quickly, and everyone started to enjoy themselves. The floor filled up with noblemen and ladies, dancing alongside Sage and Robin. In Robin's mind, Sage was no different from the others. She might not be noble, but she conducted herself in such a proper way during the dance that it was sad she wasn't wearing a beautiful gown. Still, her beauty outshined any gown she could possibly don.

"I don't feel comfortable with this," Sage said, looking up to him with those wide, innocent, pale-green eyes.

"There is no reason to feel anything but joy at the moment," Robin told her. "I assure you, we are doing nothing wrong."

"Everyone is looking at us." Her head lowered a little and her gaze swept the floor.

"And so they should. After all, you dance better than any noble, and you are filled with grace. How did you learn the dance?"

"Remember, I administer healing to many nobles. Some of

the ladies took a liking to me and showed me the dance in private one day."

"And have you ever had the chance to practice it with a man?"

"No. Not besides my brothers. And now with you, of course."

"I'm glad this happened, Sage. I wanted to dance with you."

She seemed tense all of a sudden, and Robin noticed some of the ladies watching them and talking quietly behind their hands.

"What will everyone say about this tomorrow?"

"They'll all say they wish they found the bean in their cake so they could dance with you, too."

That made her laugh. To see Sage's beautiful smile made his heart soar. He held her in his arms and together they danced the night away, over and over again. With their eyes only on each other, it seemed as if no one else in the room even existed. Robin didn't think it could get any better, until the music stopped at the end of the night, and a very drunk Oscar shouted out another command, almost as if he were reading Robin's mind.

"My sister is standing under the kissing bough," Oscar called out. "I command Lord Robin to kiss her."

"What? Nay!" Sage suddenly seemed terrified as she looked over at her brother, who was dancing atop the dais table with a tankard of Mountain Magic clenched in his fist. "Robin, no. Stop this nonsense. Please," she whispered.

"You heard the Lord of Misrule," said Robin in a husky voice, pulling her tightly into his arms and locking his lips with hers. The kiss was so filled with passion from both of them that only Robin's father clearing his throat brought Robin back to the fact everyone was watching them.

"Robin, it is time to bid a goodnight to our guests," said Madoc.

"Yes. Of course," he said, slowly releasing Sage. She turned and ran from the great hall, taking with her all the magic that had filled Robin's heart this night.

Turning back to the other noblewomen, Robin faked a smile, wondering how the hell he was ever going to be able to choose and marry one of them, when Sage was the only woman he wanted as his bride.

CHAPTER 18

Three days passed, and Sage didn't leave her healing room much at all because so many of the servants were feeling the ill effects of her brother's stupid request to give them all Mountain Magic. She administered mint and ginger for those with stomach problems. She'd made up a tincture including lavender to rub on the temples of patients to help cure dizziness. And those with headaches took her potion made of mint, rosemary, and willow bark. She was too afraid to use any foxglove again, after what happened with Lord Burchard.

Thankfully, her brother was gone for a few days, having commanded some of the knights to take him and his new peasant friends on a hunt. After Oscar had demanded that he and his friends learn to fight with swords the other day, Sage didn't think any of the nobles wanted to be around them anymore. But Oscar was having the time of his life. He'd even commanded that Amira learn to stitch in the ladies solar, and that Noel play with the noble children for the last few days.

If Sage hadn't threatened her brother, he would have most

likely commanded something for her to do again. After speaking with Oscar, she realized it was Lords Rook and Gar that told her brother to make Robin dance with her and also to kiss her. She felt like such a phony out on the dance floor with Robin. And with all the nobles staring at her, it made her want to hide away until the Twelfth Night activities were over and everyone was gone.

Finally, Sage had a few moments to herself. The sun was shining today and she decided to go for a walk to look for more herbs now that the snow had melted. She was just about to leave when a group of women came to her door.

"Yes? May I help you?" She looked up to see Lady Jocasta with a few noblewomen who Sage had yet to meet, and neither did she want to. Ladies Raven and Rose were also with them.

"Healer. I want you to remove my sling and unwrap my arm immediately. I don't believe that I need it," commanded Lady Jocasta.

"Oh, I'm sure Sage wouldn't have you wear that if it weren't needed," Raven spoke up.

"That's right," said Rose. "Sage is a healer. She knows what is best for you."

Sage suddenly felt evil. The woman never needed the sling in the first place. She'd only put it on her since Lady Martine urged her to, and because Lady Jocasta was putting up such a fuss.

"I can look at it. I'm sure you probably don't need it anymore," said Sage, removing Jocasta's arm from the sling and unwrapping it as well. "Yes, it's all better. No need for this." Sage threw the wrappings to the side. "Thank you for coming to see me."

"I don't even see a scratch," said one of the noblewomen, inspecting Jocasta's arm.

"Neither is there a bruise," said another, stretching her neck to see too.

"I told you so," sniffed Jocasta. "This girl only put that sling on me to keep me away from Lord Robin. You seem familiar, Healer. Do I know you?"

"We met a few days ago," Sage pointed out.

"No. I mean before I came to Shrewsbury. I'm sure I've seen you somewhere before."

"Nay. I don't believe so." Sage felt cornered by the nobles, with nowhere to run. If it weren't for Rose and Raven being there, she wasn't sure what would have happened.

"All that matters is that your arm is better," said Rose.

"Yes," agreed Raven. "Ladies, if you'll follow me, there is a quilt in progress in the ladies solar that I'd like you all to see."

Thankfully, Raven was able to get the nobles to leave and the accusations stopped.

Sage let out a deep breath and collapsed atop a chair.

"Lady Jocasta never needed all that, did she?"

Sage's head snapped up to see that Rose was still there. She had been so silent that Sage hadn't even noticed.

"What difference does it make?" asked Sage, feeling defeated. "No one would believe me when I said I only wrapped up her arm to make her happy."

"To make her happy?" Rose sat down on a chair across from her.

"Yes. The woman was wailing and whining and carrying on after she slipped on the ice and fell. There was nothing wrong with her at all, but she insisted she was mortally injured, so I wrapped her arm just to shut her up."

Rose laughed, breaking the tension. "Oh, Sage, you are too wicked."

"Do you think I was wrong?"

"Nay," said Rose. "Not at all. If it were me, I would have wrapped up her mouth, too."

That made both of them laugh.

"Rose, can I ask you a question?"

"Of course," said Rose with a comforting smile. "Anything at all."

"You were a commoner before you married Lord Rook, right?"

"Yes. I was naught but the daughter of the late master gardener."

"Did Lord Rook ever want to marry a noblewoman instead of you?"

"He was betrothed to a haughty French noble. He almost married her, but things changed at the last minute."

"So, then there is hope? I mean—oh, never mind."

"You are in love with Lord Robin."

Sage felt a pain in her heart when Rose said the words. "Why would you say that?"

"Everyone witnessed the dancing, and more importantly the passionate kiss you two shared."

"Robin—I mean, Lord Robin—probably kisses all the women that way."

"Well, I don't know for sure since I only recently became part of the Blake family, but I'd say by the way he was looking at you that he has eyes only for you."

"What difference does it make if it's true?" asked Sage. "Robin and I can never be together."

"Don't say never. After all, I was a commoner and married a nobleman. It seems many of the Blake siblings are marrying from below the salt lately."

"And that is why Robin would never do so. He feels as if he has to bring honor back to the family name by marrying a noblewoman."

"No. I'm sure that's not the way he feels at all."

"He told me so himself! He also said that part of the deal of him being Lord of Shrewsbury Castle was that he had to marry a noblewoman and he had to do it soon."

"Oh, Sage, I know how you feel." Rose covered Sage's hand with her own. "Lord Robin is in a tough situation. My husband Rook doesn't have a castle, just a manor house. Mayhap that makes all the difference."

"So, it's true then. Robin and I can never end up together?"

"I don't know, but I hope that is not the case." Rose got to her feet. "I think you need to talk to Robin about this."

"Nay. I don't want to burden him. He already has a lot of responsibility with his new position. And I know how important being lord of a castle is to him."

"That's true," agreed Rose. "Rook said it was all Robin ever talked about growing up. And when this castle was offered to his father and turned down, Robin's dream came true."

"Robin's father turned down the chance of having his own castle?" asked Sage. "Why? I don't understand."

"I don't know the facts, but I believe this castle has bad memories for both Lord Madoc and Lady Abigail for some reason. If you want to know more, you'll have to ask Robin about it. He can tell you. Well, I'd better go catch up to the rest of the nobles even though I'd rather spend time out in the woods."

"I'm going for a ride to look for herbs that were hidden under the snow. Would you like to join me?"

"Oh, I wish I could, Sage, but I promised Rook I'd try to blend in more with the other nobles. He doesn't want them to think he did the wrong thing by marrying a commoner. I'd better get going."

"I understand," said Sage, collecting up her bag and shears and making her way out to the stable. She walked in to hear two men arguing, and the sound of clanking and swishing.

"Quit throwing the shit into the wheelbarrow! You're going to hit me, you fool." Sage recognized the sound of Lord Rook's voice.

"Well, you deserve to be covered in dung," came Lord Gar's voice. "If you would have given the boy your sword to use in the practice yard, he wouldn't have commanded us to do such a demeaning job."

"I'm not giving my sword to anyone. I'm a noble, dammit."

Sage walked up quietly, seeing Gar shoveling manure into a wheelbarrow. Rook stood next to him with a pitchfork, but wasn't helping at all.

"Why didn't you at least let him ride your horse and try to joust like he wanted?" asked Gar.

"Me? No way. No one rides my horse but me," said Rook. "Besides, the boy would have hurt himself and I didn't want to be blamed for it. Although, right now if he were here, I swear I'd strangle him with my bare hands."

"I'd like to show the fool what it really feels like to be in a battle," spat Gar.

Sage cleared her throat to get their attention.

"Sage!" Rook dropped the pitchfork and hurried to pick it up.

"How long have you been standing there?" Gar stopped to wipe the sweat from his brow, leaving a brown streak across his forehead.

"Long enough to hear both of you threatening to hurt my brother."

"We didn't mean it," said Rook, forcing a laugh.

"Nay. Of course not." A fly landed on Gar's nose and he swatted at it, only managing to get more manure on his face.

"I'm sorry that my brother is causing so much trouble,"

said Sage. "I knew he couldn't handle the power of being Lord of Misrule. I begged Lord Robin not to let him do it."

"Your brother is doing nothing wrong." Robin emerged from one of the stalls, having heard the entire conversation. "The fact that my cousins are complaining about doing a little manual labor is what's wrong. They were given an order by the Lord of Misrule, and now they pay."

"Pay?" asked Rook. "Bid the devil, Robin, you put this idea in the boy's head, didn't you? That's why we're here doing the work of peasants."

"Nay. He wouldn't. Would you?" asked Gar.

"And who put the idea in the boy's head to have me ignore all the noble ladies and spend my time with a commoner? As well as kiss her in front of everyone?" asked Robin.

"It was Rook's idea," whined Gar. "He said you'd like it."

"I said he liked Sage," Rook corrected him. "Besides, Sage seemed to be the only one objecting to it." He looked over to Sage and she lowered her head.

"I never said I didn't like it," Robin told them. "As a matter of fact, I have both of you to thank, since Sage was the only one I really wanted to be with anyway." Robin reached out and took her hand.

"What?" snapped Gar. "Then why did you tell the boy to make us do this smelly task?"

"Yes," agreed Rook. "You're punishing us for helping you get something you wanted. That makes no sense at all."

"Stop the complaining and get back to work before I tell Oscar you need more practice cleaning out the stalls when he returns from the hunt," Robin threatened.

"You wouldn't," sneered Rook.

"He would," said Gar, throwing more manure in the wheel barrow, missing, and hitting Rook instead.

The two of them started fighting again. Robin pulled Sage along with him to get away from the noise.

"Why are you here?" he asked.

"I am going for a ride to look for more herbs since it is such a fine day."

"By yourself?" He released her hand and frowned.

"Yes. So, if you'll excuse me."

"Nay. I will not let you go outside the castle gates by yourself. It's not safe. I'll come with you." He opened a stall and started to saddle a horse.

"I don't think Lady Jocasta and the other noblewomen would like that."

"I don't care what they think. My duty as lord of the castle is to protect all who live here."

"Your duty is to choose a lady to marry, in case you've forgotten."

His hands stilled and his head turned toward her. "I'd like to forget about it. At least for today." He brought the horse out of the stable. "Up you go." He lifted her up as she protested.

"This isn't my horse. I'm not used to it."

"It's my horse, and I am used to it." He mounted right behind her. "Besides, it will be easier this way," he said in her ear.

"Easier for what?" she asked. "Kissing me? Fondling me? Teasing me when you know you're not supposed to have me?"

"Calm down, Sage," he said, directing the horse out of the stable. "I only meant it'll be easier to protect you this way if we should get into trouble."

"Oh. Yes. Of course, my lord," she said, feeling her cheeks reddening because she'd just divulged exactly what was on her mind and what she wanted him to do.

"Let's get some fresh air," he said. "Hold on, I'm going to ride fast."

They rode for a while, and little by little, Sage started to relax. It felt so good to be in Robin's arms again. They chatted about nothing important, and before long were laughing and having a good time. The sun shone down brightly for being a winter day. Sage felt warmth spreading within her. Robin made her feel so alive. He had a way of making her forget all her troubles.

"Stop over there. Down by that rock," she told him, pointing to a large boulder off the side of the road, half-hidden by fallen branches. "I think I see some yarrow."

They stopped and he dismounted, helping her to do the same. When he slid her body down his, she didn't want to step away.

"I'm sorry about all this," he apologized.

Sage pushed away from him and went to gather her herbs. "Sorry about what?" she asked.

"You know what I mean, Sage. I don't want to marry any of those noble ladies any more than you want me to."

"But you have no choice," she said, trying not to face him so he wouldn't see the tears welling up in her eyes.

"Let's sit down and talk. It feels good to be in the sun."

She thought about it for a moment, then decided that she'd like to know more about him, so she agreed.

"All right," she said, looking for a place to sit. He valiantly yanked off his cloak and spread it on the ground.

"Go on," he said with a nod.

After she sat down, he settled himself next to her.

"What did you want to talk about?" she asked.

"I don't know. I just thought we could... talk."

"Robin, are you happy you inherited Shrewsbury Castle?"

"Yes. It's a dream come true. Of course, I am. Wouldn't any man feel the same way?"

"I'm not sure," she told him. "Rose said her husband told her that this is all you ever wanted your entire life."

"It's true," he admitted. "So, when my father turned down the offer from the King when the Lord of Shrewsbury died without an heir, it was passed on to me."

"Why would your father turn down the chance of having a castle of his own?"

"Too many bad memories at Shrewsbury for him." He picked a blade of grass and twirled it around in his fingers.

"Like what? Can you tell me what happened at the castle that makes it more of a curse than a blessing to your father?"

"I don't like talking about it, but I suppose I can." He threw down the grass and scratched the back of his neck. "My mother's brother, my Uncle Garrett, was once imprisoned at Shrewsbury."

"Is he Gar's father?"

"Yes. Well, no, not really. Uncle Garrett's brother was Gar's father, but he was killed by pirates."

"Pirates?"

"Yes. My Aunt Echo, my father's twin, is Gar's true mother. She was... a pirate. Before she knew she was noble."

"I'm confused."

"It's a long story, Sage. But getting back to my father, you have probably heard he was a thief."

"Before he was noble."

"Before he *knew* he was noble," he corrected her. "He was born of noble blood, but stolen as a baby."

"And he raised and raced pigeons."

"Yes. That's right. Anyway, he has been in dungeons three times, twice in Shrewsbury alone."

"Mercy. That is horrible."

"And my mother has not only been in Shrewsbury's

dungeon, but once betrothed to a past lord of the castle, and beaten by him as well."

"I think I understand now why they didn't want the castle," said Sage, her heart going out to these people. "I'm surprised that they are even here for Christmastide at all."

"It isn't easy for them, I'm sure. But they are here to support me."

"As parents should do for their children."

"Sage, it must be so hard for you and your siblings not to have parents."

"Harder than you think."

"I want you to know that my offer for you and your siblings to live at Shrewsbury still stands. No matter what happens."

"I appreciate the offer, and that is something I'd like to speak to you about, Robin."

"What about it?"

"I'd like my siblings to stay and live here if you don't mind."

"What about you?"

"I'm sorry," she said, shaking her head. "But it would be too difficult for me to stay here, watching you with—with your new wife." She got up, not wanting to talk about this any longer. "I think we should be getting back to the castle. We've been gone for a while now and tongues will start wagging soon." She headed to the horse.

"Let tongues wag. I don't care." Robin got up, shaking out his cloak and putting it back around his shoulders. He followed her to the horse. "Sage, you can't mean you're really going to leave."

"It is exactly as I said." She mounted the horse without his help.

"But where will you go? You don't have a home." He

mounted as well. “And who will protect you from future attackers?”

“I survived before, and will again.”

They started to ride in silence. Then he asked her a question that she wasn’t ready to answer. “Those men who attacked you. They didn’t want your belongings, did they? They wanted you dead.”

“It does seem that way.”

“Why?”

“Why what?”

“You know what I mean, Sage. Why were they trying to kill you? What is it you are not telling me?”

“Nothing matters anymore, Robin. I’d rather not talk about it.”

“It matters to me.”

“Why should it?” she asked. “In another few days, you’ll be married to a noble and I’ll be gone and out of your life forever.”

When Sage said the words aloud, they hit her hard. That is exactly what was about to happen, and honestly, she didn’t know how she was going to go on without Robin in her life.

CHAPTER 19

It was near midnight the next day and everyone was still celebrating, making merry and drinking too much, as usual. Tonight was Hogmanay, as the Scots called it, or New Year's Eve. It was the time when supposedly the veils between the living and the dead were the thinnest, and dead love ones could come back to visit. Sage wasn't sure anyone really believed that, but since most everyone was superstitious, empty places were set for dead loved ones at the table, and candles burned brightly in the windows all night long. The latter part was supposed to keep evil spirits away.

More elaborate foods were served to the nobles, this time being stuffed eel, partridge with chestnuts, braised beef, and the ever-popular fowl eaten on holidays—roasted goose with quince, apple, and sage stuffing.

With everyone eating so much, many people were coming to her with their bellies aching. Sage had personally shown the kitchen how to make candied ginger and a hot mint drink to help ease all the indigestion. Sage's favorite foods were the sweets. Tonight they had served hand-sized mince pies made from dried fruit and spices. It was a custom to make a wish when you took a bite. Sage knew it was senseless, but she wished anyway for her and Robin to end up together.

Just as the hour of midnight approached, Sage, still working in the kitchen, heard a ruckus out in the great hall. Then her brother rushed in, looking panic-stricken.

"What's the matter, Oscar?" asked Sage.

"Ye canna be firstfoot! Get out!" shouted a Scotsman. "Ye'll bring bad luck upon this castle."

"Storm MacKeefe is upset," said her brother. "Firstfoot, or the person to come to the door at the stroke of midnight, is supposed to be a dark-haired man for good luck in the coming year."

"Yes, that's true. But why is he yelling?"

"It seems some lord just arrived and he has red hair. Red hair is awful! It means bad luck."

"Oh, Oscar, that is nonsense. It is just old superstitions, and they don't mean a thing."

"He looks like bad luck. Come see for yourself." Oscar pulled her along to the door of the kitchen.

Sage was laughing at the nonsense, but when she saw the man who had arrived, her eyes opened wide and so did her mouth."

"Sage? What's the matter? You look like you've seen a ghost," said Oscar.

"Oscar, hide me. Fast." She grabbed her brother's hand and hid behind a screen that separated the kitchen from the great hall.

"Sage, what is the matter?"

"I know that man. And you are right. He will bring us bad luck. Worse than you can even imagine."

"But I thought you said firstfoot was just superstition."

"Not anymore. Oscar, that is Lord Cespian of Leeds," she

said in a hoarse whisper. Her body started trembling just from seeing him.

"Who?" asked her brother.

"He is brother to Lord Burchard, the man I am accused of killing."

"Ah *ha*! That's how I know you!"

The screen was pushed aside and Lady Jocasta stepped forward. She had been listening to every word they said.

"I—I don't know what you mean," said Sage.

"I am Lord Cespian's cousin. I was there the day you killed my cousin, Lord Burchard. This woman is a murderer," shouted Jocasta, getting everyone's attention. "She's a murderer, I tell you. Put her in the dungeon before she kills anyone else."

Robin looked up to see what the shouting was all about. There was the meddlesome Lady Jocasta, telling everyone in the great hall that Sage was a murderer.

"Nay! You are mistaken." Robin walked up on the dais so everyone could hear him. The musicians had stopped playing and everyone stared directly at Sage. "This girl is my healer. She would never harm anyone. She even saved my own life."

Robin didn't like admitting that aloud, but he also didn't want trouble to come to Sage. Until he could figure out what this was all about, he had to calm down the crowd who were starting to get worked up thanks to Jocasta.

"She's right! That girl killed my brother Burchard with her herbs." The red-haired man who'd just entered the great hall pointed an accusing finger at Sage.

"Nay. I didn't kill anyone, I swear." Sage felt as if her troubles had followed her, even though she had hidden away at

Shrewsbury Castle trying to avoid the men determined to kill her.

"Tell the crowd what you gave to Lord Burchard to kill him," said Jocasta.

"I-I only gave him a slight t-tincture made mainly with foxglove for the ailing heart and his headaches," Sage stuttered. "I've used it many times before."

"Is that herb poisonous?" asked Lord Corbett.

"Only in large amounts," said Sage. "What I gave him was such a small dose that it wouldn't have done anything but stop his pain."

"She stopped it all right," said Cespian. "She killed him! I am Lord of Leeds now, and I demand justice for my brother's death."

"Do you have any proof of these accusations?" asked Lord Corbett.

"I am a witness," said Jocasta. "So is my handmaid. We were there at the castle when this girl was called in to help heal Lord Burchard," she said, walking over to join her red-haired cousin. "I didn't actually see the girl except in passing, but my handmaid spoke with her. And as Lord Cespian here can attest to, this girl named Sage used her witchery to poison and kill a noble."

The crowd went wild.

"Quiet down," shouted Robin, holding his hand in the air. "I am sure this is all a misunderstanding."

"Nay, it's not. She's a witch!" shouted Jocasta. "She made a potion that killed a noble."

"This is all nonsense," shouted Robin. "Why would an innocent girl want to kill anyone? Especially a noble? I don't believe it."

"She's not innocent like you think," said Jocasta. "I sent my handmaid to ask her for a healing potion, and she came back telling me that Sage was in love with Lord Burchard. That Sage admitted it to her, and also that she was a witch. A witch who made love potions. Sage was going to give a love potion to Lord Burchard so he'd fall in love with her, a commoner, and marry her. He had recently lost his poor wife, and this girl was going to take advantage of it."

"What? Nay! That is preposterous and certainly not true," shouted Sage. "I was asked by a handmaid to make a love potion while I was there, which of course, I refused to do. I didn't know whom she was going to use it on, but I swear I didn't make it. I never gave Lord Burchard anything but herbs to help his ailment. That is all."

"She's lying," said Jocasta. "She's a commoner who wants to marry a noble so badly that she'd do anything to make it happen. After all, everyone here sees the way she looks at Lord Robin, and the way she was kissing him and dancing with him yesterday."

The crowd started to agree with the woman.

"Now, wait a moment," yelled Robin. "Sage only did those things because it was the command of the Lord of Misrule. A game."

"The Lord of Misrule who happens to be her own brother, I might point out," said Jocasta with a sniff. "We all saw how much cake the boy ate to find the bean. I'm sure Sage told him to order her to do those things."

"Nay, she didn't," yelled Oscar.

"Oscar, please. Be quiet for now," begged Sage. She didn't want everyone knowing Rook and Gar told him to do it, because Jocasta would only turn that around too, and accuse them of something next. Sage didn't want anyone getting in trouble on her behalf.

"Well, Shrewsbury, what are you going to do about this?" growled Lord Cespian. "That girl killed my brother, and I want her punished for it. A life for a life is only fair."

"Now, wait a minute. This is all speculation," said Robin. "You have no proof."

"She's a witch and I can prove it!" shouted Jocasta. "My handmaid said Sage's mother made her mother a love potion many years ago so her parents would fall in love. Come here, Augusta. Tell them about the family of witches."

The handmaid shyly came forward. She must have been here all along with Lady Jocasta, but until now, Sage hadn't even noticed her. That is, until the girl lifted her face and Sage saw the burn scar across her cheek. She recognized it, because she'd given the girl a healing salve for it while she was in Leeds.

"Sage, have you seen this handmaid before?" asked Lord Corbett, stepping forward to take control, since he was the patriarch of the family and also the one with the highest-ranking status.

Sage looked up and her eyes met Robin's. Even from this distance she could see the concern and disappointment on his face. He shook his head slightly, telling her without words not to admit it. Still, Sage had done nothing wrong. She didn't want to lie and lose the trust of everyone when they eventually discovered the truth. And she certainly didn't want to lose the trust of Robin.

"Yes, Lord Corbett, I have seen her before," Sage answered.

"I can't hear her!"

"Speak up, wench."

Shouts came from the crowd.

"Sage, please approach the dais," said Lord Corbett.

"Sage, don't do it," whispered Oscar, gripping on to her sleeve.

"I have to, Oscar. I cannot hide away in fear for the rest of my life. I want this over with once and for all."

"But you'll be imprisoned. Don't admit to anything, Sage. Don't do it."

"Just please, promise me you'll watch over Amira and Noel," Sage said to her brother. "They will be frightened. They need you." She squeezed her brother's hand and then walked forward to find out her fate. She wished now that she had told Robin about all this, because the worst part to her was putting the man in this horrible position.

"Now, tell us again," said Lord Corbett. "Have you seen this handmaid before? And if so, where and when?"

Sage glanced around the room. Everyone was staring at her. She could already hear the wagging tongues starting to whisper. Her stomach became tight and she felt as if she were going to retch.

"Yes," she admitted. "I was called to Castle Leeds to help heal Lord Burchard's horrendous headaches, as well as his aching heart. While I was there, this handmaid told me she wanted me to make a love potion."

"Handmaid, why did you want a love potion?" Robin ground out. "And why would you think Sage even knew how to do something like that?"

The handmaid's eyes flashed over to Jocasta. Then she lowered her face and answered. "I was in love with Lord Burchard, and I wanted him to love me, too," said the girl.

Gasps went up from the crowd.

"And the nobles knew about this and yet did nothing to reprimand the girl?" asked Robin.

"We didn't know about it until after the healer killed our brother, because she wanted Burchard to fall in love with her instead," spat Jocasta.

"What?" Sage's mouth fell open. "No, I didn't. I didn't even know Lord Burchard."

"Sage's mother made a love potion for my mother years ago," the handmaid told her. "My mother told me about it before she died, and pointed Sage out to me. That is how I knew."

"Sage?" asked Robin, looking at her as if she frightened him now. "Tell me this isn't so."

Sage looked around the room once more. Then, with a heavy heart she answered.

"Yes, it is true that my mother made love potions."

"Well, surely she didn't teach you to do it," said Robin.

Sage hesitated before she answered. "I knew how to do it, but I swear I never used one on anyone."

"Now we know why Lord Robin is in love with the wench," mumbled a man in the crowd.

"Did you—did you use a love potion on me, Sage?" asked Robin.

"Nay!" Her entire body shook now. "I didn't, Robin, I swear it's the truth."

"She just addressed him not using his title," a noblewoman pointed out.

"They must have already had intimate relations," said Jocasta.

"Did you, Shrewsbury?" Lord Cespian demanded to know. "Did you couple with the witch?"

Sage froze, waiting for Robin's answer. If he said no, he'd be lying. If caught in a lie, he could lose everything, including his land, castle, and title. If he said yes, everyone would think certainly Sage was a witch, and that she tricked Robin into doing it. Things just kept getting worse and worse.

"Take her to the dungeon," said Robin, shocking Sage and making her feel worse than if he'd answered the last question.

"Th-the dungeon?" asked Sage, horrified to hear the man

she loved say this. Especially after he'd told her how horrible the dungeons of Shrewsbury were. "Nay. Please, don't send me there. Anywhere but there."

"Burn the witch," shouted someone from the crowd.

"String her up," yelled someone else.

"Stop it!" Robin's voice split the air. "This is my castle. I am Lord of Shrewsbury. Everyone will listen to me. This is the New Year, and I'll not hear another word about this until I bring it up again. We are in the middle of a celebration. Remove the girl and let the celebration continue. Take her to the dungeon, I said."

"Nay!" shouted Oscar from the back of the room.

Robin's head snapped up. Everyone turned to see who could be so bold as to go against the word of the lord of the castle.

"I am the Lord of Misrule and I say that Sage will not be sent to the dungeon at all."

"Oscar, nay," whispered Sage shaking her head, knowing her brother was being much too bold. This was not the right situation to exercise his fake powers. He would surely be punished for it along with her.

"What did you say?" asked Robin. Anger edged his voice. The room became totally silent.

"I said... you are lord of the castle, my lord," said Oscar, not sounding as confident as a moment ago. "However, until Twelfth Night, I am Lord of Misrule. My commands must be carried out." Oscar stood at Sage's side, slightly behind her. No one spoke. Griffin whined and ran over, lying down at Sage's feet.

Gar cleared his throat. "The boy has a point."

"Aye," agreed Rook. "Everyone has been honoring the Lord of Misrule's commands since Christmas."

"He's right," agreed Martine. "The Lord of Misrule's

commands must be carried out until Twelfth Night."

"Robin?" asked Lord Corbett, looking back and forth between Robin and Sage. "It's your castle. What will you do?"

Robin stared straight through Sage, making her feel like a traitor. She lowered her gaze, not able to meet his stare. It hurt too much. He seemed so betrayed by her and severely disappointed. Sage didn't like seeing the man she loved look at her this way.

Finally, slowly, Robin nodded. "So be it, Lord of Misrule," Robin answered. "The girl will not go to the dungeon, but she will stay locked in the east tower until after Twelfth Night. Then, it will be only me who decides her fate."

"Thank you, my lord," said Oscar, bowing deeply.

Robin continued. "It seems for the healer, this is her lucky night. Now, unless the Lord of Misrule disagrees with any more of my commands, I think this celebration is over. Good night, everyone."

Without waiting for an answer, Robin stormed off. Everyone split up, going to their rooms for the night, or settling down in the great hall to sleep. The joyous occasion came to a screeching halt. The happy mood of the festival of ringing in the new year was now naught but a room filled with judgements and sour dispositions, all because of Jocasta and the arrival of Lord Cespian.

Nay, Sage decided, feeling her heart breaking knowing that Robin would never trust her again. Things between them were over. This was all her fault after all.

Sage let out a deep breath, happy not to be spending the night in the dungeon. "Thank you, Oscar," she said to her brother, who bravely came to her rescue. Not hearing an answer from him, she turned around to find Oscar prone on the floor with his eyes closed. The great Lord of Misrule had fainted!

CHAPTER 20

"Get in there and don't even *think* of trying to escape." One of the castle guards shoved Sage into the dark tower room, while the other waited at the door.

"It is dark and cold in here," she said, holding her arms around her.

"Prisoners don't need light or warmth," snarled the guard. "If you were in the dungeon, the conditions would be worse, so don't complain."

"Wait!" she called as the door started to close. "I'm thirsty."

"No food or drink until morning." The door shut and closed her in all alone. It was so dark that Sage couldn't see a thing. She felt her way over to a bed and climbed atop it. Pulling a blanket over her, she cried herself to sleep, feeling so alone, and wondering if Robin would remember her once she was gone. If only things were different, she wouldn't be in this position. But being a commoner accused of killing a noble, not to mention being called a witch, wasn't going to end well for her, and there was nothing at all she could do to change it.

Robin awoke the next morning, his head down on the table of his solar where he had fallen asleep, fully clothed. Something hit him on the arm and he jumped, grabbing his sword from the table, hurriedly getting to his feet.

"Egads, Cousin, put down the blade."

When his eyes focused, he saw the outline of Gar standing there with his hands in the air.

"Well, stop startling me. Next time I might take off your head before I realize it is you!"

"Is he dressed? Can we come in now?" came a woman's voice from the door.

"Aye," said Gar, pulling out a chair and sitting down. "Just don't get too close. He seems to be in a killing mood this morning."

"Come on, girls. In here." Martine pushed the door wide open, marching into the room. Behind her was a procession of women who Robin slowly realized were his cousins.

"What the hell is this? Can't a man get a bit of privacy in his own solar?" Robin threw down his sword on the table and went over and sat on the bed.

"Open the shutter, Rose. He needs some fresh air to clear out the cobwebs of his daft head," said Martine.

Rose pulled open the shutter, letting in sunshine along with a frigid winter breeze.

"What in the devil's name is going on here?" Robin rubbed his face in his hands, trying to make sense of this situation.

"We're here concerning Sage," said his cousin Raven. "We don't like that you imprisoned an innocent girl."

"What?" Robin's head snapped up and he scowled at Raven. "She killed a man. A noble," he pointed out.

"Robin, that is ridiculous." His cousin Eleanor stood there

with her arms crossed over her chest. "Sage couldn't kill anyone. She's too kind."

"I agree," said his Scottish cousin Lark. "The lass is a healer, no' a murderer."

"You were all there in the great hall and heard the same thing I did," said Robin. "Lady Jocasta and Lord Cespian both said she used her herbs to kill Lord Burchard."

"Because she was in love with the man?" asked Raven. "That is the stupidest thing I've ever heard and it's not true."

"Aye," said Lark. "Sage is in love with *ye*, Robin."

Robin felt like he was about to retch. Everything he felt for Sage wasn't real. He knew that now. "She used a love potion on me. She betrayed me."

"The girl saved your life, Robin," Gar pointed out.

"Only so she could trick me into loving her. She must truly be desperate to marry a noble, like Lady Jocasta said." He got off the bed and started pacing. "I thought the feelings we had for each other were real. But now I see the girl only did it to make a fool of me. Or mayhap just to be the wife of a noble."

"You really are an ass if you believe that," said Gar.

Robin's temper flared. He yanked Gar up by the front of his tunic, even though the man was bigger than he. "Say that again and I really will take off your head."

"Stop it, you fool." Gar pushed Robin away from him. "You think you are ready to rule a castle? You can't even see through lies right in front of your face."

"She's a witch, Gar. You heard her admit it," yelled Robin. "And witches get burned at the stake."

"I don't even know who you are anymore, Robin." Gar held his hands up in surrender. "It's too early in the morning to try to talk sense into that thick skull of yours. I'm leaving." Gar turned and left the room.

"I didna hear her admit to bein' a witch," said Lark.

"She didn't," said Rose.

Robin felt like the women were closing in on him and he didn't like it.

"She didn't say she was a witch or that anyone was a witch at all," added Martine. "She said her mother made love potions from herbs and that the woman showed her how to do it."

"And that's not witchcraft?" asked Robin.

"Even if her mother was a witch, that doesn't mean Sage is one too," said Eleanor.

"That's right," agreed Rose. "Sage never said she used a love potion on anyone."

"What's the difference? She lied to me. She led me on and made me feel pity for her and her siblings. I should have known there was more to her story when those men tried to kill her."

"Robin, you need to talk to Sage." Martine told him, not asked him.

"Absolutely not!" He started pacing the room again. "I have nobles upset with me. I have servants and villagers scared for their children now. Even my own knights are expecting me to punish Sage. It's not like I can just let her walk out of here. She must pay for her mistake."

"The only mistake she made as far as I'm concerned is falling in love with you!" Martine spun on her heel and left the room with the rest of the women following.

"God's eyes, why me?" Robin ran a hand through his hair and sat down at the table. He heard a whining from the open door and looked up to see Griffin. "Come here, boy," he said, patting his leg to bring the dog over. The dog barked at him and turned and ran away down the hall. "Not you, too."

There was a slight knock at the door and he looked up to see his mother. "Can I come in, Robin?"

"Why not? Everyone else has already pushed their way in

and given me their opinion this morning. You might as well, too." Robin reached out for his tankard of whisky that he'd left on the table last night, raising it to his mouth. It was empty. He clunked the tankard back down on the table in frustration.

"I'm not here to tell you what to do," said Abigail, sitting across from him. "I just wanted you to know that I support you, that's all."

"Well, then you're the only one."

"Your father does, too. We both want you to be successful, Robin. And happy."

"I was happy. Until I found out that Sage lied and made a fool out of me. How can I ever forgive that?"

"Sometimes things aren't always what they seem. Mayhap you should look into this situation more thoroughly."

"Why? I have the word of nobles. That is good enough for me."

"Is it?"

"Mother, I know what you're doing. The girls sent you in here, didn't they? They like Sage and are giving me a hard time about this."

"We all like her, Robin. But do you?"

"How the hell can you expect me to believe a commoner over nobles?"

"Robin. You know your father grew up as a commoner, and even worked for one of the past Lord Shrewsburys from this very castle. Well, that Lord Shrewsbury was a noble, but not a good man."

"I know, Mother. You told me the story many times. You almost had to marry Lord Shrewsbury. He beat you, and imprisoned both you and Father, as well as Uncle Garrett."

"You still think you can always trust nobles over someone from below the salt?"

"I want to believe Sage, honest I do. But I saw the nearly

empty bottle of foxglove in her bag. And nobles were witnesses to what happened. When I asked her about the potion bottle, she became very defensive. She also never told me why the men who attacked her were trying to kill her. Now I know why."

"Are you saying Lord Cespian sent men out to kill Sage?" His mother's brows dipped. "That doesn't sound like something a noble would do. I don't know the man well, but I'd think he'd want Sage to go to trial if she killed his brother. After all, if he killed her in revenge, he'd be nothing but a murderer too."

"I didn't think of it that way," said Robin. "God's eyes, I don't know what the hell is going on. What should I do?"

"I can't make that decision for you." Abigail got to her feet. "But if you really love the girl, the way your sister says you do, mayhap you'd better talk to Sage before it is too late." She made her way to the door.

"Mother?" said Robin, causing the woman to stop and turn around.

"Yes?"

"I want to do the right thing as a noble and new lord of the castle. I want to bring back honor to the Blake name and make Father and Uncle Corbett and everyone proud of me. I want to show that I have what it takes to hold this position. I don't want King Edward to think he made a mistake by making me Lord of Shrewsbury."

"So, what is it you're asking?"

"When you and Father fell in love, did it matter that at the time you thought he was just a commoner and a petty thief?"

His mother smiled widely. "Love doesn't put conditions on people, Son. And I can honestly say that even though neither of us knew he was born a noble at the time, it didn't even matter. We were in love. We still are, and I'm sure it'll last forever."

"But nobles don't marry for love. They marry for alliances. Everyone knows that."

"If that's how you feel, then marry Lady Jocasta, if you think it'll make you happy. After all, her cousin has offered twice as big a dowry for her than any of the other suitors."

"I didn't say it would make me happy. I just said, mayhap that is the right thing to do."

"So, you're willing to put your duty over love, is what you are saying."

"I no longer know if I'm really in love with Sage or if all along it was just her love potion that made me feel that way."

"Then, mayhap before you make your final decision concerning a bride, or even what to do with Sage, you should find out for sure if you really love each other."

"If things were different—if none of this ever happened and I did end up marrying Sage, wouldn't Uncle Corbett be disappointed in me?"

"Two of his own children married commoners, if I must remind you."

"I know. And that is why he was really counting on me to marry wisely, to make up for it. To do the right thing."

"Robin, I can't tell you what the right thing is to do. That must be your decision. But now, I'm sorry your father and I ever convinced the King to make you lord of this cursed castle. All Shrewsbury Castle has ever brought to our family is sadness, suffering, and sorrow. I do not want that curse to continue with you."

"I'm starting to see what you mean. It does feel as if this is a cursed castle, doesn't it? But still, being lord of my own castle has always been my dream."

"And what about being in love?" she asked. "Are you willing to sacrifice that for this so-called dream?"

"I wish I knew," said Robin, feeling more confused than ever. "I really wish I knew the answer to that."

CHAPTER 21

Sage lay on the bed in the tower room, wishing she were dead. Her life had been going so well, but now she wished she had never even met Robin. She wished he hadn't saved her life, and she wished that she hadn't saved his in return. And falling in love with the man was her biggest mistake. At the end of Twelfth Night, Robin was sure to condemn her to death. He believed everything the nobles told him, so she had no chance to convince him of her innocence. Still, if only she had a chance, mayhap she could get him to believe that she'd never killed anyone, and that she didn't use a love potion on him, either.

The door to the room swung open, and she sat upright in bed, holding the blanket to her chest. The two guards were still outside the door. A woman wearing a wimple on her head held a tray of food in her hands.

"I brought you something to eat and drink, sweetheart."

The woman's voice sounded odd. Sage didn't remember ever seeing this kitchen maid while she helped out preparing food in the kitchen.

"Thank you," she said, watching the woman put the tray on the bed. She had big hands. And hair on her knuckles.

"Sage, there is an extra key to your door hidden in the pottage," the woman whispered when she bent over with the tray. "I lifted it from Lord Robin's solar earlier."

"What?" Sage's eyes snapped upward. The woman raised her face and smiled.

"Oscar?" Sage whispered, her eyes becoming wide. "What are you doing?"

He glanced back over his shoulder, making certain the guards were not listening from the corridor. Then he turned around and whispered again.

"I'm going to break you out of here."

"Nay." She shook her head. "It's too dangerous. I won't do it."

"Today is the Feast of Fools. The guards will leave the door for a few minutes in an hour to change posts. I'll be waiting for you under the stairs with a costume for you to wear."

"Oscar, I can't."

"Do it, Sage. This is your only chance. We'll blend in with the parade of people heading to church. Everyone will be in costume and wearing masks, so no one will recognize you."

She was about to protest again when the door opened wider and Robin walked into the room.

"Lord Robin!" she said, her gaze flashing over to her brother.

"Enjoy your food, my dear," said Oscar in his odd woman's voice. He turned so fast to leave that he tripped on his long gown, tumbling right into Robin.

"Careful," said Robin, helping to right him.

"Thank you, my lord." Oscar ran from the room, with Robin squinting, looking at him go.

"What are you doing here?" asked Sage.

Robin spoke to the guards who were watching them. "Leave us," he said.

The guards went back out into the corridor and closed the door.

"I'm here to... I need you to remove my stitches. I brought your healing bag." He untied the bag from his waistbelt and threw it down on the bed, eyeing up her food tray. "Ah, hot pottage. I could go for some right now. I missed the morning meal."

"Nay!" She jumped up from under the covers. "I mean, it's more important that we get those stitches out first." She took the tray over to the table and turned back around. It wasn't until she noticed the way he stared at her that she realized she was standing there in nothing but her shift.

"Oh!" She ran over and pulled her gown over her head. When she finished dressing, she turned to find Robin sitting on the bed with his breeches pulled down to his knees, exposing his wound. She groaned silently. Seeing him like this only brought back memories of the intimate time they'd spent together. She quickly pushed the thought from her head. After all, she must remember that this is the man who intended to send her to the dungeon and who imprisoned her in the tower.

"I think the wound is healed."

"Yes," she said, inspecting it, running her fingers gently along the stitches. "And you are right. It is time I remove the sutures."

Robin felt Sage's soft fingers running up and down his leg and it about drove him from his mind. He had come here to find out if she was really a witch. A traitor. A murderer. Now, all he could think of was kissing her. It wasn't the right thing to do. He had to forget it.

"I've never seen anyone heal as fast as you." With her head down as she removed his stitches, her hair was right under his nose. Damn, she smelled good. Like a blooming flower on a summer day.

"I do heal quickly," he said, struggling for words to say.

"All done." She stood up and moved away from him much too quickly. He longed for her body warmth, longed to touch her gently, cupping her soft cheek once again. "Will there be anything else, my lord?"

"I... I... nay."

"Then, I suggest you pull up your breeches before someone walks in and thinks I've given you a love potion to seduce you."

Her words brought him back to his senses. He stood up, pulled up his trews and tied the string at his waist. "Did you?" he asked.

She was busy putting her things back in her bag. "Did I what?" she asked, not even looking at him.

"Sage, I need to know. Did you use a love potion on me? Is that why I am so infatuated with you that I can't sleep at night? Why thoughts of your sweet lips and smiling face fill my thoughts day and night?"

"I did not, my lord."

"Really? I have to know."

"Would you like to inspect my healing bag?" She pushed it over to him, looking into it, digging around and frowning. "I see you already have."

"I took the nearly-empty bottle of the foxglove tincture, if that is what you mean. The same potion used to kill Lord Burchard."

"I didn't kill him," she said.

"I know that's what you said, but then how do you explain the nearly-empty bottle?"

Her eyes narrowed. "That proves nothing. How do you even know how much was in there at the start?"

"Sage, I talked with Lady Jocasta and her handmaid this morning," he said softly. "They verified that that was the tincture you used to try to heal Lord Burchard."

"I told you exactly what I used, it's not secret," she said, her tone telling him she wasn't happy. "I also told you that I only gave him a little. It was only enough to cure his headache and help his heart, not kill him."

"Yet, it was a full bottle when you started."

"Is that what they told you?"

"Well, was it?"

"Yes, as a matter of fact it was. But I told you, I only used a little. I don't know what happened to the rest of it."

"Sage, tell me the truth. Were you in love with Lord Burchard?"

Her face scrunched up and her mouth turned down. "Hardly. I told you, I was only there to cure him. Nothing else. I didn't even know him! Don't you believe me?"

He looked at her and sighed. "I want to, Sage. Honest, I do. My heart says you're telling the truth but my head says you are lying."

"Why would I lie? What do you think I have to hide?"

"That you're a witch? And you know witches are burned at the stake?"

"Nay! I'm not a witch. Neither was my mother."

"But your mother made love potions."

"She dabbled with it, but only because she had nobles offering her a lot of money to make one, and we were so poor we could barely afford food for the table each night."

"Who? Which nobles came to her for love potions?"

"I don't know. She wouldn't tell me."

"But you made love potions too."

"I did it only once. Just to suffice my mother. But I swear, I never used it on anyone."

"Where is it now?"

"It's gone. It was in my home, but as you remember, those assassins burned my home down, trying to kill me and my siblings. Shouldn't you be busy looking for them instead? Or is it all right with you that grown men are trying to kill a woman and children?"

"Stop it, Sage. If you would have told me all this earlier, mayhap I could have helped you. But now, after what transpired yesterday, I'm not sure there is anything I can do to help you out of this mess."

"So, you're saying I'll be condemned to death? For a crime I didn't even commit?"

"God's eyes, Sage. If only you hadn't admitted to the love potion part, mayhap I could have helped you escape a sentence."

"So I will die? You'll let that happen? That's what you're saying isn't it? Is that what you want?"

"Nay, it is not what I want!" he shouted, getting to his feet. "But I can't convince anyone of your innocence without proof. Proof which we don't have."

"Talk with the handmaid. I think she is lying. When she first came to me asking for the love potion, she didn't have that burn on her cheek. When she returned, I treated it for her. Something is odd about her. I don't trust her. I think she's covering up for someone else. Possibly the murderer."

"Are you accusing a noble of killing Lord Burchard? Possibly Lady Jocasta?"

"I didn't say that."

"Everyone knows you don't like her because you think I am going to choose her as my bride."

"Are you?" She met him in challenge.

"As a noble doing the right thing and making an alliance, it would make the most sense. Her dowry is twice as large as all the others."

"Then go to her. Marry her, if you don't believe me." She looked as if she were about to cry.

"Sage, I didn't say I wanted to marry her."

"But you will. Because it is the right thing to do, since you come from above the salt. Right?"

"I am in a trying position. You need to understand that I am expected to marry well, and someone of my own status. It is the King's rule, not mine."

"Well, I wish he were here so the Lord of Misrule could override his decision. Now go! I don't want to ever see you again. I can't believe I let myself fall in love with you when you are naught but a—"

"Careful, Sage. You are already accused of murder and being a witch. Don't add disrespecting a lord to your list of crimes."

"If it is a crime to love someone who I know would never love me in return because he was afraid to, then yes, my lord, I am guilty. Now, leave me be. You shouldn't be alone with your prisoners. After all, tongues might start to wag."

Robin found himself lost for words and feeling as if he'd only made things worse by coming here. He slowly walked to the door, afraid to look back. Because, if he did look back and saw Sage crying, he was going to want to pull her into his arms and kiss her and comfort her all over again.

And that, he was sure, was not the best thing to do right now.

CHAPTER 22

As soon as Robin left the room, Sage ran over and picked up a spoon, digging the key out of the pottage. She had to escape—she had no choice. If she didn't, she would die. And if they thought she was a witch, they would probably accuse her siblings of being witches too. It was no longer safe for them here. Oscar was right. She wasn't sure where she and her siblings would go, but she had to get her family out of here before things got any worse.

When she heard the guards changing posts, she sneaked out and hurried down the stairs. "Oscar? Where are you?"

"I'm here," said Oscar, stepping out from his hiding place wearing a mask that reminded her of the bird-beak masks doctors wore when treating plague victims. It made her jump and she held her hand to her heart. "Oh, sorry," said her brother, pulling up the mask to show her his face. "Here is your costume." He shoved it into her hands. "You'll have to dress in the shadows. Noel and Amira are already in costume. They're waiting for us in the kitchen."

"Oh, Oscar, I hope this works." Sage stepped into the

shadows and put on the costume, which made her look like a man. Her mask was equally as ugly, but she looked like a lion instead.

"Let's go," said Oscar. "I hear the change of guards coming."

They hurried to the kitchen to get Amira and Noel, then they would blend into the parade of the Feast of Fools and make their escape.

"Nay. I can't do this," protested Robin, pacing back and forth in his solar.

"Why not?" asked Gar. "Afraid you'll look stupid wearing a costume?" He held out a costume and mask for Robin to take.

"It's a damned costume," Rook told him. "Now, stop fretting and have some fun." Both Rook and Gar were dressed like women. Gar even had pillows shoved into his bodice to look like breasts. The Feast of Fools was celebrated on January 1st to ring in the new year. It was a time of much eating, drinking, and acting crazy. The men dressed like women, and women like men. Even priests and monks broke free of their inhibitions and joined in on the fun.

"I don't mean the costume," said Robin, taking it from Gar and throwing it to the floor. The headpiece he had for Robin broke in two.

"I wish you wouldn't have done that," said Gar, staring at the broken headpiece. "I had to sleep with a really ugly woman to get that. I shudder to think what she'll want me to do to make up for your breaking it now."

"I am talking about Sage," said Robin.

"What about her?" asked Rook.

"I cannot let her die. I won't. I refuse to condemn her or put her in the dungeon."

"You didn't seem to have any qualms about throwing her in the dungeon yesterday," Rook pointed out.

"I only said that to protect her," explained Robin. "And to keep from having to admit I slept with her, because that would only have made more problems. Besides, the nobles were asking about witchcraft. I had to get Sage out of there fast."

"But the dungeon?" asked Gar, faking a shudder. "Not quite the place I thought you'd send your lover."

"I purposely said she'd go to the dungeon, but only to keep her out of there," said Robin, losing his patience. "What part of that don't you understand?"

"You're making no sense at all," said Gar, bending down and picking up the pieces of the broken headpiece.

"I knew Sage's fool brother would let his power of being Lord of Misrule go to his head."

"So, let me see if I understand this," said Rook, tapping his chin with his finger. "You sent Sage to the dungeon because you wanted the Lord of Misrule to object?"

"Yes."

"What if he hadn't?" asked Gar, laying the pieces of the headpiece on the table. "I wonder if I can stick this back together somehow."

"There was no doubt in my mind that Oscar would use his power to stop it," said Robin. "After all, look at all the other things the boy commanded. I tell you, he likes having power."

"And so do you," said Rook.

"What does that mean?" asked Robin.

"You like being lord of a castle and would do anything to keep your power. Including letting the woman you love die."

"Nay! That is exactly what I'm saying. I won't let that happen."

"So... you believe Sage now?" asked Gar.

"I do. I don't have evidence that her story is true, but I believe her. I'm going up to the tower to tell her right now."

Robin made his way up the tower stairs, taking them two at a time. His heart pounded in his chest. He knew he wasn't acting the expected way of a noble, but neither did he care. All he knew was that he loved Sage, love potion or not. He wanted to not only save her from a doomed fate, but he wanted her for his wife as well.

"Open the door," he told the guards. When they'd unlocked it, he pushed the door open to find the room empty. "Damn it! Where is she?" He turned back to the guards.

"My lord?" asked one of the guards. They didn't even seem to know the girl was gone.

"She must have sneaked out when you changed posts." He hurried down the stairs, needing to find her. Because no matter how innocent Sage might be, escaping her confinement was only going to make her look guilty. Why hadn't the girl stayed put? Now, it was going to be twice as hard to clear her name, if he even could at all.

Once Robin saw the procession of fools in costume, singing and dancing as they headed for the church, he realized exactly how Sage planned to escape.

"Tobias," he called to his squire.

"How did you know it was me, my lord?" Tobias lifted up his mask.

"You have worn the same costume for the Feast of Fools for the past three years," he told the boy. "It's no surprise."

"And you haven't worn a costume yet for the Feast of Fools," Tobias pointed out, looking Robin up and down.

"I'm looking for Sage's siblings. Do you know where they are?"

"Nope. All the kitchen servants have joined the parade, so

they are probably out there." He nodded to the long line of fools dancing and jumping, heading through the courtyard to the church. "Did you want me to look for them, my lord? It won't be easy since everyone is in costume, but I can try."

"Nay. Never mind. I'll find them myself."

Robin went to the stable and got his horse, using it to catch up to the parade of fools. They were now all congregated in a circle outside of the church, waiting to go in for the mass. Robin looked from one face to another, but everyone was in costume and wore masks. He had no idea where Sage and her siblings could be.

Then he saw Griffin following a short person, and knew exactly where they were. He rode up to the group that the dog followed. "Sage. I know it is you and your siblings under those masks. Now, come back to the castle. I need to talk to you."

"Nay, it's not us," said Noel from under his mask. "Griffin, sit down, boy."

"It's no use." Sage took off her mask. "He knows it's us."

Her siblings did the same.

"What are you going to do to us, Lord Robin?" asked Amira.

"Are you going to cook us for dinner?" asked Noel.

"What?" Robin had no idea why the boy said something as absurd as that.

"He means, you're going to burn all of us at the stake because you think we are witches." Oscar removed his mask. "Leave us alone. As Lord of Misrule, I command it."

"You are only Lord of Misrule while at the castle, and we are not there," said Robin.

"It's the witch!" yelled someone, and the entire crowd went into a frenzy.

"The prisoner is escaping," called out Lady Jocasta, removing her own mask.

"Guards, catch her and bring her to the dungeon," yelled Lord Cespian. "Get the other witches too."

"We need to run," Oscar told the others.

"Nay. Don't do that," said Robin. "Go with the guards. Please."

"What?" gasped Sage. "Robin, take me, but please don't take my siblings." She pulled Amira and Noel to her. "They are just children. You need to protect them."

"That is exactly what I plan to do."

"I don't understand," said Sage.

"Sage, I believe you," he said. "I want you to know that."

"You do?"

"Yes. Everything you said. Now, I need you to trust me. I am going to help you and your siblings, I swear. But you need to do exactly as I say."

"Don't trust him, Sage," warned Oscar. "It's a trap just to catch you."

"Nay, it's all right," Sage told her siblings. "What do you want us to do?" she asked Robin.

"Go with the guards to the dungeon. You will all be safe there. I will come to you shortly with a plan to clear you all."

"How are you going to do that?" asked Amira.

"Just trust me," said Robin, having no idea what the hell he was going to do. All he knew was that he needed some time, and this would ensure Sage and her siblings stayed put and stayed safe until he could figure out how to handle this mess they were in.

CHAPTER 23

Robin paced the floor of his solar later that day, waiting for Gar to return. Tobias lounged on a chair at the other side of the room, half asleep. Finally, the door opened and Gar walked in with Raven and Lady Jocasta's handmaid, Augusta.

"My lord," said the handmaid, curtsying. "Am I in trouble?" Her face was pure white. "I heard you wanted to see me?"

"Nay, no trouble," he told the girl with a smile. "Please, have a seat at the table. I want to talk with you."

He made sure to have another woman there to vouch that he wasn't trying to bed or hurt the girl. Gar would stay as a witness, too. "Did you take care of that other part?" Robin whispered to his cousins.

"Martine and the girls are distracting Lady Jocasta and will bring her up here when I give them the word," whispered Raven.

"And Rook will be up here momentarily with Lord Cespian, Uncle Corbett, and my father, who just arrived here today," said Gar.

"Good. Good," said Robin. Gar's father, Robin's Uncle

Garrett, was the head warden of the Cinque Ports. With his high rank, he could order a death, an imprisonment, or even a release of a prisoner. "This is exactly what we need."

"I just hope you're right about this," said Gar, glancing over to the handmaid. "Because, if you're wrong, or if the girl refuses to talk, there is no coming back from this."

"Sage told me she didn't trust the handmaid and that she thought she was hiding information to protect someone. It is all I have to go on, so we will pray Sage was right."

Robin headed over to the table. "Tobias, pour us a drink," he told the boy.

He had Mountain Magic in the decanter. He figured he needed the strongest drink he could find to get the handmaid to relax. If so, she'd be more apt to spill her secrets.

"That's enough," said Robin, grabbing a cup of whisky, handing it to Augusta. "Here you go."

"Oh, nay. I couldn't drink with the nobles. It's not my place," said the girl, making Robin groan.

"Since today is the Feast of Fools, it is all right for commoners to drink with nobles," he told her.

"Are you sure?" Her eyes darted from him to the others.

"He's sure," said Gar, snatching up the cup and giving to her. "Now, have a drink."

"Yes, my lord." She took a sip and started coughing. "I don't think I am fond of whisky."

"You'll get used to it, the more you drink," said Tobias, doing his best to help out with the plan.

"That's right. Take another sip," Robin coaxed her.

She did, and put down the cup. "My, that is strong. It is making my head spin."

And hopefully her lips loose, thought Robin.

"Augusta, you have been Lady Jocasta's handmaid for some time now, right?"

"Yes," she answered. "My mother was her handmaid before me."

"I see." Robin sat down, grabbed a cup, and took a drink. He couldn't seem too eager or he might frighten the girl. "Tell me about the love potion that you said Sage's mother made for your mother."

"I don't know much about it," she said, seeming as if she truly didn't know.

"Did Lady Jocasta ever try a love potion?"

The girl remained quiet. Robin nodded to Tobias and his squire put more whisky in the girl's cup.

"I have been thinking of marrying Lady Jocasta, but I want to make sure she really likes me," said Robin, trying a different approach.

"Oh, yes, my lady would like that," said the girl. "She wants desperately to marry a wealthy, successful lord."

"Really," said Robin, picking up the cup and handing it to the girl. "So do you think she'd want to use a love potion on me so I would fall in love with her?"

"Lady Jocasta would use a love potion on anyone she could get to drink it." The girl's hand flew to her mouth and her eyes opened wide. "I didn't mean to say that."

"It's all right," laughed Robin. "I'd like to hear more about that."

"I don't know what you want me to say."

"I don't believe a girl as nice as you would need to use a love potion on a man."

"Oh, no, I don't need one. I am already married, and we are in love."

"You are?" Robin raised a brow and looked over at Gar.

"Do you have children?" asked Gar.

"Yes. I have two small children. They live with my husband in the village."

"Does Lady Jocasta ever let you go home to see them?" asked Robin.

"Not often," the girl answered sadly.

"Well, mayhap once she's married, you can go home to your family," suggested Gar.

"Nay. She'll never let me leave. And if I do, she'll hurt me." Her hand went to the burn mark on her cheek.

"Did Lady Jocasta do that to you?" Robin nodded to the girl and she slowly lowered her hand from her cheek. "It's all right. You can tell me. I will protect you, Augusta."

"I cannot speak about anything else with you." Her eyes filled with tears. "If I do, she'll hurt or kill my family."

"I see." Robin heard voices in the corridor and knew Rook was arriving with the others. He nodded at Raven to leave to get the women. "Sage never made a love potion for you or Lady Jocasta, did she?"

"Nay, my lord. She did not."

"I didn't think so. But why would Lady Jocasta even want a potion like that?"

"So Lord Burchard would marry her."

"Wait, what? Really? She wanted to marry her own cousin?"

"Yes, my lord. May I have more of that whisky?"

Tobias was about to give her more, but Robin raised his hand to stop him. It would do him no good if the girl passed out before the others heard her story.

"How did Lord Burchard die?" Robin asked her.

"Oh, my lord, I'm sorry. It is all my fault." The girl started crying.

This wasn't at all what Robin expected to hear.

"I think they're here," Tobias whispered. "Shall I let them in?"

"Nay. Not yet," said Robin. "Give me another minute."

Gar got up and went to the door, opening it a crack but not letting anyone enter.

"Why is Lord Burchard's death your fault?"

"I was supposed to bring a love potion back for Lady Jocasta. When Sage wouldn't make it, and I returned without it, Lady Jocasta burned me with the poker from the fire." Her hand went to her cheek once again. "She told me to go to the healer and not to return without the love potion."

"But you said Sage didn't make a love potion," said Robin.

"She didn't. But if I didn't come back with one, I was afraid my lady would hurt my family."

"So, what did you do?"

"When Sage wasn't looking, I sneaked a bottle out of her bag. I didn't know it was deadly, honest I didn't. I had to return with something, so I gave it to Lady Jocasta and told her it was the love potion."

"And she gave it to Lord Burchard, hoping he'd fall in love with her and marry her," said Robin.

"Yes, my lord." The girl was crying now. "I had no idea she would use so much on Lord Burchard. I didn't want the man to die, honest I didn't."

"I believe you, Augusta. And it isn't your fault. All right, Gar, let them in."

"This is preposterous," shouted Lord Cespian, barging into the room.

"We heard everything from outside the door," announced Lord Corbett.

"What is going on in here?" Lady Jocasta entered with Martine and the others.

"Cousin, how could you be so desperate that you'd actually use a love potion on my brother?" asked Lord Cespian.

"What?" Lady Jocasta looked suddenly worried when she

saw everyone in the solar and her handmaid at the table. "I don't know what you mean."

"Your handmaid just confessed everything," said Robin. "She told us how you threatened her and her family, and now we know that since you killed Lord Burchard, you needed someone to blame it on."

"So, Sage is innocent?" asked Rose from the back of the room.

"Yes. Innocent of all charges," said Robin.

"She's the one who gave me the tincture," said Jocasta, pointing at her handmaid. "She killed him, not me."

"You were the one who gave him enough to choke a horse," said Robin. "You are the only one to blame in Lord Burchard's death. The handmaid was only trying to protect her family from you, but she did not kill Lord Burchard—*you* did."

"Jocasta, I am so disgusted by your actions," said Lord Cespian. "I want nothing to do with you ever again."

"I've heard enough," said the lord warden stepping forward. "Lady Jocasta, you are under arrest for the murder of Lord Burchard of Leeds. Guards, take her away."

Robin jumped up. "So, I can release Sage and her siblings from the dungeon, right?"

"Yes," said Garret. "Go ahead."

Robin hurried to the door and stopped, turning to face the others. "I've decided on a bride," he announced to the others. "I am going to ask Sage to marry me."

"The commoner?" gasped Jocasta as the guards hauled her out of the room. "She's from below the salt!"

"That's right," said Robin. "I love her and want to spend the rest of my life with her."

"I thought the King ordered you to marry a noblewoman," said Cespian.

"He did," said Robin. "But that is not going to happen."

"Robin. If you don't marry a noblewoman, you're going to have to give up the castle and everything that goes with it," Garrett warned him. "I'm afraid even I won't be able to convince the King to let you continue being Lord of Shrewsbury if you marry a commoner."

Robin felt a pain in his heart since this is all he'd wanted for such a long time. He'd just had his dream come true, and so quickly it would be over. But Sage was his dream too, now. And he wasn't about to give her up.

"I know," he said. "I understand that."

"Robin, are you sure about this?" asked Gar. "It'll never happen again for you if you're married to a commoner. You'll never have your own castle."

"I love her," Robin told them, feeling the warmth inside his heart. "I love Sage, and if she'll have me, I'll marry her and make her my wife, no matter the consequences. That is all that matters to me anymore."

As he turned to leave, he heard his Uncle Corbett groan and complain to the others. "Not another one! And I had such high hopes that Robin would be the one to marry someone of his own status and break this awful curse."

"Curse?" asked Rook, his son.

"Father, don't speak like that," scolded his daughter Raven.

"Dear, this curse started with your parents," Corbett's wife Devon reminded him.

Everyone started talking at once, and Robin left the room smiling, heading down to the dungeon, finally knowing that he was doing the right thing.

~

"I'm scared," said Noel, clinging to Sage as she and her siblings sat atop her cloak on the floor of the dungeon inside one of the cells. Griffin had followed them into the cell and lay on the floor with his nose between his paws. Thank goodness for the dog being there. He'd already chased away half a dozen rats.

"He's not coming," said Amira sadly.

"He'll be here. He promised," said Sage.

"I'm still the Lord of Misrule for a few more days. I shouldn't even be in here at all," complained Oscar.

"Robin said to trust him, and that is what we need to do," Sage explained to her siblings.

"I don't know how you expect us to trust a man who put us in here!" Oscar jumped up and started rattling the bars of the door on the cell. "I am Lord of Misrule. Let us out of here right now. I command it!"

"Settle down," growled a guard, coming to see what all the ruckus was about. "You'll get your just rewards when Lord Shrewsbury returns."

"You heard the Lord of Misrule, Rodney. Open the door and let them out." Robin walked up, smiling.

"Robin?" Sage jumped up, running to the cell door. "What happened?"

"It's over," said Robin, taking the key from the guard and opening the door himself.

"What do you mean by *over*?" asked Sage.

"Are we still going to die?" asked little Noel.

"No one is going to die," Robin assured them. "The murderer has been caught, and all accusations against you have been dropped. Sage, you and your siblings are free to go."

"Oh, thank you, Robin." Sage fell into Robin's arms. Her siblings piled out of the cell and Griffin couldn't stop barking. His barks echoed loudly in the underground cavern.

"It is you I have to thank for giving me the clue to question Lady Jocasta's handmaid," Robin told her.

"So, who killed Lord Burchard?" asked Sage.

"I'll tell you all that later. But first, I have something to ask you, and I can't even wait until we leave this dungeon to do so."

"Robin? What on earth are you talking about?"

Robin got down on one knee, taking Sage's hands in his. "Will you marry me, Sage? Will you be my wife?"

Sage thought she'd heard Robin wrong, but there was no other reason in the world for him to be down on one knee in this disgusting place. It had to be real.

"I'm a commoner," she reminded him. "I'm from below the salt."

"Yes. Yes, you are. Will you marry me?" he asked again.

"The King has ordered you to marry someone of your own status," she reminded him, thinking he'd gone mad.

"Yes, he did. Now, will you marry me?"

"Robin, if you marry a commoner, won't you lose your castle and land and everything that goes with it?"

"Yes, I will. Now, please, don't make me ask again. Will you marry me, Sage?"

For once in her life, Sage found herself speechless. Was this really happening? Robin saved her life yet again. And on top of it, he wanted her to marry him. He was giving up everything he'd ever wanted just to make her his wife.

"I love you, Robin," she finally managed to squeak out. "But are you sure about this? I don't want you to someday regret your action."

"The only action I'll ever regret is kneeling in this cesspool. Now please, give me your answer so I can get the hell out of this godforsaken place."

"Yes," she said, laughing at Robin. "Yes, I will marry you and be your wife, Sir Robin Blake."

"Thank goodness," he said, trying to move, but his knee was stuck to the floor. "Now help me up."

Sage and her siblings helped Robin get unstuck from the floor. They all cheered and laughed and the dog continued to bark.

In all of Sage's dreams, she never expected this to happen. Her life had been a disaster until she'd met Robin. And now, because of this kind, considerate, wonderful man, she would live in love and happiness from this day on.

CHAPTER 24

SPRING—SHREWSBURY CASTLE

Three months later, Robin stood side-by-side with Sage in the courtyard of Shrewsbury Castle, just having been pronounced man and wife by the priest. They had decided to wait until spring to marry. This way, everything was cleared up before they tied the knot. Spring was also a time of new beginnings and new life. They'd been surprised to find out that Sage had a new life blooming within her as well. She was pregnant with Robin's child.

"You may kiss the bride," said the priest, closing his book.

"Gladly," said Robin, leaning over and kissing Sage so passionately in front of the crowd that Gar finally yelled out.

"Enough! I'm hungry and we want to eat. You can do that later, Cousin."

"Throw the bouquet," one of the women called out.

"Oh, I will," said Sage, taking the bouquet from Amira standing next to her as her maiden of honor. "Amira, go on out there to try to catch it."

"I want to catch it," said Noel, jumping up and down.

"You're a boy, Brother, now start acting like one." Oscar grabbed Noel's hand and pulled him to the back of the crowd as the single women came forward.

"Hurry up! I'm hungry," Gar wailed.

"I'm closing my eyes and turning around," said Sage. The bouquet was made from wildflowers, as well as herbs with strong scents, sage being the main one. "Catch it, Amira," she called out, throwing the bouquet over her shoulder.

"What the hell," she heard, turning to see Gar with the flowers in his hands.

"Give me that, Gar," said Martine, ripping it away from him.

"At least give me something to eat." Gar plucked some sage from the bouquet and stuck it in his mouth. "Yuck," he said, spitting the bitter herb on the ground. Griffin jumped up on Gar, knocking him to the ground and everyone started laughing.

"It serves you right for trying to eat the wedding bouquet," Martine told him, burying her nose in the wildflowers.

"Let the celebration begin for my son's wedding feast," Madoc called out.

"Yes, Lord Shrewsbury," said Ferdinand the steward, directing the crowd to the great hall.

"Ferdinand, I don't like being called Lord Shrewsbury. Negative memories attached," said Madoc. "Just call me Lord Madoc."

"Yes, Lord Madoc. The feast has begun," announced Ferdinand. "If everyone will please move to the great hall, we will start with serving the wedding couple."

"Robin, are you sure you don't regret giving up the castle to marry me?" asked Sage as they walked hand-in-hand to the great hall for the feast.

"Not at all," said Robin. "And since my father talked to King

Edward and accepted the position of lord of the castle after all, we can still live here."

"I thought you said this castle was cursed. And that your parents didn't want it."

"I changed my mind," said Madoc, coming up behind them. Lady Abigail, Robin's mother, held on to his arm.

"We've decided that since you and Robin fell in love here, that this castle will bring us good luck from now on," said Robin's father.

"It already has, since Sage is pregnant," added his mother.

"This just goes to show that even things that seem bad at first can end up being something very good after all." Robin leaned over to kiss Sage.

"That's true," said Sage. "After all, I thought I would be killed, but then Robin showed up and saved my life. More than once," she said, reaching up with a kiss to his cheek in return.

"And don't forget, my dear wife, I thought I was going to drown, but you saved my life as well."

"I thought you didn't like people to know that," said Sage with a giggle.

"You're right," Robin answered. "Even if I'm no longer lord of a castle, it doesn't do my reputation any good for anyone to know I've been saved by a woman."

"He'll get used to it," Lady Abigail muttered. "They always do."

"But will he get used to the fact that I am not a noble?" asked Sage.

"By marrying me, you've inherited the courtesy title of *lady,* just like Rose did when she married Rook," Robin explained.

"But I'm not really a lady." Sage felt like a fake.

"You are so much more than just a lady, Sage," said Robin, caressing her cheek and kissing her forehead.

"Well, what else am I, besides a healer?"

"You are a wonderful woman. You are strong and beautiful, and I am proud to call you Lady Blake," said Robin. "You are my love, my reason for living, and for the rest of our lives I will always consider you to be my ***Winter Sage***."

FROM THE AUTHOR

I hope you have enjoyed Robin and Sage's story and will take the time to leave a review for me. Love is a stronger power than any sword, and can make people do things or give up things they never thought they would.

Robin thought he wanted one thing his entire life, but eventually realized that the only thing that would make him happy was being true to his heart by marrying the woman he loved, Sage.

Alright, so this probably didn't happen back in medieval times, but I am a big believer of women being respected and also true love, so that is what I write. To me, this is the happily-ever-after that everyone strives to find during their lifetime.

The Below the Salt Series is about overlooking status to find true love. My main characters are all the next generation of the Blake family, who were first introduced in my Legacy of the Blade Series.

If you'd like to read about Robin's parents, Madoc and

Abigail, you can find their story in **Lord of Illusion**, Book 3 of the **Legacy of the Blade Series**.

Madoc's brother, Lord Corbett Blake, is featured in **Lord of the Blade** when he marries his thought-to-be servant, Devon.

The story of their sister Wren, the blind (at the time) Englishwoman who falls in love with that loveable but crazy Highlander, Storm MacKeefe, when he is hired to hunt down her army of women can be found in **Lady Renegade**.

And Madoc's twin sister Echo, who raised by pirates, has her story told with Baron of the Cinque Ports, Garrett Blackmore (who happens to be Lady Abigail's brother) in **Lady of the Mist.**

You can start reading this series for free (free at the time this is published) with the prequel, **Legacy of the Blade**.

You will also find that ornery old coot, Callum MacKeefe in many of my other series, including **Madman MacKeefe**, **Highland Chronicles**, and **Highland Outcasts**.

You can follow me on social media, and learn more about the books I write by using the following links:

Stop by and visit my **Website**. You can follow me on **Amazon**, **Bookbub**, **Goodreads**, **Facebook,** and **Twitter**. I also have a **Private Readers' Group** on Facebook that I invite you to join.

If you would like to stay informed of my new books and also sales, please be sure to subscribe to my **newsletter**.

Thank you,

Elizabeth Rose

ABOUT ELIZABETH

Elizabeth Rose is an award-winning, bestselling author of over 100 books and counting. She writes medieval, historical, contemporary, paranormal, and western romance. Her books are available as EBooks, paperbacks, and some audiobooks as well.

Her favorite characters in her works include dark, dangerous and tortured heroes, and feisty, independent heroines who know how to wield a sword. She loves writing 14th century medieval novels, and is well-known for her many series.

Elizabeth loves the outdoors. In the summertime, you can find her in her secret garden with her laptop, swinging in her hammock working on her next book. Elizabeth is a born storyteller and passionate about sharing her works with her readers.

Please be sure to visit her website at **Elizabethrosenovels.com** to read excerpts from any of her novels and get sneak peeks at covers of upcoming books. You can follow her on **Twitter, Facebook**, **Goodreads** or **BookBub.** Be sure to sign up for her **newsletter** so you don't miss out on new releases or upcoming events.

Click to join **Elizabeth Rose's Readers' Group.**

ALSO BY ELIZABETH ROSE

Medieval Series:

Legendary Bastards of the Crown Series

Seasons of Fortitude Series

Secrets of the Heart Series

Legacy of the Blade Series

Daughters of the Dagger Series

MadMan MacKeefe Series

Barons of the Cinque Ports Series

Holiday Knights Series

Highland Chronicles Series

Pirate Lords Series

Highland Outcasts

Medieval/Paranormal Series:

Elemental Magick Series

Greek Myth Fantasy Series

Tangled Tales Series

Portals of Destiny

Contemporary Series:

Tarnished Saints Series

Working Man Series

Western Series:

Cowboys of the Old West Series

And More!

Please visit http://elizabethrosenovels.com

Printed in the USA
CPSIA information can be obtained
at www.ICGtesting.com
CBHW030013170524
8707CB00006B/277

9 781648 395208